Addie placed the envelope on the desk, turned to go, and spotted the pedestal display case in the far corner behind the door. A red-coiled key ring hung from the lock. She peeked inside and gasped. It was empty.

"Why would you remove the book, Teresa?" She glanced around the uncluttered office. "It doesn't make sense. Why would you take it out of the case?" She dashed back over to the desk and began flinging drawers open. Nothing. She scanned the wall file cabinet and tried the drawers, all locked. She took one last look around the room and headed to the elevator.

Addie nodded at the young ginger-haired woman seated behind the front reception desk, and pressed the elevator button. The lighted floor indicator above the door didn't budge from the main floor. She pressed it again, tapping her foot, and then re-membered what Serena had said about visiting hours. She spotted the stairwell exit and quickly made her way down the four flights to the lower level, where she hoped that Teresa had made an appearance by now. When she came to the last step on the small lower-level landing, she pivoted around the handrail toward to the exit door. Out of the corner of her eye, she glimpsed a dark shape lying in a heap at the bottom of the next flight of stairs leading to the basement. . . .

Murder in the First Edition

Lauren Elliott

KENSINGTON BOOKS
www.kensingtonbooks.com

KENSINGTON BOOKS are published by

Kensington Publishing Corp.
119 West 40th Street
New York, NY 10018

All Kensington titles, imprints, and distributed lines are available
at special quantity discounts for bulk purchases for sales promo-
tion, premiums, fund-raising, educational, or institutional use.

Special book excerpts or customized printings can also be created to fit specific needs. For details, write or phone the office
of the Kensington Sales Manager: Attn.: Sales Department.
Kensington Publishing Corp., 119 West 40th Street, New York,
NY 10018. Phone: 1-800-221-2647.

Kensington and the K logo Reg. U.S. Pat. & TM Off.

First Printing: October 2019
ISBN-13: 978-1-4967-2021-4
ISBN-10: 1-4967-2021-0

ISBN-13: 978-1-4967-2024-5 (ebook)
ISBN-10: 1-4967-2024-5 (ebook)

10 9 8 7 6 5 4 3 2 1

Printed in the United States of America

Chapter 1

Addison Greyborne's eyes glistened with the reflection of the glimmering snowflakes hanging from the delicate fairy lights she'd retrieved from her aunt's attic. They were perfect. Both of her shop's bay windows resembled a winter wonderland of lights. She wrapped her arms around her middle and crossed her fingers. Hopefully, the holiday glow would beckon passersby.

"Morning, Addie," a stocky woman called as she passed along the sidewalk.

"Good morning, Carol." Addie smiled and waved.

Had it really only been just over a year since she'd established Beyond the Page, her book and curio shop? It was hard to believe given the bumps and bruises she'd endured along the way, but now she was truly a part of this town that she'd grown to love.

"Good morning, Addie," another passerby called out.

"Morning," she said, smiling.

"Your displays are looking good."

"Thanks." Addie grinned and took a step back to get a clearer view of both windows. The display of books in the right one caught her attention.

She pressed her face to the cold glass, wiped off the condensation from her warm breath, and peered at the small tree in the center colorfully decorated with antique ornaments. But it was still missing something. Tinsel! That's what it needed, and the book sets she'd wrapped with holiday ribbon displayed like gifts beneath it on a red tree skirt needed an extra splash of sparkle to make it all just perfect. She made a mental note to buy tinsel and added another package of artificial snow to her shopping list. Outdoor inspection complete, she opened the door to her store and drew in a deep breath.

The crisp smell of the New England sea air combined with the scent of old books and leather tickled at her nose, but this morning she also detected the hint of a new aroma. It appeared that Paige Stringer, her shop assistant, had placed small, festive bowls and baskets of apple-cinnamon potpourri on bookshelves throughout the shop.

The fragrance stirred warm memories of her childhood home and her family. Now, all since passed, including her beloved David. They were to have been married by now and should have been celebrating the season together, but he . . . a tear slid down her cheek. She swatted at it and forced that memory back into its box in her mind and headed for the coffeemaker on the far end of the long, antique Victorian bar she used for a sales counter.

Paige poked her blond, curly head out of the storeroom, grinned, waved, and disappeared back inside. Addie shook her head and tossed her purse and red wool coat on the counter. Dropping a coffee pod into the machine, she sorted through the previous day's receipts as the aroma of fresh-brewing coffee taunted her. Paige reappeared, wearing an "I 'heart' the Cook" apron and carrying two steaming mugs in her hands.

"What are you up to?"

"Well?" Paige waved a mug under Addie's nose. "What do you think?"

"I think I smell my grandmother's Christmas apple-spiced punch?" Addie clasped the cup and waved the fragrance toward her. She took a sip. "Yes, perfect." She beamed over the rim.

"Good." Paige gave a toothy grin. "After you told me yesterday that your grandmother's punch was one of your fondest Christmas memories, I worked most of the night perfecting the recipe."

Addie took another sip. "You've done well, thank you."

"I brought in a small cook plate so I can prepare it in the back room, and a large coffee urn that we can refill as needed. I thought it might be a good idea to have it up here on the counter for customers. You know, as an alternative to coffee for the holidays. What do you think?"

"I think"—Addie set her mug down and crossed her arms, looking hard at Paige—"that you come up with some"—Paige sucked in a sharp breath—"of the most . . . outstanding ideas."

Paige's cheeks flushed with a rosy glow. "You always get me."

"Just keeping you on your toes." Addie winked, grinning. "I don't want all your brilliant ideas going to your head."

"No risk of that happening with you as my boss."

Paige returned an exaggerated wink. "I'll fill the urn and set it up." She swung on her heel and headed to the back room, straightening bookshelves as she went.

Addie smiled at her protégé. She really had turned out to be the perfect employee despite her best friend, and the local tea merchant, Serena's initial misgivings as to where Paige's loyalties might lie. Would they be with Addie, her employer, or the tyrant baker next door, Martha, her mother, but time proved Paige most adept at finding a balance between the two of them.

Addie scanned the store. A large wreath and a few more lighted green garlands to wrap around the pillar posts would complete the holiday ensemble. Now to only find time to shop. When she glanced past the window, she spotted a man dressed in a black trench coat and black hat with the brim pulled down covering his features. He stood across the street seemingly staring at her store. A shiver traveled up her spine. She moved closer to the window for a better look, but a large delivery van pulled up, blocking her view of the man.

The courier driver hopped down from his truck and scurried to her front door, yanking it open. The bells attached to her door protested with a merry jingle. Within thirty seconds, he had delivered a package, asked for a signature, and left with the same force, bells still echoing from the first time. She peered across the street after Mr. Speedy screeched away. The man in black was gone.

Addie shrugged and glanced at the large envelope. From Boston. With a smile, she placed it on a shelf under the front counter. The door chimes rang. She looked up, a welcoming smile forming on her lips. The color drained from her face, and the smile faded. The man in black removed his hat, ran a leather-gloved hand over his silver hair, and stood silently staring at her.

She grasped the counter edge to keep her wobbly knees in check. "Jonathan?"

"Hi, Addie." A smile tickled the corners of his mouth.

She swallowed hard to release the lump growing in the back of her throat.

He shuffled his weight from one foot to the other. "Maybe I should have called first?"

"No." She shook her head and walked around the end of the counter. "You just surprised me. That's all. Come in, please have a seat." She motioned to a counter stool. "Would you like some coffee, or hot spiced Christmas punch?"

He shook his head and slid onto a stool. "Coffee's fine. Just a quick warm-up and I'll be on my way." He pulled off his gloves.

"You're leaving?" From the coffeemaker, she glanced over her shoulder. "But you just got here."

"Afraid so, there's a big storm coming tonight or tomorrow, and I'd like to get past it before the highways are closed, but I'd heard you'd moved to Greyborne Harbor, and well . . . just stopped to say hello."

"Five sugars, right?" She grimaced as she passed him his coffee. "This is hardly on the interstate running to and from anywhere?"

He nodded, lifting the cup to his lips. "Exactly what I needed, thanks." He set it down. "No, it's not, but I'm on my way home from a business meeting in Boston and am living north of Albany now. So, before the forecast changed, I'd already decided on a short detour to drop in to wish you a Merry Christmas." He reached over and clasped her hand, guiding her to the

Lauren Elliott

stool beside him. "But now it appears it's going to have to be a shorter visit than first planned."

"I'm glad you stopped by anyway." Her throat tightened. "It's wonderful to see you again." She released her hand from his.

Paige coughed and placed the large urn on the end of the counter, glancing at the stranger.

"Paige, this is—"

The bells over the door chimed. "Morning, Addie." Catherine Lewis swept toward the counter. She pulled off her gloves and slid onto a stool.

"Good morning, Catherine." Addie rose to her feet. "You're out and about early today."

"Yes, lots of shopping to do, and my car's in the garage. So, I'm on foot today and have a lot of ground to cover. I thought I'd better get an early start and headed right here for one of your delicious, fresh-brewed coffees to get me going." She nodded at the silver-haired man seated beside her.

"Paige, Catherine, I'd like you both to meet my . . . umm, David's father. Jonathan Hemingway."

"Hemingway?" Paige's brow creased. "I thought David's last name was Armstrong or something?"

Addie nudged Paige with her elbow.

"Yes"—Jonathan cleared his throat—"it was Hemingway. His mother and I divorced when he was quite young, and she remarried."

"You're a relative of Addie's?" Catherine turned to him, her hand outstretched. "How wonderful."

His eyes and hand held fast with hers. "I must say your husband is a very lucky man."

"I'm . . . I'm not married." Her porcelain complexion turned a shade of peach.

"Jonathan, this is Catherine Lewis. She's a good

friend of mine and was also a close friend of my father's."

"It truly is a pleasure to meet you, Catherine." He brought her delicate hand to his lips and kissed the back of it. "Any friend of Addie's, and the late Michael Greyborne's, is a friend of mine, too."

"Hemingway, like the author?" She all but purred when his thumb began stroking the back of her hand.

Paige looked at Addie, who was in the midst of an involuntary eye roll.

"Yes, he's a distant relative and may be the reason my son had such a fascination with books and women who love books." He glanced at Addie, but then caressed Catherine with another gaze. "Do you love books, too, Catherine?"

Catherine let out a breathy sigh and pulled her hand away. Her already flushed cheeks brightened with an intense fiery hue. She straightened stray strands of her brown shoulder-cropped hair, slid off her stool, and backed toward the door. A shy smile graced her lips. "It . . . ah . . . was wonderful to meet you. I hope . . ." She swallowed. "I hope I run into you again, Jonathan, before you leave." She studied the tips of her toes before bolting out the door.

Addie looked at Jonathan from under a creased brow. "I see you haven't changed at all." She clucked her tongue.

He tossed his head back and released a barrel-chested laugh. Addie gave Paige a dismissive head tilt, and after the girl retreated with the book trolley into the back room, Addie glowered at him.

He smirked. "What?"

"I see you're still up to your same old tricks. I thought you promised David that was all in the past."

He looked up at her and set his cup down. "And I see you have carried on the same grudge my son held against me for years. He forgave me in the end, Addie. Why can't you?"

She threw her hands in the air. "I did, and I tried for David's sake, but what do you expect after that seduction I just witnessed?"

"Really? Just exactly what did you see? Me being kind to an attractive woman? I didn't see her complaining. Did you?"

"I saw the same thing I saw for the five years David and I were together. Something he'd lived with his entire life."

His eyes narrowed. "And just what was that?"

"Every time you dropped in out of the blue, there was a different woman on your arm. You'd deposit her on our doorstep and disappear, leaving us to entertain your flavor of the month and then not return for hours, acting all nonchalant like you'd just popped down to get something from your car." Her knuckles whitened when she gripped the edge of the counter. "You never showed any regard for the emotional havoc those visits created, leaving me to try to put him back together after you'd disappear again for months without another word."

"I didn't realize that my family visits were such an imposition on you?" His lip twitched.

"They wouldn't have been except for the fact that you never spent any time with your son, and left us to make small talk with your . . . your . . ." Her whole body vibrated.

He shrugged. "They were all in a similar line of work as you were in and even a few who were in David's line. So, you had something in common with them." His hand clasped hers. "Look, I was busy. Working."

"Working?" Her eyes widened. "The visit was just a cover for having us babysit your latest piece of arm candy."

"Addie." He squeezed her hand. "David eventually came to understand the hours my work demanded, and he didn't let it stand in the way of our relationship the last few years." She yanked her hand out of his. "Why can't you let the past go, too?"

Her chin jutted out. "Because you kept lying to him, and it broke my heart."

Jonathan's shoulders stiffened. "I never lied to my son."

"But you did, every time you'd tell him this wasn't like the old days. This woman was serious, but it never was because he saw the same old revolving door of your women friends as he had his whole life. Then you'd promise him that the next visit would be longer, and you'd spend more time with him." Her eyes flashed. "Did you know that after one of your later visits, he started to become withdrawn? He seemed worried and wouldn't even talk about you to me anymore."

"I see." He stood up and collected his hat and gloves from the counter. "Just remember that everything is not always as it appears. David came to know that." He placed his hat on his head and nodded, pulling one glove on.

"Look, Jonathan, we're like family, and I want to believe in you, but Catherine is a good woman, a nice woman, but she's emotionally fragile because she's been hurt more than she ever should have during her life. Stay away from her, please. She doesn't need you and your old philandering ways only to have her heart broken again."

He tilted his head. One corner of his mouth twitched. "Give me more credit than that, will you?"

"I know you, Jonathan."

He leaned over the counter, fixing his steel-gray eyes on hers. "Do you?"

She crossed her arms and nodded. "I just saw it with my own eyes."

He straightened and pulled on his other glove. "Don't worry about Catherine. I'm pretty sure she's a big girl and capable of making her own decisions." His brow rose, and he smirked. "I have a lunch date, so if you'll excuse me."

"I'm warning you. Stay away from her, please. For me. I don't want to have to clean up another mess in the wake of your visit."

To her surprise, he smiled just a little, revealing a suggestion of dimples in both his cheeks. Addie wavered. Everything about his features reminded her of David, from the set of his jaw to his magnetic gray eyes and the way he held his head. David had looked exactly like a younger version of him.

"Don't worry," his throaty voice softening, "I'm not about to go chasing down the street after Catherine. My luncheon is with an old friend who lives in Greyborne Harbor now."

"Who's that? Another friend of mine I'll have to warn about becoming involved with you?" She searched his face for a moment. "Although, if she knew you before, I'm pretty sure she knows what you're all about."

His eyes twinkled with a hint of mischievousness. "She does, don't worry. Teresa Lang is very familiar with my ways."

"Teresa Lang." Her eyes flashed.

His lips turned up at the corners.

"You don't mean the same Teresa who's the Charity

Fund-raising Coordinator for the Hospital Foundation, do you?"

"Yes, why, do you know her?"

"I have an appointment with her today after lunch about the Christmas Charity Auction."

"Then you'd better not plan on her being there until at least mid-afternoon. You know, in case our lunch date goes as per usual." He gave her a sly wink and then added, "Merry Christmas." The door closed behind him, the bells seemingly singing with joy at his departure.

Chapter 2

Addie settled onto a chair behind the desk in the back room, slid an antique letter opener along the edge of the manila envelope, and envisioned it was Jonathan's black heart. A low growl escaped her throat. Hoping for happy news to distract her, she blew a wayward strand of honey-brown hair from her eyes, slid the enclosed papers out, and grinned. At last, it was the final report from her old coworker Kate at the Boston Library. The appraisal for Charles Dickens's *A Christmas Carol* and the last thing Addie needed for the auction. Apparently, a certificate of authentication trumped her skilled knowledge of antique books.

The book itself had since been returned, but for the auction, Addie needed this current market report and Kate's certificate so the foundation could make as much money as possible from its sale. The report contained one surprise, but otherwise it was exactly as she thought it would be. Addie was pleased to see that she really hadn't lost her touch. It was only too bad that she'd allowed her appraisers' association membership to lapse. It wasn't a requirement for appraisers to belong, but a member's number on the documents added considerable credibility to an appraisal. Nonetheless, it was done now, and Teresa Lang would be more than pleased with the results.

When Addie discovered the 1843 first edition book tucked in a box of Christmas decorations in her aunt's attic, she knew then it was special. She was a little confused at the time as to why her aunt stored it in there, but knowing she was eccentric and did love hiding things, Addie shrugged it off. When she heard about the desperate need for donations this year to the annual Christmas Charity Auction fund-raiser, she decided, why not? It was perfect for the season and might bring in more money for the auction just because of that. Well, if truth were known, it took a little bit of persuading by her good friend the coroner, Dr. Simon Emerson, but once she'd offered it up as a donation, she had no regrets. As Simon had pointed out, Dickens himself was actively involved in social issues his entire life, so it seemed like the right thing to do.

She glanced at her phone clock and entered Serena's number, tapping her pen on the desk, waiting for her friend to answer. "Hey, where are you, we have to get moving. We have to meet Teresa at one."

"I'm on my way." Serena's voice echoed through the speaker.

Addie held the phone away from her ear and looked at it. "Are you in a tunnel?"

"No." Serena's whispered voice reverberated around her. "I'm right behind you."

"Ah!" Addie jumped in her seat when Serena placed her hand on her shoulder. "You nearly scared me to death." Wide-eyed, she shut her phone off and tugged playfully on a handful of her friend's red hair.

"My, my, aren't we jumpy today. Have you been reading ghost stories again?" Serena smirked, pulling away, and leaned on the edge of the desk.

"No, but a ghost of my past has come to pay a visit." Addie slid the documents into the envelope and waved off Serena's look of concern. "It's not that serious, really. David's father blew into town this morning for one of his *quickie* visits." She pulled on her coat, grabbed her purse and the envelope from the desk.

"I didn't know you and Philip Armstrong were still in touch, after the rocky relationship he had with David when he didn't take the teaching position at the university that Philip arranged for him," Serena said, following Addie out the door into the shop.

"No, it wasn't Philip who dropped in. It was Jonathan Hemingway, David's natural father."

"But I thought you liked him?"

Addie stopped and smiled at a customer over the top of Serena's head. "I do." Her voice dropped. "I do, basically. I don't like his lifestyle, but deep down, he's a good guy. I think. He has to be. After all, he's David's father, and David was a great guy."

"So, what's the problem? He dropped in before the holidays. You should be happy. He's probably missing David as much as you are, especially at this time of year. I can't wait to meet him." Serena swept past her toward the front door.

"You're not going to meet him."

Serena skidded to a halt. "Why not? Are you ashamed of your best friend?"

"Of course not." Addie grabbed Serena's coat sleeve. "He dropped in for one of his usual flyby visits and is off again, and—"

"And what?"

"And it kind of hurts, especially since I was on my

own for Thanksgiving." Her eyes cast downward. "When I saw Jonathan, I was hoping just a teeny-tiny bit"—she squeezed her pointer finger and thumb together—"that he was here for Christmas."

Serena placed her arm around Addie's shoulders. "You weren't exactly alone on Thanksgiving. You were with your new family here."

"You're right. It was a wonderful day and nice to be surrounded by such great people. Between you and Zach, Simon and his sister Carolyn's crew, it really was a special dinner." She took a deep breath and pressed her lips tight.

"If it was so great, why such a glum look, then?"

"I don't know. I guess it's just the time of the year, and I'm missing my real family and David and, well, having Jonathan here would have helped. After all, he is the last connection I have to David, and I guess I don't want to lose that. But on the other hand he never was much of a family man, anyway, and after this morning, when he made me so mad . . . I think I really blew it. I doubt we'll ever be close now."

"No matter what happened this morning, he's still part of your family, and any issues can be worked out, just like in other families. You'll see. Remember that you both have to learn now how to have a relationship without David around. Just give it time."

Addie's eyes scanned the store on the lookout for listening ears. "Yes, but I don't know if I can because he hasn't changed in all the years I've known him. In the few minutes he was here, he managed to turn poor, innocent Catherine into a swooning teenage girl. Yeah"—she let out a deep breath—"it's for the best that he's gone. If he stayed, he'd only end up hurting her and ruining my Christmas, too."

Serena shrugged. "If he's gone, there's no harm

done, and maybe Catherine enjoyed the attention, even though fleeting."

"By her reaction, I'm pretty sure she did enjoy it, although I think his overt displays of affection toward her scared the heck out of her. But the whole thing, his visit, his interest in her, was all too contrived on Jonathan's part for my liking. I get the feeling he's up to something."

"Like what? No one's died lately. Don't you think it's time you stopped treating everyone as a suspect in some sinister plot."

"You're right," Addie said. "I guess I can take off my certified amateur sleuth hat. It's just that, well . . . after my father died, and I found out that he had broken Catherine's heart years ago, I somehow feel I have to watch out for her. That means keeping her out of the grips of the renowned silver-haired fox, and I threw her right in his path."

"You did no such thing. You didn't ring her up and invite her over to meet him, did you?"

Addie shook her head.

"There you go. As usual, you're overthinking again. Catherine's a big girl. Now let's go. We're going to be late."

"You're right. It's just that it was that same behavior on his part that broke up his marriage to David's mother in the first place, and I guess there's some things I find hard to get past. But if I'm going to have any future dealings with Jonathan, I'll have to learn to accept him for what he is because David eventually did."

"Yes, you do, but I'm sensing there's something more to all this, isn't there?" Serena stood with her hand on the doorknob, studying her friend.

"You can read me so well."

"Spill."

"It's just that every time I look into Jonathan's face since David's murder, all I see is David reflecting back at me, and it's—"

"Haunting? Is that the word?"

Addie pressed her lips tight and nodded. She waved at Paige over her shoulder as they stepped out into the cool afternoon air. "Where's your box of donations?" Addie looked at Serena. "I thought that's why you were going over to the hospital with me."

"In my car. I thought we could drive over. I really don't feel like slogging through the snow. The box is *really* heavy."

"A large donation, is it? Well, aren't you the philanthropic donor?" Addie laughed, then opened the passenger door and slid in.

"Not really." Serena plopped into the driver's seat of her older model Jeep Wrangler. "I usually do up a large gift basket filled with teas, a teapot, cups, strainer, and other small stuff for the auction every year. People seem to like bidding on it, and it's good advertising, and besides, the money goes to a good cause."

"Yeah, there's no better cause than being able to help the hospital upgrade the pediatric wing." Addie smiled and checked her reflection in the sun visor mirror. "I just hope my donation brings in at least what the appraised value is."

"So that means you got the appraisal back?" Serena pulled out and headed toward Main Street.

"Yes, and it was even a bit higher than what I had originally estimated. The book must be in better shape than I'd given it credit for. I guess my skills have slipped a little not being in the loop of daily market updates."

"You have been out of the business for a while. It's lucky you still have connections you can turn to."

"That I am, and I'm glad that I already told Teresa that she needed to set a reserved starting bid of at least thirty thousand. It might even go as high as fifty to sixty thousand. I had thought only forty to fifty."

"Wow," Serena whistled. "I hope there's enough money in town for someone to bid on something that expensive."

"I suspect that it may come from outside the community. Teresa told me that within hours of her posting a list of the items for auction on their webpage, she had calls from rare-book brokers all over the world wanting tickets for the event."

"Yuck. I mean great for the auction, but"—Serena pulled into a parking space by the hospital main entrance—"I hope us poor local folk will still be able to buy tickets."

"You don't have yours yet?" Addie frowned at her as she stepped out and then cringed when icy slush ran over the top of her ankle-high boot and oozed between her toes. She shook the remaining snow from her pant leg and hopped one-footed over the curb to the cleared sidewalk.

"No, guess I'm a typical small-town girl." Serena cocked a questioning eyebrow at Addie, who stood crane-style on one leg. "I don't plan ahead and buy at the last minute."

Addie wiped the remaining slush from her boot with her other pant leg. "You should at least ask Teresa to hold two tickets for you. You are taking Zach, aren't you?"

Serena nodded, grinning, and pulled a large box out of the back of her Jeep and shuffled it from hip to hip.

"Want some help?"

"No, it's just awkward. I can manage." She panted into the lobby. "There's the elevator. Hurry, I don't want to have to wait for the next one; they get so slow during visiting hours." She rushed in and pressed the lower-level button.

"But Teresa's office is up on the third floor." Addie peered at the numbered circles and moved a finger toward the number 3.

"Yes, but the auction and dance are on the lower level." Serena swatted away Addie's hand, and the elevator dipped and journeyed down.

"The basement?"

"No, that's a level below." The door opened and they stepped out.

"Now I'm confused." Addie frowned. "This is the floor the lab, X-ray, cafeteria, and Simon's office is on." Addie eyed the signage hanging overhead in the wide corridor. "Is the auction in the cafeteria, then?"

"No, there are the two wings. All that other stuff is in the north wing, and the south one is mostly classrooms and conference rooms with folding dividers between them that can open up into one large space." She waved her hand like a game-show hostess. "This is where the auction and dinner dance are held every year."

Addie stopped at the conference room entryway. The winter wonderland scene in front of her was breathtaking. A smile touched the corners of her mouth when her head bobbled back and forth as she glanced over the richly decorated space. Serena led the way to table number 5, set her box down, and scanned the room.

"There's Patrick. I'll just let him know I've finally

brought in my donation," Serena said, and sauntered off across the large room.

Addie took one look at Patrick, Teresa's frazzled-looking assistant, and thought that if he wasn't already balding, he would be by the time this event was over. She willed herself not to laugh, but it was hard given the fact that he kept scouring his hand through what little hair he did have left. Not trusting herself to behave, Addie shifted her attention from Patrick by browsing through the silent auction items displayed on the tables around the room's perimeter.

It impressed her to see that aside from local businesses, there were donations from all over the eastern Massachusetts area, including a few from Boston. She glanced around the room and found it curious, though, that she didn't see the pedestal book display case she had borrowed from the Boston Library to safeguard her donation. When she spotted Serena and Patrick chatting in the far corner, she headed toward them.

"Hi, Addie." Patrick's eyes lit up when she joined them. "As you can see it's pretty crazy in here today. The volunteers are still hard at work adding glitter and glam"—he cleared his throat and glanced sideways at Serena—"and the last-minute items are being delivered."

"Hey, I've been busy." Serena pouted.

"Never mind, your baskets do bring in some nice, high bids, so we are grateful regardless of how tardy you are."

"Well, I do have a reputation I have to uphold. It takes me months and months to put one together." She placed the back of her hand across her forehead as if in a swoon. "I don't know how I manage it all."

Addie guffawed at her friend's theatrics. "I don't

see my donation, Patrick." Her gaze darted around the room again.

"No, it's still up in Teresa's office. She thought that since it's the only live auction item, and that you'd set a reserved starting bid on it of thirty thousand dollars, she wasn't exactly comfortable about keeping it down here."

"That's a good call. I have the paperwork for her now, which will help the auctioneer drive up the price. My estimate may have been a little on the conservative side, though."

"Really?"

"Yeah, my ex-coworker at the Boston Library informed me that in today's market, it could bring in a sale price of well over sixty thousand."

Patrick's face paled. "Wow. That would really help pay for the wing renovations, maybe even the operating room." His hand swept around the room. "Combined with the other money raised by all these, we should be in great shape to meet our goal."

"Let's not get our hopes up too high," Addie said, "but you never know these days. A copy apparently sold at a Sotheby's auction a few years ago for one hundred and sixty thousand." Patrick's eyes popped wide open. "But it was an inscribed copy. So, it's hard to know ahead of time what my copy will go for, but it might be higher in the market today than first thought, especially this time of the year." She looked around the room at the array of twinkling Christmas trees placed between the display tables.

"We can only hope." He held up his crossed fingers.

"Where's Teresa? I haven't seen her yet to give her these." She tapped the envelope she held to her chest.

"She had a luncheon"—Patrick looked up at the

wall clock—"but that was hours ago, and it's almost one thirty. I haven't seen her down here, so I'm not sure she's back yet."

"Maybe she's in her office. I'll just run these up and see."

"Don't trouble yourself. I can give them to her." He held out his hand.

"That's okay." She danced a step backward. "I need to talk to her anyway. I'll head up there."

Addie made her way toward the door, the inside of her boot sloshing with every step. She cringed as the water squirted between her toes. She stepped off the elevator on the third floor and headed toward the north wing, where Teresa's office was located, along with the hospital chairman's and the other executives. She paused at the reception desk, noted the BE BACK IN ONE HOUR sign, made her way to the far end of the long hallway, and knocked at the closed door. No answer. She knocked again. "Teresa, are you there?" She jiggled the handle and frowned when the door opened freely in her hand.

She peered inside. "Teresa? It's me Addie. I've just come to drop the appraisal off." She stepped into the empty room.

Two coffee cups sat on either side of the desk. One had the unmistakable trace of Teresa's trademark red lipstick on the rim. The other? She peered at the thick brown goo sitting in the bottom. She picked it up and sniffed. Her nose wrinkled. There was no mistaking that sickening, sugar-sweet scent of Jonathan's favorite drink, sugar with a splash of coffee. She shook her head and set the cup down. "Well, Jonathan, you weren't joking about holding off until mid-afternoon, as it appears your luncheon date has gone as per usual."

Addie placed the envelope on the desk, turned to

go, and spotted the pedestal display case in the far corner behind the door. A red-coiled key ring hung from the lock. She peeked inside and gasped. It was empty.

"Why would you remove the book, Teresa?" She glanced around the uncluttered office. "It doesn't make sense. Why would you take it out of the case?" She dashed back over to the desk and began flinging drawers open. Nothing. She scanned the wall file cabinet and tried the drawers, all locked. She took one last look around the room and headed to the elevator.

Addie nodded at the young ginger-haired woman seated behind the front reception desk, and pressed the elevator button. The lighted floor indicator above the door didn't budge from the main floor. She pressed it again, tapping her foot, and then remembered what Serena had said about visiting hours. She spotted the stairwell exit and quickly made her way down the four flights to the lower level, where she hoped that Teresa had made an appearance by now. When she came to the last step on the small, lower-level landing, she pivoted around the handrail toward to the exit door. Out of the corner of her eye, she glimpsed a dark shape lying in a heap at the bottom of the next flight of stairs leading to the basement.

She paused, staring down the long cement staircase. "What the—?" She dashed down the steps. "Teresa!" Addie's stomach lurched at the sight of the odd angle of her head. She placed two fingers at the side of her neck to check for a pulse. The skin was still warm to her touch. The unmistakable pong of whiskey hung heavy in the air. "Help!" Addie screamed. "Someone help!"

Chapter 3

Addie leaned forward on the bench in the main lobby, elbows on her knees, her fingers clasped around a vending machine cup. Her gaze drifted from the floor toward Marc Chandler, Chief of Police, who was engrossed in conversation with Simon, the coroner, and Jerry, one of the officers with whom Addie was well acquainted from previous cases. Their faces looked grim. She knocked back a gulp of the rancid coffee and choked.

Serena reached over, took the half-empty cup from her hands. "Wait until you can have a good cup." She tossed it into the trash can at the end of the bench. "I just don't get why my brother's treating us like suspects and forcing us to wait here. He already has our statements."

"He's just doing his job." Addie leaned back against the wall, stretching out her long legs, tapping her ankle boots together. "At least my boot dried out," she snickered.

"What do you think they're talking about?" Serena whispered.

Addie shrugged. "They're probably comparing notes. You know, making sure that there are no glaring discrepancies in anyone's statements."

"But we didn't even see her today, so why are we being detained?"

Addie let out a sharp breath. "Well, I did find her body." She straightened up when Marc walked in their direction.

Her shoulders slumped when he walked past without even a sideways glance and pressed the elevator button. She heaved out a deep sigh and bit the inside of her lip. She glanced back at Simon and Jerry, who were looking at the photos Jerry had taken of the crime scene. One, in particular, appeared to hold their attention. Simon raised it closer to his face. He looked over his shoulder at Addie. His brow creased; then he looked back at the photo. Jerry clicked on his police radio. His eyes held fast on Addie's.

She grimaced. "That can't be good."

"What?" Serena scanned the lobby. "What can't be good?"

Addie shook her head and scrubbed her hands over her face.

"What happened? What did I miss?"

"Wait for it."

As if on cue, Jerry marched toward them, unclipped his handcuffs from his police belt, and came to a stop directly in front of Addie. "Miss Greyborne. I'm afraid I have to take you in." He dangled the cuffs in front of her.

She rose to her feet. "Those won't be necessary, Jerry."

"Standard procedure, miss." His feet planted squarely.

"Come on, you know me. I'm hardly a danger to you or a flight risk."

His cheeks flushed. "I know, but—"

"This is ridiculous, Jerry." Serena shot to her feet. "What's going on here?"

His eyes flashed an apology at Addie. His shoulders twitched with a slight shrug. "Chief's orders, sorry."

"Addie?" Serena grabbed her arm. "What happened that I don't know about?"

"Nothing, it'll be okay. I'll call you later, promise."

Jerry looked from Addie to Serena, refastened the cuffs to his belt, stood back, and allowed Addie to walk out the door in front of him.

"Thanks for not cuffing me in the lobby, Jerry."

"I'm going to have some explaining to do later, but—" He placed his hand on the top of her head and steered her into the backseat of his patrol car.

Jerry ushered her up the back stairs into the police station and led her past Carolyn, the desk sergeant, who was also Simon's sister, and escorted her into Marc's office. "Have a seat. The chief will be along shortly." He left, closing the door.

Addie slumped into a chair, drumming her fingers on the wooden arms. Moments later, the door burst open. She jumped when Marc strode in, slamming it behind him.

"You really ordered Jerry to handcuff me?"

He stomped toward his desk. The dark look in his chocolate-brown eyes sent a shiver through her. He sat down and folded his hands on the desk in front of him, fixing his cold gaze on her. "I didn't think you'd come willingly."

"What? Did you think I was going to bolt and dash when I hadn't done anything wrong?" She leaned forward, matching his gaze.

His eyes flashed, and his jaw tensed. "I've seen some stupid things in my life, Addie," he spat out between clenched teeth, "but you doing what you did beats them all."

"I didn't do anything."

He shook his head and stared down at a file folder clutched in his hand. "Obviously, you did. Your prints are all over Teresa's office. I thought you knew better and were smarter than that?"

"Yes, they are, and I am." She rose to her feet. "Remember, that was before I knew Teresa was dead and it was a potential crime scene."

"Sit down, Miss Greyborne."

"Miss Greyborne? We're back to that, are we?" She touched her lips where he'd last brushed his with hers, and bit her tongue, holding her thoughts in check. That was a long time ago.

He studied her face. "You're right." His lips pressed into a straight line. "But I do have some questions for you." He leaned forward on his elbows, raking his hand through his thick chestnut-brown hair. "And the truth is, it's not really a crime scene yet, either. At this point it looks like her fall was an accident."

"I guess it could have been. She did smell of alcohol."

"Exactly, so if she was drinking, she may have stumbled and fallen down the stairs, but until the autopsy is done, we won't know for certain. That's why not contaminating the scene is imperative. You know that."

"Except you're missing one important fact, and that's a book that I had donated to the auction worth over sixty thousand dollars is missing." She leaned across his desk. "That's why my prints were all over the room. I couldn't believe she'd removed it from the case. I was looking for the book. I hope you've asked Patrick if he knows where she put it."

"We've also brought Patrick in for questioning, so I'll ask him about the book, too."

"Patrick was downstairs, and had been for a while by my understanding. He was the one who sent me up to her office to see if she'd returned from lunch. Why bring him in?"

"Because"—he leafed through the folder on the desk—"as far as any witnesses are concerned, he was the last person to see her alive before lunch."

"I don't think so." She tapped her fingers on the chair arm. "I think it might have been Jonathan Hemingway who last saw her."

"Who's Jonathan Hemingway?"

"He is . . . was David's father." Marc's jaw flinched. "He told me this morning that he had a lunch date with her, and I know he'd been in her office."

"Did you see him in there?"

"No, but two coffee cups were on the desk, and one was no doubt his."

His brow ticked up. "How do you know?"

"Because not many people take their sugar with a dash of coffee, and let's just say that over the years, I've had to soak enough of his cups in hot water to get all the crusty goop out."

He pulled out a yellow notepad, clicked his pen, and poised it on the paper. "What else did you notice when you were in her office?"

She scrubbed her hands through her hair, adjusting the elastic on her long ponytail. "Nothing, really. Well, except I remember wondering why she was concerned about displaying the book downstairs before the auction for fear it would be stolen and then would leave it in her unlocked office."

"So, the door was unlocked? Is that all you noticed?"

"No, I also thought she must be Wonder Woman because her office looked a little too neat and orderly for a woman who was in the final stages of hosting a large silent auction and dinner gala."

"How so?"

"It's just that over the years, I've done appraisals for tons of these charity events, and usually the coordinator's office looks like a hurricane just swept though as the date gets closer. Her office was pristine."

"She was"—he jotted something down—"a rather particular woman."

"I know. She only shopped at New York's Fifth Avenue." Addie's lip curved in a twisted smile. "But this was more than immaculate." She shrugged. "It all looked like it had been staged. As if someone had ransacked the office, maybe looking for the key to the bookcase, then tidied up, but too much."

"First, we don't know if it was stolen and that she didn't move it, and if it was, why wouldn't the culprit just do a smash and grab?"

"Because the top of the case is shatterproof glass." She leaned forward, twisting her fingers together in her lap. "Maybe I'm overthinking it, though."

"You probably are"—he gave her subtle wink—"but it is worth noting."

Her chest constricted with an involuntary heart flip, or had her eyes and ears deceived her. She watched him continue to scribble in his notes. Had he really offered her a word of kindness, a friendly wink? Was the old Marc she knew and cared for deeply finally reemerging? The person she knew before that life-changing day when she'd uttered that one word that tore them apart. She wiped her damp palms across her knees. Maybe he was seeing his way around to being able to forgive her.

"Tell me more about this Jonathan Hemingway," he said without looking up.

"There's not much to tell. He is, was David's natural father. I haven't seen him much since the"—her words caught in her throat—"the funeral. Actually, just once since then, I think."

"And he showed up today? At your house, your shop, where?" He paused and looked up at her.

She fidgeted with her bottom jacket button. "My shop, first thing this morning."

"And he said what?"

"Not much, really. He met Catherine Lewis when she came in, had a coffee, and left, saying he had a lunch date with Teresa Lang, and that she was an old friend of his."

He stared down at his pad, tapping his pen. "Where is he now?"

"On his way home, I suppose. He said he was leaving right after lunch because a storm was coming in."

"Where's home?"

"Not sure. He moves a lot, but he did mention he was living north of Albany, New York, now."

"Okay." He pushed the pad of paper away and rose to his feet. "I think I have all I need right now."

"So, I can go?" She picked up her purse from the floor and stood up.

"Yes, but"—he walked around the desk toward the door and opened it—"don't leave town. I may have some more questions once we get the autopsy report back and talk to Patrick about that missing book."

She rolled her eyes. "Yeah, I'm such a flight risk."

She shook her head and stalked out, tempted to slam the door in his face.

So, that was that. The Marc Chandler she knew was still gone. He was the cop, and she was a . . . what? Was she a witness or a suspect? She buttoned up her coat to ward off the chill and headed across the waiting room to the front door. It flew open, and Serena bolted right into her.

"There you are. Sorry, got here as soon as I could. Both stores are closed and secure against the impending storm. And Paige has been delivered safely home by yours truly. It's really kicking up as you can see."

Addie pulled her collar up and stepped out into the howling wind. "Thanks for that and for this, but you didn't have to come. It's late. You should have just gone home."

"Nonsense, I didn't know what was going on. No one would tell me anything at the hospital, not even Simon." She steered Addie toward her Jeep.

"I can walk. It's not that far to my shop."

"Not in this weather. With this wind and now the snow starting, it looks like the nor'easter came sooner than expected, and they say it's only going to get a lot worse." Serena pulled her collar up over her face. "Besides . . ." Her voice was muffled by the wind and her wool coat. "I'm starving, so we need to eat before we get snowed in tonight."

Addie dropped into the passenger seat, shivered, and brushed the snow from her hair. "Me, too. Where do you want to go?"

"Mario's, it's close."

"Come in, come in, Signorina Greyborne, Signorina Chandler." Mario's glistening teeth beamed through a broad smile. Addie figured the smell of the food would entice her even if Mario lost his smile and booming welcome. "I have a table for you right this way."

He took Addie's arm and swept them to a table at the back of the restaurant. Short room dividers topped with potted plants created smaller intimate dining areas in the large room. Addie settled into a chair facing the main room. Serena took the seat opposite looking toward an Italian garden wall mural.

"May I take your jackets?" He filled their water glasses.

"Maybe in a few minutes after I've warmed up, thanks." Serena rubbed her hands together, shivering, and smiled up at him.

He bowed, clicked his heels, and headed back to the front counter.

Addie stood up and removed her coat. Her face turned ashen.

"What's the matter?"

She dropped into her seat and leaned forward. "Look, there by the front corner table."

Serena spun around in her chair and stood up to see over the leafy planters. "It's Catherine. I wonder who she's with."

"That"—Addie picked up her water goblet and took a long sip—"is Jonathan Hemingway."

Chapter 4

Addie slid her red and white Mini Cooper into a parking space behind a black Land Rover with New York plates. Her fingers clutched hard around the steering wheel. "Well, Jonathan, by the looks of that high-end vehicle, business must be good, whatever business it is these days." She jammed her car into park and slammed her door for emphasis. Picking her way through the wind-swept snowdrifts, she finally made it to the front door of Catherine's nineteenth-century two-story, salt-box-styled house.

Catherine answered the doorbell, a glass of white wine in her hand. "Addie, what on earth are you doing out in this storm? Come in, come in." She stepped back for her to enter.

"Thanks, it is rather nippy out there. I just wanted to make sure you got home all right." Addie peeked around the corner into the living room. She looked coolly at Jonathan reclining on the sofa in front of the window. "But I see you're home safe and sound."

"Yes, thanks to Jonathan rescuing me," Catherine

giggled. "I was trudging up the hill loaded down with my parcels, and he offered me a ride."

"I see." Addie glanced back at him. The sparkling lights from the Christmas tree in the corner reflected a rainbow pattern over the surface of his wineglass.

"Yes, then after he unloaded my bags and we ran a few errands, he invited me out to dinner." A smile spread across her face.

"How thoughtful of him." Addie's gaze drilled into his. He nodded, raising his glass to her. If he would have winked, she would have smacked the smirk off his face, too.

"Yes, we had a most enjoyable meal."

"I guess it's lucky for me that I didn't miss you, then." She returned her gaze to Catherine. "I would have been beside myself with worry if you weren't home yet."

"We've just gotten back. So, this was good timing. But come in, please. Join us for a glass. It might warm you up." Catherine motioned toward the living room.

"I don't mind if I do." Addie swept past Catherine and dropped into a chair across the coffee table from Jonathan.

"Good to see you again so soon, my dear."

"I bet you are." She smiled sweetly at him, hoping the sugar shock alone would render him mute. "So, tell me, Jonathan, I thought your plan was to leave right after lunch to stay ahead of the storm. Now it appears you're in the middle of it." She removed her jacket and laid it across her lap.

"Here, let me hang that up for you." Catherine took her coat.

"What are you doing here?" Addie leaned across the table and hissed.

"He's here because I invited him," Catherine called

from the hallway. When she returned, her cheeks had taken on a flushed hue. "This afternoon after we unloaded my shopping, we went to the hotel to book a room for Jonathan until the storm passes, but by then they were full up. Jonathan was kind enough to bring me home while we figure out his options for the night."

Addie's brows shot up. "Really, and what have you come up with?"

Jonathan's lips twitched, and Catherine clapped her hands. "Red or white?"

Addie looked at her.

"Wine?"

"Umm, white please, thanks."

When Catherine left the room, Addie leaned closer to him. "What are you doing here?"

"You heard her. I gave her a lift, and then we had dinner."

"And?"

"And nothing, Addie. It's all completely innocent."

"With you? Never," she snorted, and slumped against the back of the chair, crossing her arms.

Catherine swept back into the room, handed Addie a glass of wine, and made herself comfortable on the sofa. "Jonathan and I were just talking about you." She smiled at Addie. "He commented on my wide range of books, and I was telling him that since you've taken over as chair for the book club, you've gotten me interested in so much more than those steamy novels I used to read." She took a sip of her drink and gazed into Jonathan's eyes.

Addie cringed when he reached over and patted Catherine's hand. She stood up and walked over to the bookcase. "Yes, it is very diverse. We have everything from *Wuthering Heights, Madame Bovary,* and *Lady Chat-*

terley's Lover"—her fingers traced the spine titles—"to Agatha Christie, Poe, Nathaniel Hawthorne, and everything in between." She spun around, smiling at Catherine and ignoring the fact that Jonathan was now holding her hand. "I'm glad the club has taken some of my suggestions." She made her way back to her seat, trailing her fingers over the piano keys on her way past, and flopped down in her chair beside it. "So, if the hotel is full, where are you planning on staying? I hear the Grey Gull Inn is lovely."

"No, it's full, too," Catherine said. "When we were at the hotel, I had them check around for us and"—she shrugged—"there's not a room anywhere within two hundred miles."

"So, then where are you going to stay?" Addie's eyes narrowed.

He looked at her, swirling his wine in his glass and peering at her over the rim. "If the storm lasts longer than one night"—he glanced at Catherine—"I honestly don't know."

"What do you mean?" Addie leaned forward, setting her glass down.

"Catherine was such a dear and just offered me one of her guest rooms for tonight."

Addie leapt to her feet. "You can't be serious." She glanced at Catherine's shocked expression and sat back down. "Wouldn't you be more comfortable at my house? Being family and all, you should have called me." Her voice dripped honey. He hadn't become speechless as she'd hoped earlier. Maybe he just needed a little extra dose of sweetness. But maybe that was impossible given how he took his coffee.

"That's very kind of you to offer. Perhaps tomorrow." His thumb stroked small circles over the back of Catherine's hand. "I've had a few of these"—he tipped

his glass—"and have settled in nicely for the evening."
He leaned back on the deep sofa.

"It's just that your longer visit comes as such a nice
surprise, and we do have so much catching up to do."
Addie's jaw twitched. "I'm sure Catherine has other
things to do besides entertain a house guest. Didn't
you tell me you were busy preparing for family coming
for the holidays?" She looked at Catherine.

Catherine waved her hand. "It's no trouble, really. I
have plenty of room and generally end up spending
my evenings just sitting and reading. It's wonderful to
have a house guest who's so well versed in the classics
to discuss them with. In fact, I was just thinking that
Jonathan would be welcomed to stay as long as he
needs to. You know with the weather and all." She took
a sip of her wine. Droplets dribbled down her chin.

"Here, let me get those for you, my dear." Jonathan
reached over and traced his finger over her lips, re-
moving the trickles of wine.

Addie rose to her feet. "No, really, Jonathan. I insist
you stay with me. Besides, Police Chief Chandler will
want to speak to you."

He looked at her. "The police? Why?"

"Because . . . you had lunch with Teresa Lang today."
Her jaw flinched and she glanced at Catherine.

He edged to the front of the sofa. "So? That's not
against the law. We're old friends."

"It might be against the law if you were the last person to see her alive."

"What?" He jumped to his feet. "Teresa's dead?"

Addie nodded. "And you had lunch with her right
before her body was found."

"But we didn't have lunch." Addie's brow arched at
Jonathan's outburst. "Honest, we only had coffee, and
then she got a call and said she'd have to take a rain

check on lunch. I left right after that. I swear she was alive, in her office, when I left."

"Did anyone see you leave?"

He pressed his lips together and shook his head. "There wasn't anyone at the reception desk. On my way by, I noticed a sign saying, BE BACK IN ONE HOUR."

"What time was that?"

"About eleven."

"I think the police are going to want to speak with you anyway. Maybe I should drive you to the station."

"Surely it can wait until morning." Catherine stood up. "I can vouch for the fact that Jonathan picked me up shortly after that, so he wasn't at lunch with Teresa."

"Okay, I guess since you plan on staying in Greyborne Harbor for the night, Jonathan, it probably won't hurt if you go by first thing in the morning." Addie jumped at the sound of a sharp crack against the window.

Catherine pulled back the curtain and peered out. "It's just the wind, looks like my old maple tree will be lucky to survive this storm."

"Yeah." Addie took a slow, deep breath, bringing her breathing back to normal. "It's probably not a good night to go out anyway, but you'd better both go in tomorrow and make a statement. Marc will want you to corroborate Jonathan's whereabouts."

"We will"—Catherine glanced at Jonathan— "won't we?"

He ran his fingers through his thick hair. "Yeah, we will."

Addie wanted to check if he had crossed his fingers while fussing with his hair. "I guess I'd better be off before the roads get too bad. Are you sure I can't change your mind about you staying with me?" She steadied her gaze on Jonathan's expressionless face.

He shook his head.

"No, it's fine." Catherine took her arm and steered Addie toward the front door, retrieving her coat from the closet. "Really. Don't worry. I'll take good care of him for you. He's your family after all."

"Not really. David and I were only engaged when—"

"I know"—Catherine's voice lowered, and she squeezed Addie's hand—"but family nonetheless." She kissed Addie's cheek. "Drive safely. Call if you have any problems on the way home." Addie nodded and pulled her collar up, braced against the wind, and made her way through the snowdrifts to her car.

Addie hopped in and sat staring at the house. The blood boiling in her veins took away the chill of the storm raging outside her windshield. She pulled her phone out of her purse and sent a text to Marc.

Jonathan still in town, staying at Catherine's. I'm just leaving there in case you want to talk to him.

She started her car and began to pull out onto the road. Her text alert pinged, and she stopped.

Can you stop by the station before you go home?

She typed, **On my way**, and headed for the police station.

Addie parked as close as she could to the main doors and cringed when the knee-high snow covered her legs. "Skinny jeans and ankle boots just aren't the thing to wear in this." She stomped her feet all the way up the stairs to the door and stumbled into the waiting room.

Carolyn lifted her head. "Addie, the chief's waiting for you, go on in."

"Thanks."

"Are we still all on for Christmas dinner?"

Addie stopped. "As far as I'm concerned, we are. Is it still good for you and Pete?"

"Yeah, I'm planning on cooking a small ham to go along with the turkey. I hope that's okay with you?"

"My mouth is watering already." Addie grinned and headed into Marc's office.

"Close the door." He never bothered to look up from writing in his notebook. "So, a family dinner, hey?" He set his pen down and looked at her.

"You heard that?"

"Couldn't help it. You and the good doctor seem to be seeing a lot of each other lately."

"Have you been spying on me?"

"Nope, just seen the two of you out and about." She squirmed in her chair under his gaze. "Tell me, have you called him David yet when he kisses you?"

A hot flash raced up from under her collar to her cheeks.

"I'd say no, or there wouldn't be a family dinner planned." His gaze never cut away.

She flung her hand up in a stop motion. "That's not fair. How many times do I have to apologize? It was a slip of the tongue."

"Was it?" He leaned forward on his elbows.

"Yes, David and I had been together for years. We were engaged. You knew that. It just slipped out, force of habit, I guess. I've told you that." She stiffened her shoulders and met his hardened gaze. "So, what's up? Why did you call me in? Just to ask me about Simon?" She rubbed her rapidly freezing hands together.

He pursed his lips and leaned back in his chair, tapping his pen on the desk. "How much do you know about Jonathan Hemingway?"

She shrugged and blew out a quiet breath of relief over the change of topic. "I told you most everything I do know. He's David's father, he's divorced from Mary,

David's mother, has been for years. Umm, I don't know where he lives other than what I said earlier. Why?"

"Where does he work?"

"He worked for years as an antiquity and rare-book retrieval specialist, like David, but every time he visited, he seemed to be working someplace new." She shrugged. "I'm not sure what his latest job is. He never seemed to be able to hold one down." She edged closer to the front to her chair. "Why all the questions? Did you find out something about him I should know? God"—her hand shot to her mouth—"Catherine's alone with him. Is she in danger?"

"I don't think so, but I'll dispatch a car just to keep an eye on things there tonight. We won't bring him in until morning. I doubt he'll be going anywhere in this weather. Besides, the area highways are all closed."

"Marc, you're scaring me. What's going on?"

He blew out a deep breath and tapped the corner of the envelope on the desk. His jaw soon ticked in unison with the thumping of his finger.

"Tell me what you found."

"It's what I didn't find." He stood up and came around the desk, leaning against it.

"That's good, isn't it?"

"Not if the person you run a background check on didn't exist before 1977."

"What?"

"There are no records of this Jonathan Hemingway before that date."

"Then you didn't trace the right guy. Maybe there's another one, someone born that year?"

He shook his head. "We triple-checked every database we have access to. There's nothing, no birth certificate, no school records, no social security number, no driver's license, nothing before 1977 when all those and a marriage certificate were issued."

"That's impossible," she croaked.

"Nope, before that, he's a complete ghost."

Chapter 5

A tantalizing smell tickled her nose. Addie snuggled deeper into her pillow and downy comforter. Her eyes flew open. The light through the window seemed unusually bright for an early winter morning. She bolted upright and looked at the bedside clock. Nine a.m.

She grabbed her robe from the foot of the bed and headed downstairs toward the unmistakable aroma of bacon cooking. The clanking of pots and pans coming from the kitchen hastened her steps, and she grabbed a candlestick from a side table in the hallway, brandished it over her head, and peeked around the doorway into the kitchen. Immediately she recognized the intruder's chiseled profile framed by shocks of black wavy hair dangling over his brow, and her hand dropped to her side. "Simon? What on earth are you doing here?"

He looked up from chopping onions on the island, tears streaming from his eyes, and beamed at her. "Good morning, sleepyhead. I was afraid you'd sleep right through breakfast, but you're just in time. Voilà." He waved his hand.

She crept over to the counter and peered at the delights laid before her. "Wow, this looks amazing, but I can't possibly eat that much first thing in the morning."

"I have it on very good authority that you can." He dumped a pan of scrambled eggs into a serving dish.

"Who's good authority?"

"Mine." Serena popped her red head out of the pantry door. "Surprise." She carried over a box of table salt in her hand.

"When did you get here?"

"About thirty minutes ago."

"But shouldn't you be at your store?" Addie glanced at the wall clock.

"Nope." She set the box down beside Simon. "I thought I told you that I hired a friend of Paige's to help out over the holidays."

"If you did, I don't remember, sorry."

"Yeah, pretty sure I did, but it doesn't matter. There's been a lot going on lately. But I decided that if you can afford an assistant, then I should be able to, as well, and she's working out great. I might just keep her on after the holidays."

"That's good." A beat of silence filled the air. "Crap. Paige. I should text her and tell her I'm running late."

"Already done." Serena smiled.

"You did that?"

"Yup, it's the least I could do when I saw what Simon was up to here."

"I just can't believe I missed hearing all this"—Addie's hand swept over the food—"and you coming in?"

"You were sleeping rather soundly." Simon cocked his brow and looked at her. "Did you know that you snore, just a wee"—he pinched two fingers together—"bit."

"I do not."

"You do, too." His sea-blue eyes creased up around the corners. "I checked on you a couple of times just to make sure you were still breathing, but only had to go halfway up the stairs and I knew you were fine."

Addie flopped down on a counter stool, certain she was still dreaming. "What are the two of you doing here, and why"—she waved her hand over the spread of food—"all this and calling Paige for me? Do you both think I need a babysitter?"

"No, but you have to admit that you had a pretty rough day yesterday, finding a dead body and then discovering your sixty-thousand-dollar book was missing."

Simon came around the island and kissed her cheek. "Besides, I missed seeing you last night. This case is turning out to be quite a puzzle, and I ended up working late in the lab."

"And I didn't hear from you and was worried. Simon was already here cooking up a storm and invited me to stay for breakfast. How could I refuse an invitation like that?"

Addie shook her head. "You guys are really too much. Thank you."

Simon passed Addie a fresh-brewed coffee. "I must admit, though, that I was afraid you were going to sleep right through until lunch, and then Serena and I would have to eat all this by ourselves. Then we'd have to start all over again preparing lunch."

"No worry there." She picked up the coffee and took a sip. "I've never slept until noon in my life."

"Now taste this"—he held a forkful of scrambled eggs to her lips—"and tell me these aren't the best eggs you've ever had. They have my secret ingredient in them."

Addie clamped her lips over the eggs and swallowed.

Her eyes lit up. "Mmm . . . they're delicious. What's the secret ingredient?"

His usual bright blue eyes darkened. "I'm sorry. If I told you . . . then I'd have to kill you."

Addie's eyes flew wide open. "What did you say?"

"Too soon?" He quipped and fed her another fork-ful of eggs. "It was a joke. I would never—"

"Isn't that saying from a spy novel or movie?"

"Yeah, I remember hearing that line in an episode of"—Serena scratched her head—"I don't remember, but it was that television show about the crime-solving author who worked with the pretty police detective."

"I remember that." Addie snatched a piece of bacon from the platter and chewed thoughtfully. "Isn't there a scene where the author finds out his father was a se-cret agent or a spy or something?"

"I think so."

"What does this have to do with my award-winning eggs?" Simon frowned.

Addie studied her forkful of fluffy eggs before shov-ing it in her mouth. "You won a cooking award for eggs?"

"My mom made one and posted it on the fridge." He thrust out his broad chest. "So, yes."

She rolled her eyes and snorted. "Serena, what in most every movie or novel is a secret agent called?"

Serena frowned and shrugged her shoulders.

Simon whirled an eggy spatula about. "A spy?"

"No, a ghost." Addie clapped her hands together. "That's it. I have to talk to Marc." She snatched two more pieces of bacon and raced out of the kitchen.

"But what about breakfast?" Serena called.

"Enjoy it," she hollered back over her shoulder as she took the stairs two at a time. In record time, Addie washed, dressed, grabbed her purse and keys, and flung the front door open. "Jonathan? Catherine?"

"Morning, Addie," Jonathan nodded. "I hope you don't mind us dropping by. Paige said you were running late today, so we might still catch you here."

"No, come in." She stepped back from the door. "The more the merrier," she mumbled, closing the door behind them.

Simon walked out from the kitchen. "Good morning, Catherine," he nodded, "and . . ."

"Simon, this is Jonathan, David's father."

"Nice to meet you, sir." Simon shook his hand. "Are you hungry? There's lots of food. Come on back to the kitchen, Serena's already in there."

Addie waited for her uninvited guests to wander off to the kitchen and then whispered, "Glad you've made yourself so comfortable in *my* home."

"You gave me a key and said I was welcome to use your kitchen anytime, remember?"

"Yes . . . but for emergencies only. It's not my fault your new apartment comes with nothing but a cook plate in it."

"Well, this was an emergency. You needed a proper meal, and I needed to see you." He kissed her brow.

She opened her mouth to speak, but he pressed his finger over her lips. "And as far as me inviting them in, I was just being friendly. You might try it some time." He kissed her gently on the nose this time.

She screwed up her face and gave him a sidelong glance.

A laugh bubbled up in his chest and he swatted her butt. "Come on, your guests look hungry."

"*Your* guests," she mumbled under her breath, and followed him into the kitchen.

Serena had already set the kitchen table with two more settings and directed Jonathan and Catherine to their seats. "You guys sit here." She glanced at Addie and Simon as they entered and then produced serving plate after serving plate of scrambled eggs, bacon, sausages, flapjacks, and toast.

Addie's eyes widened with each platter deposited. "This is really too much food, Simon. How will we ever get through it?"

"I don't know about you"—Jonathan took a forkful of pancakes from the platter—"but I'm starving."

"This looks wonderful." Catherine buttered a slice of toast. "Talk about perfect timing to drop by."

Addie set her fork down. "Jonathan, did you happen to speak with Marc this morning?"

"I did"—Jonathan popped a slice of bacon into his mouth—"and everything's fine. All cleared up."

"All cleared up, huh?"

His hand stopped, a scoopful of eggs trembling in midair. His eye slightly twitched at the corner. "Yes, all cleared up." He dropped the eggs onto his plate.

"That's good to hear." She went back to her plate, trailing the food in circles around it with her fork. "I was just worried because—"

"Like I said," his tone sharpened, "all cleared up."

How had such a great man like David come from the loins of the . . . the . . . Addie couldn't think of a harsh enough word, but still wondered on David's paternity. The lively conversation around her pulled her from her funk. Simon and Jonathan appeared to hit it off, and Serena and Catherine had a tug-of-war going on between the two of them over who could mother hen the group best. Addie's eyes darted back to Jonathan whenever he laughed or spoke. What was it about him that bothered her? She wasn't sure, but she couldn't shake the feeling.

Finally, when coffee was served, Addie couldn't hold her tongue any longer. "So, Jonathan, tell me. When you were having coffee with Teresa in her office, did she show you the copy of *A Christmas Carol*?"

"Why, yes, she was most proud of it. Very excited about the rather large donation, too. Why?" His gaze never wavered from hers.

"It's just that the book is in such fantastic condition. I know you'd appreciate seeing it." Addie fidgeted with her napkin on the table. "It's just too bad that it's gone missing now."

"It has?" His jaw flinched.

"Didn't Marc mention that when you saw him?"

Jonathan looked back at her. "No, he didn't. Perhaps they found it."

"Yes, that must be it." She returned his hardened gaze.

He pushed his chair away from the table. "Are you done, my dear?" He held his hand out to Catherine.

"Yes, I suppose so." She set her coffee cup down.

"I think then we'd best be off. We've kept these good people long enough, and I'm sure they all have their *real* jobs to get to." He glanced at Addie. "It's been wonderful, truly." He looked at Simon and Serena. "Thank you. I can't say how long it's been since I've had such a fantastic home-cooked meal with such pleasant table companions."

Simon glanced sideways at Addie, who made no effort to rise. "Um, I'll walk you out, then."

The trio made their way out of the kitchen door.

"What just happened?" Serena whispered. "Why did he nearly bolt out of here?"

"That's what I'd like to know."

Chapter 6

Addie drummed her fingers across the front counter. She peeked around the corner into Marc's office. He sat hunched over his computer, a cup of coffee steaming in his hand. She maneuvered around the empty reception desk and rapped on his partially open door.

"Miss Greyborne, what can I do for you?" The corners of his lips lifted in a smile.

"Hi, sorry to drop by, I was just on the way to my store. If you're busy, I can come back."

"No." He waved her in. "Come in, please. Have a seat."

"I was wondering if"—she blew out a quiet, pent-up breath and settled on the edge of a chair—"if Jonathan had come in this morning to talk to you?"

"As a matter of fact, I did want to talk to you about him. There are a couple of things we need to clear up."

"Okay . . ." She eyed him. "But I've told you everything I know."

"It's what I know now"—he pulled a file from the

basket on his desk—"and I thought I should tell you since he is . . . kind of family to you."

"I must admit I am surprised to hear he actually did drop in and see you. He told me this morning he had, but sometimes I'm not sure whether to believe him or not."

"He did. First thing, too, and it's all good now."

"That's exactly what he said. What was his explanation for the missing years of his life?"

"It appears to be an ongoing problem he's had."

"How so?"

Marc leaned back. "Well, I guess his earlier records were filed under a misspelling of his name, and it wasn't corrected until 1977."

"And you believed him?"

"He called his lawyer and had me speak with him to confirm. It sounded legit, so I guess, yeah, it does happen."

"He dialed the lawyer or you did?"

"He did. Why does it make a difference? I spoke with him."

"Could you do me a favor?"

"What's that?"

"Check out the number and the lawyer."

He crossed his arms and studied her face. "What's up, Addie?"

"Nothing, just my stomach acting up again, I guess."

"Acting up like in one of your gut feelings?" His gaze dropped to her lips, being chewed quite diligently. "Okay, I will, but it won't lead to anything. I can tell you that right now."

"Yes, but how can you be certain you spoke with his lawyer, and it wasn't someone pretending to be his lawyer?"

"Because he gave me his Bar Association number

along with other credential information, and after we'd hung up, he e-mailed me all the records I needed. Jonathan's birth certificate, school records, driver's license, everything we couldn't find before showing Hemingway with two *m*'s and then the 1977 correction to one *m*. Mystery solved."

"That's very convenient of him to have all those at his fingertips, don't you think? Are they real government-issued documents or forgeries?"

"As real as the government seals stamped on them."

"Marc, I know that forged seals on scanned copies can easily pass as legitimate ones when you don't have the original document to compare it to. My father came across it plenty of times in his work. Unscrupulous brokers and criminals do it all the time on certificates of sale and authenticity and Lord knows what else."

"I do know how to do my job." Tiny shivers raced up her spine. The piercing look in his eyes on hers told her she'd overstepped. "But if it makes you feel better." He shrugged. "I'll dig deeper. I have a friend with the FBI who I can call."

She blew out a silent breath of relief. "What about the phone number, do you still have it?"

"He made the call on his phone." Marc tapped his pen on the desktop.

"Can you run a trace on his phone?"

"I can, but I'd need a court order to do that."

"See if your friend at the FBI can help with that, too?"

"Addie." He leaned forward across the desk, his eyes searching hers. "I think you're looking for villains where there are none."

"Maybe, but I think I might be on to something. I think he's a spy or a secret government agent."

Marc's grin matured into a full-blown smile. "Look at it this way, Miss Snoopy. If he were a government agent, why would his target objective be a local charity foundation coordinator who poses no threat to national or international security?"

"We don't know that for sure, do we?" She shifted in her chair.

His smile grew, and he sat back. His fingers interlocked behind his head. "You've been reading those Jason Bourne novels again, haven't you?"

She ignored his comment. "But if not that, then maybe he's part of an international crime ring. I have wondered about that before with all his jobs." She quashed his sigh with a glare. "That fellow you spoke with on the phone might have been a mob lawyer trying to cover Jonathan's true identity." She sat back, crossing her arms. "Did you think about that, Mr. Smarty-pants?"

"He was David's father, and if the David you loved was anything like him, I doubt he's a bad guy or a spy, whatever it is you're thinking. It's nothing more than a simple clerical error."

At the mention of David's name from his lips, again Addie gulped, and looked past him out of the window, biting the inside of her cheek so the sting in his words didn't develop into tears in her eyes.

"Addie, I'm sorry—"

"Don't be, you're right. Like father like son. I suppose it's just my imagination running wild again. Forget what I said."

Without saying a word, he rose and walked around the desk, dropped into the chair beside her, and took her hand in his. Goose bumps erupted on her arms. After all this time, she couldn't believe this man still had the same effect on her. She took a deep breath to try to put her erratic beating heart back where it belonged: in her chest.

He leaned closer. "Is there anything else I can help you with?"

There it was again, the wild pounding in her throat. If they were as they had been before, she'd have a witty comeback, but now . . . she had nothing. "Um, yes." She turned to him, their eyes locking. Heat crept up from under her collar as her mind attempted to come up with something that would give her a reason to stay and wouldn't break this moment between them. "Do you have the results of Teresa's toxicology screen back?"

He dropped her hand. "Isn't that a question you could have asked Simon, your boyfriend?"

Not the response she'd hoped for. "I've told you before, he's my friend, not my boyfriend. I don't have a boyfriend." The words burned in her throat.

He stood up and perched on the edge of his desk. "Does he know that?" His eyes never wavered from hers.

"What does that mean?" She studied the wood grain in the armrest.

"Nothing." He sucked in a sharp breath. "The tox screen." He reached behind him and picked up a file, flipped through the papers, and pulled a page out. "Here it is. Tell me, why should I share this with you?"

She squared her shoulders. "If I remember correctly, I was consulted in another case the DA felt you needed my help with"—his mouth dropped open—"and if I'm not mistaken, I am still on your suspect list for this one, at least I haven't been told otherwise."

"Which is exactly why I can't share the contents of this report with you." His eyes bore into hers.

"I see." She picked up her purse and stood up.

"Wait." He raked his fingers through his hair, causing brown tufts to stand straight up. "I will tell you she had been drinking as you suspected when you found her body."

"Really, so it was an accident? Am I cleared, then?"

"I didn't say that." He tossed the file back on his desk.

"Then what are you saying?"

"I'm just telling you everything I can right now, and by the way, as it stands, this is still not a murder investigation until proven otherwise."

"I see. So, for now, I remain on your potential list in case you do discover it to be murder?"

His jaw flinched. She headed for the door and stopped. "Did you find the book by chance?"

"Not yet."

"What did Patrick say about it?"

"He said the last time he saw it, it was in the case in her office."

"When was that?"

"Yesterday morning"—he walked toward her—"before he went downstairs to coordinate the convention room setup."

"He doesn't know if she moved it?"

"No, he has no idea where it might be."

"Did he know where she kept the key for the case?"

"He said she always had it with her and wore it on the key ring on her wrist, the same one that was found in the case. If that's all, then?" He motioned to the door, his eyes softening.

Her breath caught in her throat, and she could only nod. She opened the door and then paused. "Did you check all her locked file cabinets and—"

"Of course." His eyes narrowed. "I'm a trained police officer." He mumbled something under his breath that sounded suspiciously like "unlike you," but she couldn't be certain and decided to ignore his pouting anyway.

"I know you are, but . . . I have to be certain. That book is worth a lot of money. Did you find any notes in her office about it, something in her desk drawer, anything that might lead to a special hiding place she might have had in the office or at home?"

"Are you insinuating that you, an amateur detective, knows the job better than my highly trained crime-scene investigation team does?" The corner of his lip twitched.

A cough came from behind her. She glanced over her shoulder at Jerry, one of Marc's officers, red-faced, sitting in the desk sergeant's seat. She leaned her hand against the doorframe and glared at Marc. "Of course not. Your team is excellent, but I think that book has been stolen because there are too many coincidences. Like Jonathan with his mysterious past showing up and him being an old friend of Teresa's, and now she's dead. On top of all that, a sixty-thousand-dollar book has been stolen."

Mark let out a long, slow breath. "First, the mystery around Jonathan has been answered. Second, Teresa had been drinking, and she obviously took a fall down the stairs. Third, we don't know if the book has been stolen, or if it's just missing because the key ring she always wore was in the lock. She probably moved it because there is no proof to the contrary." His hand scoured through his hair. "You're not going to let this go, are you?"

She shook her head. "My gut tells me Teresa's fall wasn't an accident, and Jonathan's arrival in the Harbor a week and a half before the auction is all connected to the missing book."

"Your gut feeling again?"

She nodded.

"I'll keep that in mind, but for once and for all, please leave police work up to the *police*. Have a good day, Miss Greyborne."

"Well, I never," she huffed out a breath as his office door closed. She glanced sideways at Jerry, who sat silently watching her and leaned over the desk. "You know," she whispered, "what I said was in no way implying you and your team—"

"I know, miss." His lips twitched up at the corners.

"You're a great officer and very good at your job. I just don't want there to be any hard feelings."

"No worries, miss."

"Good." She pulled her gloves on and headed for the door.

"Miss Greyborne," he called out behind her, coming around the desk. He glanced around the empty waiting room and at Marc's closed door before leaning toward her. "There were two coffee cups."

"I know." She frowned. "I saw them on the desk."

He shook his head. "Not the ceramic ones. I probably shouldn't tell you this, either, but there were two paper cups in the waste basket under her desk."

"So, she liked coffee. I do, too."

"The interesting thing is one cup had the same red lipstick markings as the one on the desk, but the other one . . ."

"Yes, what are you saying, Jerry?" she prodded.

"That it also had lipstick marks on it, but it was a different color. It reminded me of the shade my wife wears." He stuck his hand in his pocket, pulled out a piece of paper, and handed it to her. "When I went home, I smeared some of my wife's on this napkin. Apparently, the shade is Dark Honey-Peach. Although I've never seen a honey peach before. Have you?"

She turned the napkin over in her hand. "Any finger-prints on the cup?"

He shook his head. "Sorry, only smudges. But I gave the cups to Doc Emerson to test."

"Interesting." She bit on her lower lip. "What did the lab test show about the contents?"

He shuffled from one foot to the other and glanced back at Marc's door. "As the chief said, she'd been drinking, but that's all I can say. You'd have to ask Doc Emerson about anything else."

"Okay, I will. How long till the DNA results come back?"

He shrugged. "It takes a few weeks, but I thought you might be interested to know that your relative wasn't the only one there, and his cup did only contain coffee and a lot of sugar."

"Thanks for letting me know." She laid a hand on his upper arm. "I hope you don't get into trouble on my account."

His neck above his collar turned red. "It's no trouble." But his gaze flicked to Marc's office door.

She bit the inside of her cheek to keep a smile from forming. "How often does the housekeeping staff clean the offices? Is there any chance the cups might have been in the trash can for a few days?"

"Nope"—he rocked back on his heels and tucked his thumbs in his belt—"they're cleaned every night. So that means—"

"Besides Jonathan, she had a female visitor bearing alcohol yesterday." Her eyes lit up. "Thanks, Jerry, for everything." She kissed his cheek, shoved the napkin in her pocket, and dashed out the door.

Chapter 7

Addie checked her phone clock, sent a quick text to Paige, and made her way through the slush across Main Street to Fielding's department store. The scent of a pungent perfume cocktail assaulted her nose, even before she saw the COSMETIC DEPARTMENT sign. She made her way past the jewelry department and smiled at the familiar face behind the counter. It was refreshing to see Ida in her natural work environment. Usually, Addie was only exposed to her birdlike features peering at her over the top of a book at one of their monthly book club meetings. "Good morning." Addie pulled off her gloves, rubbing her chilled hands together.

"Addie, what a nice surprise." Ida glanced at her watch. "Shouldn't you be at your store? Is everything okay?"

"I'm just running a few errands. Paige is there. All's fine."

"Good, with this storm brewing, one never knows. What can I do for you today?"

"I'm interested in some lipstick."

"Then you've come to the right place." She reached under the counter and produced a sample tray of lipstick shades.

"Excellent." Addie scanned the color palette tray. "I'm thinking this one." She pointed to the Dark Honey-Peach shade Jerry had smeared on a napkin. She put her hand in her coat pocket and fingered the scrap of paper and hoped her hunch was right.

Ida shook her head. "That's not really a good one for your coloring. Can I suggest something in a muted plum or wine shade?"

"Thanks, but"—Addie tapped her finger on the palette—"I'm just interested in this one."

"I know it's a popular shade right now. Everyone is wearing it . . . even those who shouldn't." She pinned Addie with a knowing look.

"I didn't realize it was the season's hottest color."

"Yes, and it's perfect on Serena with her skin tone, Catherine, too, in fact. They both bought some recently, but trust me. It's not the right shade for you. Try this one." She dipped a brush into the pale strawberry-wine shade and held it up. "It's made for a cooler skin tone, like yours."

"That is very nice, but I really want to buy the peach one. It's . . . ah . . . for . . . Serena."

Ida's brow creased. "But she just bought one."

"Yeah . . . but she dropped it in the gutter slush and asked me to pick her up a new one while I was out." Addie pasted a smile on her face.

"Okay." Ida shrugged. "I'll ring it up. Are you sure I can't interest you in the—"

"No, I have lots at home, but thanks." Addie's cheeks began to ache from grinning.

"Here you go." Ida handed her a small bag. "See you at the next book club meeting."

"Yes, right after Christmas, isn't it?"

"Is it that far away? I thought it was next week?" Ida's short, graying cropped hair lay as motionless as a helmet even through her chicken-like head bob. "Silly me, I remember now. We changed the date. So, I guess if I don't see you before then, have a wonderful Christmas."

"You, too, and thanks for this." Addie held up the bag and then stuffed it in her purse.

She made a mental note to tell Serena about the lipstick ploy. She had to cover her bases in case Ida said anything to her. Addie tiptoed across the road through the rapidly building snow back to the hospital entrance and made her way to the elevator. Her eyes focused in on the lips of every woman she passed. Ida was right: It was the season's most popular shade. Then Addie remembered what it was like after she'd bought her Mini Cooper. All she saw were Minis on the road. Perhaps this lipstick shade was acting in the same way, where the mind sees what is familiar and personal, or was everyone actually wearing it?

On her way down the corridor to Simon's office, she passed two nurses and swore they were both wearing the lipstick shade in question. It seemed finding the woman who had been in Teresa's office with her was going to be a much larger task than she'd thought.

Simon's office door flew open. He stepped out and crashed into her. "Addie"—he grabbed her arm to steady to her—"I've told you before we have to stop meeting like this."

"I think you have it planned," she mocked. "Do you have a camera out here so you can see when I'm coming?"

"Hardly, I think all these collisions we have are your way of getting my attention." His warm hand remained on her forearm. Stillness surrounded them. He was the first to break it. "Look, I just have to run this down to the mail room in the basement." He held up a shipping box in his free hand. "I'll be back as soon as I can. Go in and have a seat." He gestured toward his office and disappeared down the hall.

Her arm still tingling from the glow of his touch, she rubbed it, smiling, and made herself comfortable in one of the two leather chairs facing his desk. Simon's office was exactly as he was. Warm and comfortable, sophisticated but not pretentious, and held just the faint hint of his aftershave. The wall behind his desk was a floor-to-ceiling bookcase. She walked toward it and examined the titles. Naturally, most were medical journals and textbooks. She patted a book spine and shuffled back to her chair. Her gaze fell to a file folder on his desk. *Teresa Lang Preliminary Autopsy Report.* She took a quick look at the door, inched sideways toward the document, and flipped it open. Her eyes focused on the entries that had been highlighted.

Blood Alcohol Level: 0.045 – Low

Stomach Contents: There was a long list of chemical and scientific terminology that Addie could make neither heads nor tails of, but the final words she understood clearly. *Probable Sushi Ingestion.*

Cause of Death: Due to blood anomalies and multiple trauma fractures evident on the skeleton, Undetermined at this time.

Addie continued to scan down the page. The office door creaked. The fine hairs on her arms stood upright, and she sprinted around the desk back to a chair, glancing at the door, and noticed her purse propped against the leg of the chair beside her.

Simon's voice echoed from the hallway, the door remaining partially open. "Sounds good, Walter, we can go over it then, thanks."

Addie slipped over to the chair beside her, strummed her fingers on the arms, squelching the guilt manifesting itself as acid rising in the back of her throat.

"Sorry about the delay." Simon stepped inside and closed the door. "The hospital chairman caught me in the corridor and wants to discuss department budgets later." He kissed her cheek on his way to his desk chair. "What do I owe this surprise visit to?"

Addie shifted in her seat. "It's just that after this morning's incredible breakfast, I wanted to see you, and thank you again." Her gaze flicked to the open folder on his desk. Had it been open before or had she opened it before snooping? She couldn't remember. Panic caused her tongue to trip. "And . . . and . . . ah . . . I was just in the neighborhood."

"You already thanked me, numerous times, and you work a block away and rarely drop in for a visit. So I'm guessing this is really about the case." He rested his elbows on the desk. "Am I wrong?"

She let out a deep breath and shook her head. "You're like Serena. You know me too well." Her cheeks grew warm.

"Okay." He cupped his chin in his hand. "What can I help you with?"

"I was wondering if you have the results of Teresa's blood work." Her eyes dropped to the open folder and quickly back to his.

"I hope you made yourself comfortable while you

waited for me." His eyes narrowed as he closed the folder, tapping his fingers on the cover.

She swallowed hard. The heat from her neck crept up to her face. Tiny beads of perspiration formed on her brow.

"Have you been officially consulted in this case?"

"No." Her chin jutted out. "But I found the body. Doesn't that count for something?"

"And . . . your fingerprints were all over the office."

"I know, but I have a witness that I was in my shop all morning and with Serena right up until I found the body."

"Yes." He sat back, his eyes narrowing. "But there is still the case of the missing book."

"Really? You think I stole my book from her?" When he remained silent, she blurted, "If I'd changed my mind about donating it, I'd just have asked for it back and given her another book instead for the auction."

His eyes held fast on hers. "As you are obviously aware"—his cheeks sucked in like he'd just bitten into a lemon—"I have my preliminary results right here."

"Why preliminary? It says . . ." Her voice faded at her blunder. Well, when one stumbles, one must make it look good at least. "Her blood alcohol level was low, wasn't it? Which means it's highly unlikely that she fell, at least on her own."

He tapped the corner of the folder on the desk. "But as I'm sure *you* read, it's what else I found that stumps me."

She gave her most winning smile. "You couldn't understand the words, either?" She stifled a giggle and stopped when she saw the glacial look in his eyes.

"I'm familiar with the words, but they don't make sense in this context."

"I see." She pursed her lips. "Could it be a poison? You know, from the sushi?"

"I don't think so, at best an early case of food poisoning. However, and this is what has me stumped, if it was contaminated sushi, any symptoms would have taken hours to develop not minutes."

"Would early food poisoning symptoms like dizziness have caused her to trip on the stairs?"

He shook his head. "Not that soon after consuming tainted food. The autopsy indicates she had only recently ingested the fish, and her time of death wasn't long after that. You yourself said her skin was still warm when you took her pulse. At that stage, she might have had very mild stomach discomfort or indigestion, but that's all."

"Hum." She shifted in her seat. "I was told that two cups were found in her trash can. Any chance her coffee was spiked?"

"Didn't you read that?" He shoved the folder to the side. She dropped his gaze and shook her head. "They didn't contain coffee. The contents of the cups showed a common whiskey."

"What about the lipstick markings on the rims?"

"Who have you been talking to?"

"A friend." *And his unknowing wife.* She pressed her lips together.

"As a matter of fact, I've sent the cups for DNA analysis to the lab in Salem."

"What about the color of lipstick? I know the red one was Teresa's because she always wears the same shade, and it was on the ceramic cup"—she pulled the small bag out of her purse—"but the other one is closer to this shade from what I was told. Is this any help?" She held up the tube of lipstick.

"Unless it's a custom-made shade, it doesn't tell us much."

"Yeah, it seems it's the hottest color this season." She shoved the lipstick back in her handbag. "So, with all this, we still don't know if she slipped or miscalculated the landing on the lower level or—"

"It all takes time, but time will help determine the actual cause and not speculation."

"I know, but there're just so many weird coincidences that don't add up. It makes me feel there's more to this than her opening the exit door, her shoe heel catching on the top basement step, and falling backward."

"And that's a good possibility, except I have scientific proof"—he tapped the folder—"that the angle and placement of her injuries suggests a face-first fall before her neck was broken."

"Which means she had to have been pushed, right?"

"Not necessarily." He rubbed his eyes. "In this report there are too many other anomalies. So, I can't make a final determination right now on the exact cause of death."

"What's next, then?"

"I've just couriered her blood and tissue samples to an old colleague of mine at the major crime's lab in New York to see if he can find something I can't." He shrugged. "Now we wait and see."

She let out a sharp breath. "That means I remain on the suspect list."

He grinned. "You might be on the list, but I don't think the chief sees you as much of a suspect."

"I hope not." She looked at him. "Do you?"

"Addie." He got up and came around the desk. "Of course not." His lips swept lightly over hers. "I think you are way too smart to kill someone and then be the one to find the body."

He sidestepped her playful jab. Chuckling, she picked up her purse and looped it over her shoulder.

"Where are you off to now? Your store, I hope? I think you've done enough sleuthing around here for one day, don't you?" His narrowed eyes fixed on hers.

"Not quite yet, I have one more stop to make."

He twirled a piece of her hair around his finger. "You aren't going against the chief's orders, are you?"

"What orders?"

"The orders he's decreed about you not doing any investigating?"

"Moi?" She patted her chest and fluttered her lashes. "Not at all, I'm just going to see a man about a book." She pawed at his chest and traipsed to the door.

"Addie? Stay out of trouble."

"Really, how much trouble can I get into at the hospital?" She glanced back over her shoulder, grinning.

Chapter 8

Addie poked her head into the event room in the south wing and spotted Patrick chatting with the ginger-haired woman she remembered seeing at the reception desk on Teresa's floor. He handed her a clipboard and made his way in Addie's direction. "Good morning. As you can see, we're in the final throes here."

"Yes, it looks like you have your hands full."

"You have no idea." A low whistle escaped through his puffed-out cheeks. "So, what can I help you with today?"

"I was hoping to chat for a minute." She glanced around the room swarming with volunteers adding final touches to the setup and decorations.

He swept past her. "Sure, but it'll have to be up in my office. I have a few minor crises to work out."

"No problem." She quickened her pace to keep step with him as he lunged through the stairwell exit door and took the steps up two at a time.

When they reached the third-floor landing, Addie seized the railing, gasping for air. For a stocky man, his short legs could really fly up the stairs. He flung the door open, stepped back, and bumped against her. She teetered backward on the top step, one hand clinging to the rail, her other arm flailing through the air. His hand caught her wrist, and he pulled her safely toward him.

"Now, now." His dark eyes narrowed. His hot, sour breath wafted across her cheek. "We don't need someone else taking a tumble, do we?" His thin lips twitched at the corners as he squeezed her wrist and then let go.

"We certainly don't." She glanced down to the landing below and shivered. She straightened her jacket, took a deep breath. Willing her shaking legs to behave, she followed Patrick down the hall to the offices.

They made their way past the door with the nameplate with PATRICK BARTON – ASSISTANT FOUNDATION CO-ORDINATOR engraved on it and stopped at the end of the hall. He fished a set of keys out of his trouser pocket and swung Teresa's office door open. "Come in." He waved toward a chair as he made his way around the desk and took a seat. He sat back, stretched his short neck, and locked his fingers behind his head. "So, what is it that you wanted to talk to me about?"

Addie gave a tight-lipped smile and perched on the edge of a chair. "I wanted to talk to you about the missing book if you have a few minutes."

"Sure, but I've told the police everything I know."

"I know you have, but I was wondering"—she glanced around the room, noting a change in the decorations since she was last in here—"in your change of office locations, have you come across *A Christmas Carol*?"

He shook his head. "Teresa probably took it home. I know she was concerned about keeping it here after you told her the estimated value of it."

"But didn't you tell the police you'd last seen it in the case the morning she died?"

"I don't remember. It might have been the day before." He started to stand. "Is that it?"

"Not quite." She narrowed her gaze. He returned to his seat. "You told Chief Chandler's men that she always wore the key to the bookcase on a stretch-coiled wristband, is that right?"

"Yes, I saw it on her wrist yesterday morning. Why?"

Addie absently tapped her fingers on her purse. "Well, when I saw the ring, there were two other keys on it aside from the one for the case. Do you happen to know what they were for?"

"Yes, her house key was on it if I remember correctly."

"And?" She leaned forward.

"I don't remember the other one." He shrugged. "Is that important?"

"It could be." His jaw flinched. Her gaze never wavered from his. "That key interests me."

"Why?" His right eye twitched, and he toyed with a file folder on the desk.

"Because if she took the book out and left the key ring with her house key on it in the lock, she obviously didn't go home and take the book with her. So where would she have put the book? That third key must be for another locked compartment close by or even here in the office."

He stood up and leaned across the desk. "You certainly ask a lot of questions for a bookseller, don't you?" He glared down at her. "I have no idea where the book is."

Her eyes widened. "I wasn't saying you did, but I hope you can understand my concern. That book is worth a fortune, and it's missing."

"Yes, I know what you told her it was worth." He stroked his baby-smooth chin, looking more like a pudgy eight-year-old than a man in his mid-thirties.

"According to the certificate of authenticity"—she shifted in her seat—"it's worth even more than I originally calculated, as I told you, and I'm sure you saw that in the documents."

"No, I never saw them." Small beads of perspiration formed on his brow.

"But I left them in an envelope on her desk yesterday just before I found her." She rose to her feet.

"I never saw it."

"Hum, I guess the police must have it for some reason." The door flew open. Addie jerked and spun around, facing the ginger-haired woman.

"I'm sorry, Patrick. I didn't know you had company."

"That's fine, Crystal. Miss Greyborne was just leaving. What can I do for you?"

"It's just that we seem to have a major issue." Her face flushed and she glanced at Addie, her tight-lipped expression noticeably lipstick-free. "And I don't know how you want me to handle it."

Patrick shrugged. "It can't be that bad."

"The highways in the area are still closed, and there's talk of closing the Boston airport, too. I have e-mail inquiries from the out-of-state dealers who'd purchased tickets for the auction. What do I tell them?" She handed him a sheet of paper.

He glanced over it, flung it on the desk, and then walked her to the door. "Tell them we are monitoring the situation closely and will keep them updated when we know more."

Addie pulled her phone from her pocket, leaned over the list, and snapped a photo, just as he closed the door behind Crystal and returned to his seat.

"But you don't have the book." She pointed to the list. "The reason they're all coming."

"I know. I know." He scoured his face with his hand. "I'll figure something out." He tapped his fingers on the arms of his chair. "Look, you have a huge collection of rare books, don't you? Do you have another book of equal value you could donate?" He shook his head when she opened her mouth with a retort. "Never mind. Just trying to problem-solve." His flushed face dripped beads of perspiration.

"If the book doesn't turn up soon, you'll have to tell them the live auction of the book is canceled and refund their ticket money."

"I will, but it will bankrupt the entire foundation if I have to refund two hundred and fifty dollars a ticket. We're in too deep now with our suppliers to even consider that."

"If you don't have the book, you can't keep the ticket money under false pretense. They have a right to know."

"I'm well aware of that." He shot to his feet. "Now, I have work to do as you have just witnessed. Unless there's anything else?" He glowered at her across the desk.

She walked out without a word and then paused mid-step upon hearing Patrick's raised voice echoing through the closed door. She shook her head. He must be on the phone attempting to straighten out the mess the foundation had found itself in. In passing the front desk to the elevators, she noted Crystal gazing in a compact mirror, applying honey-peach lipstick.

"That's a nice shade on you." Addie rested her forearms on the counter. "It really complements your skin tone."

"Do you think?" Crystal snapped the compact mirror closed and dropped it along with the lipstick tube in the top drawer of her desk. "I wasn't sure, especially since after I bought it I found out *everyone* is wearing it this season. So, I'm having second thoughts."

"Nonsense, it looks great on you, and to be honest, not everyone else can pull that color off like you can." She hoped her smile looked more genuine than it felt.

"Thank you so much. I really needed a pick-me-up today."

"I can only imagine. Teresa's death must be hard on everyone."

"Yeah," she shrugged. "I guess so."

Addie flinched with her callous tone. "It's just that"—she glanced back down the empty corridor—"it looks like Patrick is running you ragged to help him pick up the slack. I saw you working downstairs a while ago, and now this." She pointed to the computer.

"Yes." Crystal rolled her eyes. "I was supposed to be flying to the Cayman Islands yesterday to meet my sister for a holiday." She checked over her shoulder and dropped her voice. "But when he found out I was stuck here because the highways to Boston are closed and I couldn't get to the airport, he actually put me to work as *his* assistant of all things."

"That's too bad, about your trip, I mean." Addie eyed the young woman. "You must be really disappointed. All this has changed *your* plans."

"You have no idea. My sister's going to be furious.

She's flying all the way from Sydney to meet me, and I won't be there." Her lip jutted out in a pout.

"Does your sister live in Australia?"

"Yeah, she's just finished her PhD there."

"Nice place to study. What field is she in?"

Crystal squinted and focused on the computer screen.

"Crystal?"

"Huh?" She looked up at Addie blankly. "What?"

"I asked what field she was in."

"Right, sorry. Um . . ." She swallowed. "I don't know." Her shoulders twitched with a slight shrug. "Some nerdy science stuff."

"At least she gets to do *whatever* it is someplace without snowstorms."

"Yeah." Crystal stared at the screen, toying with her cell phone beside her on the desktop.

"But I can see you're busy. I hope you get lucky and the storm passes soon, and this whole mess with Teresa's death and Patrick now using you as his assistant sorts itself out."

"Me, too. It's a pain and definitely not what I signed up for."

"Yes, of course, you wouldn't have." Addie studied Crystal's flat expression. "I'd better be off, too. Good luck with your vacation plans."

"Thanks." She refocused on her computer screen, not giving Addie a second look.

Addie headed down the hall. *Self-centered little . . .* She scoffed and glanced back at Miss Perfect Receptionist, only to see her in the midst of a selfie photo shoot. She snickered and punched the button. The elevator stopped at the second floor. A group of visitors rushed in, pushing Addie against the back wall. She collided with a man jostling to squeeze in behind her and squirmed when his hot breath caressed the back of her neck. When the doors opened on the main level, he shoved forward, propelling her into the lobby. She fought to regain her footing and glared at him as he pushed past her. Out of the corner of her eye she glimpsed a man in a black trench coat slip into the elevator just as the door closed. "Jonathan?" She gazed up at the floor indicator until it stopped at level three.

"What are you up to?" She punched the up button for the elevator, but it stalled in its descent on the second floor. Addie glimpsed the stairwell sign behind her and took the stairs two at a time. The text alert pinged on her phone, and she paused on the second-floor landing.

Powers out at the store, filled with customers, can't open the cash register, do you want me to close?

I'll be right there.

She tapped her reply to Paige on the keypad. The lights in the stairwell flickered; then it went black.

Addie sucked in a deep breath and clutched the handrail. From the floor above, heavy footsteps echoed down the darkened stairwell. Her heart beat a staccato rhythm in her chest and then the emergency lighting switched on. She rushed back down to the first floor, fingers clenched around her purse. She burst through the exit door and rushed into the lobby, taking a quick look over her shoulder. Her eyes locked with Jonathan's as he pushed through the staircase door behind her. Caught up in the wave of visitors heading for the main entrance, she glanced back, but lost sight of him in the crowd stampeding for the street.

Chapter 9

Addie gasped when the frosty air bit into her lungs. The intersection streetlights on Main were flashing in all directions, and traffic was at a standstill. She buried her face in her coat collar and headed next door to the police station parking lot, where she'd left her car earlier. One look at the snowdrifts piled up past the windows of her Mini told her it wouldn't be going anywhere for a while. She braced against the wind and made her way on foot through the knee-deep snow on the sidewalk back to her shop, thankful she'd traded in her ankle boots today for the higher ones.

By the time she reached her shop, she was chilled clear through to the bone. A fiery sensation had crept over her numbed cheeks, the tips of her ears, and her nose. Even so, her heart at least quickly warmed by the delightful cinnamon-spiced Christmas fragrances and the magical ambiance of candles that greeted her. Once again, Paige had demonstrated her resourcefulness and had arranged the reading spaces into neat conversation areas with candles dispersed in strategic locations around the large room. Customers closer to the windows were curled up in the overstuffed leather armchairs, sipping on steaming mugs and quietly reading.

Paige caught sight of Addie and slid up beside her. "I hope you don't mind that I used the candles from the curio shelves and took the three lanterns from the window book display?"

"Heavens no, it's beautiful. Thank you for thinking of it." She looked around the bookshop. "Exactly as it should be and probably would have been a hundred years ago." Addie frowned. "But why is everyone still here? You'd think they'd want to get home in a blackout."

"A few tried to leave and then came right back. With this"—she gestured to the gridlocked street—"they can't even get their cars out of the parking spots right now."

"Of course." Addie rubbed her cold, stung hands together. "Okay, what we need to do now is figure out something about sales since we can't get the cash register open."

"I had a few from people who happened to have exact change, and I told everyone else to sit tight until you got here."

"Right, well, for those who can't or don't want to wait until the power's restored, let's just take hold orders and store them for now."

"Sounds good." Paige began making her rounds, visiting with each customer to explain the checkout plan.

Addie noticed Catherine hunched over at the counter reading a book by lantern light. "Find something good?" Addie leaned over her shoulder.

Catherine stuck her finger in the binding and showed Addie the cover. "Yes, in fact, I did. I found *A Holiday for Murder.*"

"Ah yes, Agatha Christie."

"I'd only read a couple of her books years ago and had no idea what I'd been missing all this time. I love this."

"Are you aware that book you have had at least three title changes over the years?" At Catherine's head shake, Addie pulled up a nearby stool. "It was first released in England as *Hercule Poirot's Christmas* back in 1938. Then the American publisher changed the title in 1939 to *Murder for Christmas.* The copy you have was a paperback version put out in 1947 under a completely new title."

"I don't care what it's called," Catherine laughed softly. "I love it and am glad Jonathan recommended it to me."

"Jonathan?" Addie made an effort to appear that she was scanning the store. "Is he here, too?"

"No, actually he ran out to buy some cigarettes"— she shuddered—"but I thought he'd be back by now."

"Don't worry. The roads are near impossible with all the traffic and with the power out, cash registers won't be working, either. I'm sure he won't be much longer." Addie shrugged.

"You're right. At least it gives me time to read some of this, and then I can discuss it half-intelligently with him tonight."

"Tonight? So he is staying with you again?"

Catherine's lips turned up slightly at the corners, and she returned to her reading.

Addie bit the inside of her cheek. "Catherine, I'm—"

"How wonderful to find the two most beautiful women in the world here together." Jonathan kissed

Catherine's cheek and slid onto the stool beside her. "What have you got there?" He took the book from her hands. "Ah, yes, Dame Agatha Mary Clarissa Christie."

"Did you get your cigarettes?" Catherine looked at him under a raised brow.

"Yes." He patted his coat pocket.

Addie's lips twitched. "That surprises me."

"Why?"

"With the power out, how did they ring in the sale? And besides, I thought you quit that disgusting habit years ago." She bit her bottom lip between her teeth. "At least you told David you had."

He handed the book back to Catherine. His hand cupped hers, but his eyes fixed on Addie's. "Some habits are hard to break."

She looked at Catherine's sparkling eyes and back at him. "Yes, I can see that."

He patted Catherine's hand. "So, tonight, my dear, when I start carrying on about the world's greatest fictional detective of all time, Hercule Poirot, you'll understand who I'm referring to. Because as we all know"—he glanced at Addie—"that's where the best detectives are found, isn't it, between the pages of a book."

"Of course." Addie held his gaze. "But don't forget about Jessica Fletcher and Nancy Drew." Her lips twisted up at the corners in a smirk.

He tossed his head back, laughing.

"Now those are two fictional detectives I do know." Catherine erupted in laughter, joining Jonathan's horselaugh in a disharmonious chorus.

Paige dropped an armful of books on the counter. "There. I've attached sticky notes with the name and phone number of the customer. Now we need a handy place to hold them. Any room under the counter?"

"I've got the perfect thing. Mind if I borrow the lantern, Catherine?" Addie dashed to the back room, returned with a clear plastic bin and lid, placed the books inside it, and shoved it out of the way with her foot. "Done." She smiled at Paige.

The overhead door chimes rang, and Addie glanced up as Marc made his way toward them, a wide grin across his face. "I see you've made the best of the situation here." He glanced around the candlelit room.

"It was all Paige's idea." Addie smiled at her beaming assistant. "She had everything under control by the time I got back from the hospital."

Marc looked at her as the corner of his mouth twitched. "What were you doing there? Never mind, I know what you were doing there. How *is* Simon today?"

Addie's cheek burned. "No, I was checking on a few things. You do remember a very expensive, rare book is still missing, don't you?"

"How many times do I have to remind you not to play detective and leave that up to the police?"

"Funny." Jonathan swung around in his seat toward Marc. "We were just speaking of that and how the best detectives are found between the pages of a novel."

"Well, then." Marc squared his stance. "Please keep reminding our friend here of that because I think she has fact and fiction confused."

Addie scowled at both of them.

Marc's eyes twinkled, and his lips creased up at the corners. "I've just come by to check on everyone who's still open and make an announcement." He nodded at her, turned, and spoke to the remaining customers. "Could I have your attention, please. The traffic exiting the town center has thinned out now; but so you know, the power is out across town. I strongly urge you all to start making your way home before it gets dark."

There was rumbling among the customers, and two people's hands shot up with questions. He held up his hand. "Greyborne Harbor is not the only affected location. The storm has swept across the entire eastern seaboard. Although we are luckier than most as their phone lines are also down. Ours aren't, plus we still have cell tower service, so the Internet is working. However, please do consider heading home now and be careful. Should you require assistance tonight, please continue to call nine-one-one as all lines are operational, at the moment." He tipped his hat rim and glanced over at Addie. The suggestion of a smile pulled at the corner of his lips, but it was quickly replaced by a curt nod, and he left.

"I guess that's our cue, my dear." Jonathan rose to his feet and held Catherine's jacket.

"Can I have you put my book on hold, please?" Catherine slid her arms into the sleeves. Jonathan's fingers lingered on Catherine's neck as he held it for her. Addie's jaw clenched.

"You can take it now. It will give you something *constructive* to do tonight." She glanced sideways at Jonathan, who challenged her with a steady gaze. "Wait, though. Before you go, Jonathan, can I ask you a question?"

"What's that?"

"When I was at the hospital a while ago . . ." His shoulders squared, and his eyes went blank. "I got to thinking. Did Teresa say who called her or why she canceled your lunch?"

"No." If he felt relief over her question and her not calling him out about deceiving Catherine with his actual recent whereabouts, he masked it well. He was good at not expressing a tell. She'd give him that. Not even an unconscious cheek tic, or lower-lip chew like she, according to her friends, reverted to when thinking or stressed. "Teresa just said there were a few issues she had to take care of and she'd have to take a rain check. I told her I'd call her later and left."

"That's it?"

"Yes." He paused buttoning his coat. "But on my way out, her phone rang again, and I overheard her tell the caller, 'That sounds perfect, see you then.' "

"But you don't know who either caller was?"

He shook his head. "She never mentioned any names."

"And you say you left at . . . ?"

"Just after eleven. Why is that important?"

"And you only had coffee with her, nothing stronger?"

"No. Why do I get the feeling I'm being interrogated?"

"Sorry, just trying to figure out why she had an elevated blood alcohol level in the morning. Was she a heavy drinker?"

"No more than most people. She liked a cocktail and maybe a glass of wine with lunch, but nothing more as far as I'm aware." He gave her a crooked grin. "Is that all, Nancy Drew?"

"Yes, sorry. Drive safe." She waved as they left.

Addie walked through the shop, blowing out candles as Paige tidied the front counter. A redhead appeared at the end of a bookcase and Addie jumped. "Serena, you nearly scared the life out of me."

"Are you almost ready to go?"

"Yup, and you?"

"Yeah, I can't wait until I can take a hot bath and finally warm up. My shop furnace is electric, that's why I popped in here for a minute, to thaw out." She shivered and rubbed her hands together. "Where's your car? I didn't see it out back?"

"Oh no," Addie groaned. "I forgot. It's still in the police station parking lot, where I left it this morning. I don't think I'll be able to get it out. Minis weren't made for this weather."

"I'll give you a lift. At least my vehicle is made for this. What did I tell you about cute vehicles?" She grinned and playfully shoulder-bumped Addie.

"No, that's okay. Your bath is waiting. Carolyn's off tonight, and she has a pickup. I'll see if she can give me a lift home."

Serena shook her head. "Afraid not. Marc pulled her off desk sergeant duty and put her in the field tonight. She's working storm patrol."

"Really?"

"Yeah, she was just in my shop giving me a weather and power update. Didn't she come in here?"

"No, Marc came in."

"Oooo, personal service by the chief." Serena nudged her arm.

Addie's chest constricted. Had she received preferential treatment? She shook it off. There'd been too many snide remarks to let her hopes take over her common sense now. Time to move forward and forget about the past. . . . She took a deep breath. "I'll just lock up the back." She checked the alley door and headed toward the front. "Paige, are there any more matches up here?"

"Yeah, I found three boxes under the counter. We got them for the Halloween displays."

"Great, let's each take one. We'll need them at home. I'll pick up more from the store tomorrow in case we still need the candles."

Serena wrapped her scarf around her throat. "I told Paige we'd give her a lift, too."

Addie pulled her gloves on and looked at Paige. "What about your mom? Does she need a ride?"

"No, she closed the bakery right after the power went out and went home. As I still had customers, I told her she didn't have to wait for me."

"Did she actually come in and ask you? I think that would be a first since I opened. You know, her crossing my threshold."

"No, she tapped on the window and made me go out to talk to her." Paige shrugged. "She can be a tough nut to crack sometimes."

"I wonder if she'll ever be able to accept me," Addie chuckled.

"I think she's slowly coming around. She just doesn't like change, and you have brought a lot of changes to her sleepy little town." Paige laughed.

Serena pulled the door open. A blast of whirling snow pushed her back. "Wow, it's getting worse. Heads down, ladies."

They dropped Paige off and headed up the hill toward Addie's house. At the top of her driveway, Serena stopped. "Were you expecting a visitor?"

"No, why?" Addie wiped the condensation from her side of the window. "Tire tracks?"

"Well, it does make the drive in easier, but I'm not leaving until I know if it's friend or foe." The headlights bounced off a light-colored, older-model Lincoln. "Anyone you know?" Serena shifted the Jeep into park.

"No, I have no idea whose car that is." Addie opened her door, flipped on her phone flashlight app, and shone it through the driver's side window. "Patrick?"

Chapter 10

"Okay, what's so important that you had to talk to me tonight?" Addie kept a wary eye on Patrick as she dug through her purse, produced the box of matches, and lit the candelabra on the foyer side table.

Patrick flicked snow from his jacket shoulders. "I was hoping to talk to you, alone." He darted Serena a suspicious look.

"Not a chance that's going to happen." Serena crossed her arms and planted her feet. "As a matter of fact, I'm staying the night to ride out the storm with Addie."

Addie glanced sideways at her. A smile tugged at the corners of her lips. "Yes, that's right. Anything you say to me, you also say to Serena."

"Okay." He stamped the snow from his dress shoes, sighing like a sulky child.

"We can at least get comfortable." Addie picked up the candelabra and walked into the living room.

Serena waited and followed Patrick, then stood at the door, arms still folded. Addie had to bite the inside of her cheek to keep from laughing. Serena was the spitting image of her brother when he went all Robo-Cop on her.

Patrick eased onto the sofa and laid his gloves on the coffee table. "This is hard for me"—his eyes met Addie's—"but I don't know what else to do."

"Just tell me what it is." She took a seat on the chair opposite him.

He wrung his hands. "I wasn't joking when I asked you today if you had another book you could donate to the auction." Addie's eyes flashed. He held up his hands as if deflecting a blow. "I know. It's a lot to ask, but . . . I'm desperate."

"I can't. No, I won't donate another book. I understand it's for a worthy cause, but until we know what happened to *A Christmas Carol*, I won't risk the chance that another rare book could get lost." She ignored his tight white lips. "I hope you understand that until we know if Teresa's death was an accident . . . or something else and locate the book, I just can't."

"It's not like you don't have others," he snapped, gesturing toward the bookshelf. "They just take up space, anyway."

"She's already told you no." Serena followed his gaze to the bookshelf. "And in case your desperation has given you any ideas, she also has a state-of-the-art security system."

He leered at Serena. "Not much good in a power outage."

Addie nonchalantly studied her cuticles. "It runs off the telephone lines and Wi-Fi, which are both still operational."

A bulge moved inside his cheek. Addie shivered with the thought of his tongue touching anything.

"Look, I need a book in its place because if I have to refund ticket money, it will bankrupt the foundation."

"You may have to give those refunds, anyway, with the highways closed." Addie tapped her fingers on the chair arm. "You'll still have to postpone the event. But this storm won't last forever, so pick another future date, and then contact the ticket purchasers. Offer them the choice of a ticket refund or attending on the new date."

"What about the book auction?" Patrick squirmed in his seat. "As you pointed out today, many are coming just for that, and I still won't have the book."

"Perhaps by then we'll find it and—"

"What if we don't?"

Addie cocked her head and pierced him with a gaze. "What makes you think it won't show up?" His hand scoured over his head, wilting under her gaze. "Look," she continued, "it might yet, and if it does, then nothing's lost. But if it's not found by early next week, then you'll have to inform the out-of-town dealers that *A Christmas Carol* isn't available at this time and offer them a ticket refund, anyway. Before they spend the time and money to get here and then end up suing you."

"But I've paid out too much in invoices to do that." He shot to his feet. "If I had another book of equal value, that would solve the problem."

"No, it wouldn't, because there's still the matter of the roads and airports being closed, and no one from out of area, or state, for that matter, will be able to get here, anyway."

"The long-range forecast is for this storm to pass by the end of the week, so that's not an issue."

"It could be if the forecast is wrong," Serena interjected, grabbing a blanket from the back of the sofa and draping it over her shoulders. "After all, the storm hit a day before they thought it would. It's probably better if you officially postpone the entire auction now and pick another date later when you know for certain about better weather conditions."

"Postponing is out of the question because the Christmas decorations will be useless on another date. There's no money to start over again." His face took on a bright-red hue, and Addie feared he might explode. "And the only alternative would be to hold the auction closer to Christmas, but people are too busy to attend then and will want a refund, anyway."

"What about planning it at or around New Year's; that way you can still use the Christmas decorations, and most people can spare the time once Christmas Day's over with?" Addie nabbed an extra blanket and cuddled inside it.

"But I still won't have a book," he barked.

"You seem awfully sure that the book won't be found by then."

"Never mind, I just thought you cared more about the charity work the foundation does, but I see I was wrong. You're actually very heartless." He grabbed his gloves from the table, brushed past Serena, and slammed the front door behind him.

"Am I heartless?" Addie toyed with the fringes on her blanket.

"Absolutely not." Serena slumped onto the sofa. "I don't blame you. How do we know that he didn't steal the book and is looking at getting his hands on another one before he bolts out of town after the roads reopen?"

"I just can't bring myself to donate another book until we know what happened to this one."

"That doesn't make you heartless it makes you . . . well, you."

Addie snorted, stifling a laugh. "And what exactly does that mean?"

They jumped at the banging on the front door.

"Crap, he's back for another go-around." Serena seized a marble statue from the coffee table. "Grab that letter opener." She pointed to the desk.

Addie peeked out the curtain and laughed. "Relax. It's Carolyn, her truck's out there." She made her way to the foyer, Serena at her heels, carrying the candelabra. Addie swung the door open. "Simon? What are you doing here?"

He stepped in, brushing snow off his jacket. "I wanted to make sure you got home. I can't even get my Tesla out of the alley behind my apartment, and Carolyn got called in to patrol and was kind enough to loan me her truck." He removed his coat, snow falling to the floor in a mini-blizzard.

"That was nice of her," Addie said, and hung his parka on the coat rack. "It's probably only jeeps and trucks that are getting through tonight. My poor little car is still snowed in at the police station from this morning."

"I know. I saw it there when I drove by and went in. Marc said he hadn't seen you for hours. I got worried and thought I'd better check." He rubbed his hands together. "I don't suppose you have a Wi-Fi–operated coffeepot, do you?" He cackled, grinning, and headed for the living room. "I could kill for a coffee right now."

"Long day?" Addie stood at the end of the sofa as he made himself comfortable.

"Mostly slips and falls, nothing horrific. People seem to be staying off the roads tonight, which is good." He smiled up at her. "When I got to the top of your drive, I saw a car leaving. Did you have visitors, or was it someone turning around?"

"We had a visitor all right." Serena slumped onto the far end of the sofa. "Patrick just left."

"Patrick, Teresa's assistant? What did he want bad enough to bring him out on a night like this?"

"He wanted her to donate another book for the auction." Serena nearly spat the words.

"You're kidding?"

"Nope." Addie offered him a patchwork quilt that still smelled faintly of mothballs. "And he seems desperate. He says the foundation will go bankrupt if he has to refund ticket money."

"Still, I hope you told him no." Simon sniffed the edge of the quilt draped over his back.

"Of course she did. Addie's smarter than that. Besides, I don't trust him. He even tried to make her feel guilty when she said no."

Simon shook his head. "I know the auction is for a good cause, but for heaven's sake. A woman just died, and he's worried about refunding ticket money?"

"Yeah, I'd say if anyone is heartless, it's him." Serena jutted her chin toward the outer walls of the house as if Patrick were still lurking outside in the storm.

"It's done now. He knows my answer. Let me see if I can do something about that coffee." Addie smiled at Simon. "Why don't you build a fire, and I'll be back in a minute."

"Sounds mysterious. Are you going to work your magic on the electricity?" He laughed and swatted at her butt.

She zigzagged out of his reach. "Got to be quicker than that if you want to catch me," she quipped with a sassy grin before grabbing a candle and sashaying from the room.

Minutes later, she returned bearing a coffeepot, juggling three mugs, the candlestick, and a kitchen towel draped over her shoulder.

"What on earth?" Serena took the candle from her hand.

"No electricity magic but maybe the next best thing." She placed the cups on the table and held up the coffeepot. "I found this old camping percolator in the pantry and thought at the time that I'd better hang on to it in case of, well, this, I guess."

"I'm glad you did." Serena poked at the ancient contraption. "But how do we perk it?"

"Voilà." Addie pulled a small, barbeque grilling pan from under her arm. "Let's see if this works." She slid the pan grate over the wrought-iron log holder in the fireplace, set the coffeepot on top, and sat back on her haunches. "Okay, fingers crossed."

"Brilliant," cried Simon. "You are amazing in a pinch, I must say." He kissed the top of her head.

A loud knock came from the door. Simon squeezed Addie's shoulder. "I'll get it, just in case it's Patrick not understanding what no means." He grabbed the candlestick and headed to the foyer. Marc's voice echoed into the living room, and Addie groaned. Simon poised himself behind Marc in the doorway, his arms crossed, his square jaw set.

"Evening, Serena, Addie." Marc nodded. "I see you're all safe. I saw Carolyn's truck outside and wondered why she wasn't out on patrol." His cheek twitched. "Now I see why it's here." He spared Simon a glance.

"Are the roads still bad?" Serena sank into a chair in

front to the fireplace. "It doesn't look like the snow's let up."

He shook his head. "And, Addie, your car is nearly completely covered by now. It's really coming down hard."

She collapsed on the sofa. "I guess I'll be digging out tomorrow."

"Maybe not even then. They're forecasting another couple of feet before tomorrow night. Don't plan on going anywhere in the near future, and they're not sure when electricity will be restored."

"I guess I'd better text Paige and tell her the shop's closed tomorrow." She eyed her friend, snuggled so deep in a blanket that only her face poked out. "Serena, you should do the same."

"You are a wise one, Sherlock." Serena buried her face in her blanket, sniffled, and then sneezed. "I will later. Right now, I just want to hibernate," she said, pulling the blanket over her head.

Addie sniffed the air. "Ah, the smell of success. Marc, we've just put a pot of coffee on, would you like a cup before you head back out?"

"I'd love that. With the power out I haven't had coffee all day." Marc sat on the sofa, tossing his cap on the table. He looked at Simon looming in the doorway. "Aren't you going to join us?"

Simon stiffened and slid past him, taking a seat beside Addie. She could hear him grinding his teeth. *Good grief, men!* An eye roll would only give her a headache, so she ignored them both.

"I'll get another cup." Serena's gaze ping-ponged between the love triangle on the couch; she grabbed the candlestick and fled for the kitchen.

Simon edged closer to Addie and draped his arm over the sofa back, his fingers lightly resting against her shoulder. Addie curbed the smile that was forming on her lips and glanced past Simon to Marc. Simon's arm placement apparently didn't go unnoticed by him. Marc's eyes narrowed and then fixed to the flickering flames in the fireplace.

Serena swept back into the room, set down the extra mug, and stared at the three silent statues. She took her seat back in the chair, drew her knees up, and looked from one to the other. "Well, this is cozy, isn't it?" Marc grunted. Simon shifted in his seat. Addie stifled a giggle. "Or not," Serena smirked.

The fire hissed. Addie jumped to her feet, whipped the kitchen towel from her shoulder, wrapped it around her hand, and snatched the bubbling coffeepot off the grate. "Ah, just what we all need, a cup of strong campfire coffee."

The room settled into a more peaceful silence. Addie settled back into her spot and sipped her much-needed caffeine fix. She peered at Marc. "There's something I want to ask you about the case."

"Of course there is."

"I just wanted to know if you were finished with the envelope I left on Teresa's desk the morning she died."

"What envelope?"

"The one with the certificate of authenticity in it and my colleague's remarks about the open-market prices."

He shook his head. "Never saw it."

"But I left it there right before I found her body."

"Sorry, when we went in, there wasn't anything on her desk but the coffee cups. Pristine as you said, I think."

Addie slunk back into the sofa. "Well, that is interesting."

"How so?" Simon slinked his arm on the back of the sofa again, his fingertips making swirlies on her shoulder.

"Because Patrick told me this morning that he never saw an envelope on her desk after he was allowed back in. I figured that the police must have taken it for some reason."

Simon's finger paused for moment. "Why is the envelope so important?"

"Because if a book is sold with Kate's association number on the documents it proves the book was appraised by a reliable source. It will usually bring in a higher sale price."

"I'm thinking"—Serena drew her legs up, resting her chin on her knees—"that we need your crime board right about now."

Chapter 11

"I think I'll let you three get on with your . . ." Marc cleared his throat. "Investigating? Of what, I don't know, because so far there's no crime." He set his empty cup on the table and stood up. "Anyway, thanks for the coffee"—he adjusted his holster—"but I'd better get back out there." He glowered at Simon's hand placement still resting on Addie's shoulder. "I have real police work to conduct tonight."

"It's a shame you have to run," Simon sneered, "and just when we were all having *so much fun*. Here, let me show you out." He steered Marc toward the door and banged it closed behind him.

"Simon!" Addie cried out. "That was rude."

"I didn't like his condescending tone, did you?"

"No, but—"

"Then we all agree."

Addie glared at Serena, who mutely agreed with a nod and salute with her coffee cup.

"Okay." Simon rubbed his hands together. "One

makeshift crime board coming up." He turned on his phone's flashlight and dashed up the stairs.

Serena sighed, tapping her fingers on the arms of her chair. "I don't know what you think, but I'd say he just made it clear to Marc that this, and you, are his territory now, and Marc wasn't welcomed."

"What shocks me is that Marc didn't turn around and pop him a good one."

"Yeah," Serena stifled a laugh, "me, too."

Simon thumped down the last step into the foyer, darted past the living room French doors, and headed down the hall toward the kitchen, the sound of banging and clanging echoing through the main floor. Moments later, he returned, waving a pair of scissors, with a roll of tape clenched between his teeth and a roll of brown shipping paper tucked under his arm. He dropped the scissors and the tape on the coffee table. "I remembered seeing this in the attic once when we were looking for pirate books to sell in the shop." He presented Addie with the roll of paper.

"Perfect." Addie jumped to her feet. "Yes, we can make this work." She cut off a large piece. With Serena's help, she secured it to the wall with the masking tape.

Serena dug around in her large hobo handbag and produced a black marking pen. "Here, this should work."

"Now we're in business." Addie propped her hand against the paper. "Okay, where do we start with this whole missing book thing and Teresa's timely fall?" She tapped the pen on the paper, waiting for a reply. The room was silent. "Anyone? No? All right, I'll start, then." *Jonathan*, she wrote.

"Jonathan? But you know him, and he's David's father. Why would you suspect him?"

"I agree with Serena." Simon's fingers stroked over the stubble on his five o'clock shadowed chin. "He really can't be on your list of bad guys, can he?"

"As a matter of fact, he's—" She drew a number *1* and circled it. "Think about it. He arrived in Greyborne Harbor the same day as I received the certificate of authentication. He also knew Teresa previously. They obviously had talked before his arrival because they'd arranged a lunch date, so he might have been aware through her that the certificate was due anytime." She looked from one blank face to the other. "The book and the documents might be his real reason for coming here, and saying he came to visit me was just a cover."

Serena's eyes widened. "You don't really think he's that blackhearted, do you?"

"Yes, because he was also the first name on the list of out-of-town ticket buyers, which, by the way, he purchased the same day Teresa released the auction information on the website."

Simon chuckled. "I'm afraid to ask, but how do you know that?"

"Because," Addie preened, "I saw the list of collectors and brokers who are attending."

"When?"

"In Patrick's office." She waved him off. "I have a copy. I'll show it to you later." She wrote, *sketchy past, police couldn't run a complete trace and*—

"Why couldn't they?" Serena stepped up to the crime board. "You've known him for years. Anything that made you suspect him before?"

"Not really, just a gut feeling, but Marc said he couldn't find any records of him existing before 1977."

"You're kidding." Simon sat down on the coffee table.

"No, although Marc said they discovered the issue was only a clerical error before it was found and corrected. Apparently up until 1977, he was listed in all public records as having Hemingway spelled with two *m*'s instead of one, but I don't buy it."

"But just a minute here." Simon raked his hand over his face. "Like Marc said, so far there hasn't been proof of a crime being committed. I can't even draw a conclusion with the autopsy results yet."

"That's right," said Addie, "but you have to admit there are too many weird things going on not to consider that there is one. It's just that no one has put all the pieces together yet."

"If we're just throwing ideas out to see where they fall—" Serena took the pen from Addie's fingers and wrote *Patrick*. "He showed up here, demanding another rare book to replace *A Christmas Carol* for the auction, and said he'll get it one way or another."

"That sounds like a desperate man." Simon tapped the scribbled name written in thick black.

"Yes, it does, doesn't it?" Addie took the pen back and marked a number *2* beside Patrick's name.

Serena eyed the list of names. "What about Crystal? You said she was his assistant now? Should we add her?"

"I don't know how suspect she is." Addie rubbed her chin. "From what I saw today, she's too self-centered and doesn't seem to be bothered by anything other than the weather changing her vacation plan and how Patrick is actually making her work as his assistant. Teresa's death seemed more like it was just an inconvenience for her."

Serena shrugged. "Maybe they weren't close?"

Addie studied the names. "Maybe, but one thing

that does bother me is the lengthy lunch break she took that day."

"How so?" Simon looked from the board to her.

"For one thing, Jonathan said she wasn't there when he left Teresa's office around eleven, only a sign stating BE BACK IN ONE HOUR, but that same sign was still there when I arrived at one thirty."

Simon rubbed his neck. "Yeah, but that could have been anything. You said her flight had just been canceled and she was upset." He shrugged. "Maybe she was just busy trying to book another one."

"You're right. It could have been anything, especially this time of year." Serena flopped down on the sofa. "So, we really have nothing on her."

"She does wear the same shade of lipstick that's on the coffee cup." Addie wrote next to her name. "That's something."

"But apparently so do half the other women in town," Simon muttered, and joined Serena on the sofa.

"Forget about Crystal for now. Let's focus on what we do know." Addie's hand hovered over the paper.

"I've got nothing," Serena murmured.

"Me neither," Simon echoed.

Addie wrote, *foundation broke, unable to refund ticket purchasers*. She tapped the board. "Now, does anyone besides me think that's curious for a multimillion-dollar charity agency?"

"But"—Simon's eyes locked with hers—"he had a plausible explanation, didn't he?"

Serena tapped her finger on her chin. "Yes, he said because he's had a lot of accounts payable due to the high cost of decorations. I'm sure he would have had to pay advances to the caterer, photographer, and whatever else, too."

Addie twirled the pen in her hand. "But, in truth, how much would that be? Enough for the foundation to be left completely broke?"

"Come, sit down." Simon patted the sofa beside him. "You're making my head spin."

Addie growled, tossed the pen on the coffee table, and dropped onto the sofa, putting her feet on the table.

Simon's hand landed lightly on hers. "When I sit here and see it all in black and white—"

"Don't you mean black and brown?" She playfully slapped Simon's knee.

"Okay, black and brown," he snickered. "I don't see anything that points to an actual crime having been committed. The book is missing, yes, but it could have just been stored in a hiding place Teresa had. There's no proof of theft. The only fingerprints on the case were hers and yours."

"Yup, I'm thinking we need to add your name up there," giggled Serena.

Addie slammed her head against the back of the sofa. "You're right. If there is a crime, I look guilty." She sat up and glared at the board. "Problem with that is lack of motive. Why would I steal back a book I do-nated?"

"If we were looking at any other suspect"—Simon's brow rose—"then you'd be guessing they changed their mind once they found out the actual worth of the book."

"Or they were drunk when they donated it, but then changed their mind." Serena imitated a drunk trying to pour a drink and then giggled. "Maybe the person asked Teresa for the book back, and she refused so that said person pushed her down the stairs"—she flailed her arms out—"took her key ring from her wrist"—Serena pretended to snatch something from her own wrist—"and went back and reclaimed her book."

"That's it." Addie jumped to her feet.

"I was joking. Although I do have to say my charades were spot-on." She smiled at Simon. "Wouldn't you agree?"

Addie waved her hand. "Yes, yes, your charades were lovely, but maybe that's exactly what did happen, only not that silly scenario involving me."

"Who do you think would do that?" Simon reclaimed her hand after she finished gesticulating with it.

"I don't know yet, but we have to think along the lines that it was murder and the book was stolen."

"I still think it might have been an accident." Serena crossed her arms. "Marc and Simon both said there was no proof of murder."

"But what if it was a murder made to look like an accident. Remember, I told you how when Patrick opened the door to the third floor, it almost knocked me down the stairs. What if he or someone else did the same thing when they were on the staircase with Teresa, only it wasn't an accident when she did fall? What if it was the only way that person could get the key ring off her wrist, so they could nab the book? Patrick told me she always wore it, so that must be it." She stabbed the pen tip into the paper.

"Perhaps, but only if she spun around frontward to try to save herself from falling. Remember, I said the main damage was to the frontal bone and tissue, so a backward fall doesn't fit the evidence."

"But it is possible, right?" Addie asked.

He nodded. "I guess. It makes more sense than her shoe slipping off the top step and falling backward."

Serena's face scrunched up. "But if it was . . . say

Patrick, and he was trying to make it look like an accident, wouldn't he have called for help or report it to cover up that it was intentional?"

"Not if he had to get the key off her first." Addie's eyes lit up. "He probably had to run back upstairs, take the book out of the case, and hide it somewhere. He might have planned on coming back down and reporting the fall, but I found the body before he could."

Simon crossed his arms and looked at Serena. "Serena, didn't you tell the police that you were downstairs talking to Patrick while all this was going on?"

She shook her head. "Not all the time. I was visiting with some of the volunteers I know, too."

"Then he could have slipped out at any time." Addie circled Patrick's name. "He stays on the list for now until we know for sure. If he was downstairs the whole morning, and others can account for that, and if he left, given how busy it was, surely someone would have noticed he wasn't around."

Simon sighed. "We really don't have much other than guesses, do we?"

"No, but those guesses as you call them have been helpful in the past, haven't they?" Addie reminded him.

"You're right, but I think now we also need to identify who Teresa had lunch and drinks with. Given the lipstick on the cup, I doubt it was Patrick."

"Maybe Jonathan was lying about what time he left." Serena pointed to his timeline comment.

Simon coughed. "Does he wear lipstick, Serena?"

"No, but—"

"Catherine does," Addie said, looking from one to the other.

"And so do I, like half the women in town right now. You can't seriously think Catherine had anything to do with this, can you?"

Simon backed away from the two glowering women.

Addie turned toward her. "I hate to think it, but she is Jonathan's only alibi for what time she said he picked her up after his visit to Teresa's office. You have to admit they have gotten pretty chummy in a short period of time. What if she is one of the many women from his past?"

"Think about what you're saying. You know her, and I've known her my whole life. There is no way she would be involved in anything like this."

Addie gestured toward the board. "There's just too many coincidences."

"Not in this case. What I think is we're all tired and need sleep before we go down too many more rabbit holes." Serena grabbed her throw blanket from the chair and headed for the stairs. "Since we seem to be snowed in, I'll be sleeping in the yellow guest room. If and when you ever come to your senses, we can revisit that stupid theory," she called down the stairs, and slammed a door.

Chapter 12

Addie expelled a frustrated breath. "I'm sorry you had to witness that."

Simon placed his hands on her shoulders. Her skin quivered under his touch. "I understand that we were just throwing out theories, but Catherine and Jonathan working together to commit murder and steal a rare book? That one seems farfetched even for me."

"I know, but my gut tells me he's involved in this somehow. Look at the evidence." She pointed at the board. "And we know Catherine does wear that shade of lipstick."

"All true, but she is an attractive single woman, and he's an attractive single man, and perhaps their relationship is just two people who made a connection." The soft candlelight reflected in his eyes. "Not everything is some dark conspiracy plot."

"You're right." She pursed her lips. "I'll apologize to Serena in the morning." She gazed into his eyes. A smile tugged at the corners of her mouth. "I guess I do tend to get carried away when there's a knot to be un-raveled."

"Actually, you become like a dog with a bone." He kissed the tip of her nose. "Serena is right about one other thing."

"What's that?"

"We do appear to be snowed in."

"I guess that means you'll need a place to sleep?"

He held her gaze.

She sucked in a sharp breath. "Well . . . I . . ."

"I'm just guessing"—his eyes flashed with amuse-ment—"but I think that in this big, old, rambling house, you do have more than one guest room?"

"Yes, of course." Her racing heart decelerated. "You even have your choice of blue, green, beige, floral, or the old servant's quarters in the attic."

"That many? Wow, but I think I'll pass on the attic. It sounds . . . lonely." He played his fingers down her arm. "What color is yours?"

"Mine?" The roguish expression in his eyes left her in-capable of thinking. "It's . . . ah . . . cream." She pressed her trembling lips tightly. "It was my aunt's. I've only re-cently had the nerve to move into it." How was it that he rendered her speechless? "I used to sleep in the blue room."

"Is it called the blue room because it's sad?" His fin-ger stroked the line of her jaw.

"No"—she glanced downward—"it's nice, and it's soothing, and comfortable." She looked up into his eyes. "Just like you."

"Okay, the blue room it is, then." He lifted her chin. His lips brushed across her cheek. "Is it close to your room?" His warm breath caressed her neck. Her chest tightened. She nodded, her lips parting. "Good, because I really do love the sounds of rattling walls all night."

She growled. "I should know better by now." She pushed his arm away. "And I told you before, I don't snore."

He howled and attempted to pull her into his arms.

"I don't see the humor in any of this, but don't worry. I won't disturb you." She spun out of his reach. "I won't be sleeping much tonight, anyway. I feel sick about *everything* that's just happened here."

Addie checked her phone clock every hour, but at some point, she must have slept because she vividly remembered a vision of Jonathan as a cartoon character rolling around on a stack of blood-covered books. It was then she jerked fully awake and gave up any further hope of sleep. She pulled her robe from the foot of the bed and tiptoed into the hallway. The thought of starting the fire to make a pot of coffee was her only focus. The bathroom door opened. She stopped short. Quite certain she must still be sleeping. She rubbed her eyes. Silhouetted by golden light was what she could only describe as another figment of her dream state. Clad in a pair of snug-fitting boxer briefs, she allowed her gaze to wander from the figure's broad shoulders to his muscular chest, ripped stomach, and down to his perfectly developed calves. Any words that might have come to her caught at her throat. She was thoroughly convinced this wasn't real. There was no way Simon looked like this beneath his hospital scrubs, or sport jackets and blue jeans.

"Good morning," he murmured, holding her gaze, "as you can see the power's back on."

Her gaze snapped back up to meet his. She sucked

in a sharp breath. Oh, dear! It wasn't a dream. He'd actually witnessed her gawping at him. She pulled her eyes away, focused on her morning coffee mission, and fled down the stairs without a word.

The image of his lithe body clearly visible in her mind, she stumbled into the kitchen and plopped a pod into the coffeemaker, grateful that she didn't have to build a fire right now to heat the percolator. She gazed down the hallway toward the stairs, and was a tad disappointed when he appeared at the bottom fully clothed in a sweater and blue jeans.

His hand brushed a stray lock of hair from her eyes. "I'd say good morning, sunshine, but by the look of those dark circles under your eyes . . ." He was not deterred by her low, guttural growl. "You're up earlier than I thought you'd be. I was going to surprise you with breakfast."

"Coffee?" Her voice cracked. She shoved a mug and a coffee pod at him, forcing him to occupy his hand elsewhere. After last night, she wasn't going to let her guard down again and become the focus of one of his boyish taunts. "Fool me once," she muttered.

"Is everything okay?" He studied her.

"Yup." She stirred cream into her cup.

"Okay, if you say so." He shrugged and dropped the pod into the machine.

She studied his broad back. A quiver raced through her. He turned, their eyes locked. She exhaled loudly, barely aware she'd been holding her breath. He removed his cup from the coffeemaker and sat down on a counter stool, never taking his eyes off hers.

He raised his mug to his lips and took a long, slow sip. "Anything you want to talk about?"

She shook her head.

His eyes remained fixed on her over the rim of his cup.

She clenched her fist and took a deep breath. "Okay, there is one thing. Last night . . . I felt something stir inside me that I haven't felt in a long time." His brows rose, but she plunged on. "I thought you felt something, too, but then you turned it into a joke just like you always do. I don't know what to think anymore. One moment you act like there's something more than friendship between us, and the next you're teasing me like you would if I was the little girl next door."

He came to her side. She exhaled when he laced his fingers through hers. "Sit down, Addie." He eased her gently onto the kitchen stool. His hand left hers and stroked her cheek. "I do feel it, and there's nothing I want, desire more than to take you into my arms and kiss you like neither of us has been kissed before."

Butterflies exploded in her chest. "But why, then?"

He leaned over and kissed her forehead. "Because you're still chasing ghosts." He held on to her when she attempted to stand. To run. To escape. "Not only David's, that's understandable, but I also see you still trying to recapture what you and Marc once had." He placed his warm hands on her cheeks when she shook her head. "Yes, I've seen the way he looks at you and you at him. I know that memory still haunts you."

Tears burned in her eyes. "But . . . ."

"No buts." He kissed the tip of her nose. "Until you've exorcized *that* particular ghost, as much as I don't want to, I'm willing to wait. Because like I've said before, I think Marc, and what you felt for him, is a rebound after David. So, until you decide if that's true or not, we'll just have to stay friends. It makes things less complicated if it ends badly for us." His lips weakly turned up at the corners.

"Isn't this cozy," snarled Serena, plugging in the kettle, "I hope I'm not intruding."

Addie jerked. "Not at all." She wriggled from his grasp.

"I hope you slept well, Serena." Simon walked to the sink and rinsed his coffee cup. "I was just going to start breakfast. I hope you're hungry."

She ignored Addie and smiled innocently at Simon. "Truthfully, I'm starving. We missed dinner last night." She gave Addie a sideways glower.

"Serena, I'm sorry. I crossed a line when I brought Catherine's name into it, and I know that hurt you." Addie touched her shoulder.

Serena shrugged off her hand.

"I really am sorry. We were just brainstorming, and I got carried away."

Serena dropped a tea bag into a cup. "I guess I'd feel better about that if you had also written your name up there since you are the only one who does have hard evidence against them."

"You're right." She looked back at Serena. "I'll put my name up, too. It's only fair if we're just throwing ideas out." Serena gave Addie a tight-lipped smile. "After all, if we look hard enough, maybe we can see that I was actually set up to be a suspect, or even possibly that the lipstick on the cup was planted to lead the whole investigation on a wild-goose chase."

"Interesting theory." Simon tapped his fingers on the counter. "Yes, we hadn't thought of that, but . . . well, who knows what the three of us can come up with if we work as a *team*."

"Yes, much like three pairs of hands making breakfast." Addie grinned at Serena and retrieved a frying pan from the cupboard.

*   *   *

Addie had only just bitten into her toasted scrambled egg sandwich when a loud rumble rattled the windows. She choked on her mouthful. Simon patted her back and offered her a glass of orange juice. "Thanks," she sputtered. "I'm fine, but what on earth is that noise?"

"I'll go see." Serena dashed down the hallway to the living room. "We're being rescued," she called.

Addie and Simon joined her and peered out the window.

Simon grinned. "It's Carolyn and Pete with his dad's snowblower."

"She must want her truck back," Addie laughed.

Carolyn waved at the three grinning faces in the window and stumbled through the snowdrifts to the door. Addie flung the door open and hugged her, dragging her into the foyer. "You're a lifesaver. I was afraid the three of us were trapped here together for eternity."

"I know one person who wouldn't mind that." She slid a sly look at Simon.

Simon coughed loudly, his face red.

Addie, sensing the tension, broke the silence. "Can I make you and Pete some coffee?" She glanced out the door sidelight window at the tiny snowstorm Pete created with the snowblower.

"No, thank you. We have a huge Thermos in Pete's truck."

"Do you need your truck back today?" Simon asked over Addie's shoulder.

"No, we're just clearing a few friends' and families' driveways until I'm back on shift at three. I was worried that you might get called into the hospital sometime today. I know they were hopping last night. So were we. It was crazy out there."

"I can imagine." Addie shivered at the thought of

having to work in the storm. "I don't ever remember seeing this much snow in my life, and it's darn right freezing out there. I don't know how you haven't turned blue yet."

"I'm tough stuff," Carolyn laughed, flexing her arm.

Simon leaned his hand against the doorframe. "Just so we're clear. You don't need your truck? I don't want any surprises."

"No, keep it. Pete's truck is just as good on these roads. We're fine, and he can drop me off at the station later."

"Thanks." Simon drummed his fingers on the door casing.

"Yeah, anytime. You'd think my older, wiser brother would know that a fancy-dancy sports car doesn't cut it in these winter storms."

Simon flicked the ball of fur at the top of his sister's woolen hat. "Just remember that 'wiser' part later."

"I see you guys have electricity, but so you're aware if you do head out today, the power's still out in town center, well, in most of the harbor, actually." Carolyn glanced through the window at the snowblower when it backfired. "That thing really is as old as the hills. I hope it gets through all the snow we're planning on feeding it."

"If the power's still out, I guess we definitely won't be opening our stores." Serena pulled her phone from her pocket. "I'd better text Elli since I forgot to give her a heads-up last night." She walked back into the living room.

"Who's Elli?" Carolyn asked.

"Her part-time assistant, I think." Addie shrugged.

"Elli Hollingsworth?"

"Maybe? Do you know her?" Addie stifled a laugh when the snowblower seemed to let loose a belch.

"Only through dealings with her mother, Maggie. She's the real-estate agent we bought our house through."

"Right, I know her, too. She's in my book club."

"As far as I know Elli is, or at least was, a handful. You'd better warn Serena to keep her on a short leash, as her mother says."

"I will, thanks." Addie looked into the living room at Serena busily sending a text.

Hearing another mechanical belch, Carolyn sighed. "I'd better go help Pete. He'll be cursing my disappearance by now." Her cell phone rang. She removed her glove and fished around in the pocket of her parka. Holding up a finger, she walked toward the kitchen, leaving Simon and Addie in the foyer. Simon shrugged his shoulders and mouthed "crazy morning, huh?" Addie grinned. When had one of her mornings not been crazy?

Carolyn reappeared. "It seems we have an incident."

"Is someone lost in the storm?"

"What?" Serena planted herself between Addie and Simon. "Who's lost?"

Carolyn drew a notepad and pen out of her inside chest pocket. "The chief said that Patrick Barton dropped in to talk to you last night?" At Addie's nod, she continued. "What time did he leave here?"

"Just past six, I think." Addie's senses tingled.

"That timeline would work." Carolyn scribbled on her pad.

"I can verify that," said Simon. "I was arriving when he left."

"Good." She continued to write.

"What happened, Carolyn? Did he say something about it? Did he accuse us of something?" When she didn't look up from her notebook, Addie forced the spiral book down, forcing Carolyn to look at her. "Why the questions?"

"Have any of you seen this man before?" Carolyn opened a sketched photo on her phone.

Simon and Serena peered at it and shook their heads. Addie sucked in a breath. "Yes, I think I have. I know him, but his name escapes me. . . ." Addie opened her phone to the photo she snapped in Patrick's office of the list of presold ticket purchasers. She scrolled through the list of names. "I'll remember it when I see it . . . yes, here it is. His name is Marvin Gibson."

"How do you know him?" Carolyn asked.

"My father and David had past dealings with him. He's a relic and book broker, works mostly out of Italy and New York, I think."

"Anything else you can tell me about him?" Carolyn's pen kept scribbling.

"It has long been speculated in the rare-book and artifact community that he brokered some pretty suspicious deals for a lot of shady collectors."

"What's he got to do with Patrick?" Simon asked.

Carolyn glowered at Simon. "You know I can't give information to the public about an ongoing investigation."

"We are hardly the general public. I'm the district coroner, and Addie's the . . . the . . . whatever she is. But she's the only lead you have right now and your best chance of getting information about this guy for whatever this is all about."

She tapped her pen on the coiled notebook. "Okay, but don't tell the chief I told you any of this." Seemingly satisfied with their head nods, she continued. "It seems that Patrick's assistant, Crystal Parker, filed a missing person report this morning. Apparently, Patrick hasn't been seen and no one's been able to reach him since last night about seven. That's when witnesses saw him arguing at the hospital with the man described in this police sketch."

Addie glanced at the crime board in the living room. She was definitely going to need another sheet of paper to keep up with the growing list of suspects.

Chapter 13

"So, what are you thinking, Nancy Drew?" Simon stood, hands on hips, beside Addie in front of the board.

"I'm thinking . . ." She let out a deep breath and wrote, *Marvin Gibson number 1A*, and circled it, stabbing the pen tip on the paper.

"What was it you were saying before about him and shady dealings?" Serena leaned against the doorframe, a plate in hand, shoveling what looked like cold bacon and scrambled eggs into her mouth. At Addie's laugh, she looked at her plate. "I told you I was starving, and breakfast was kind of interrupted."

Simon guffawed. "Yummy, why don't I make you some fresh ones?"

"No, I'm good, but thanks." Serena wiped a chunk of egg from her chin. "So back to this Marvin guy."

"Right." Addie looked back at the board. "Rumor is that he has close ties with organized crime syndicates."

"Like the Mafia?" Serena's fork dropped on the plate.

"As the rumors go."

Simon's eyes widened. "And he worked with your father and David?"

"No, they definitely didn't work *with* him, but they had a lot of dealings with him over the years, though. His specialty as a broker was to launder money for some of the most ruthless crime bosses in the world."

"It sounds dangerous." Serena flopped onto the sofa, scooping the last of her breakfast into her mouth.

Simon lightly touched Addie's hair. Her scalp tingled. "You actually met with this guy?"

"Once." Her mind flashed to the night she and David attended a small reception and auction in Boston. After David had left her to get them each a drink from the bar, Marvin had approached her, his smile as oily as his face. Apparently, he'd heard a lot about her appraisal skills and wondered if she would do some private work for him. He'd guaranteed good, fast money. David quickly rescued her with a warning to stay far, far away from that man.

"David told me to watch out for him in the future and to report to him if I ever saw him again, especially at small auctions. He said his offer of employment was probably to legitimize the sales he made from stolen or ill-gotten books."

"Why the small auctions? Wouldn't he do better going after books and relics worth millions rather than something with an appraised value of, say, sixty thousand dollars?" Simon rubbed his hands over his throat. He looked wan and overtired. She stifled the urge to run her thumb over the dark circles bloating under his eyes.

"Because"—Addie shook her head and forced her focus to the present situation—"the purchase of lower-priced items doesn't attract the same public attention that the higher-priced ones do. His employers aren't interested in what they are buying, anyway, but use the purchases only as a way to launder their money."

"I guess I don't understand this whole money-changing thing. It's so confusing, but what about all these multimillion deals and art thefts we read about?" Serena asked.

"Sure, there are some big arms dealers and the like who are on the lookout for the multimillion-dollar pieces because they don't resell them usually. They trade those on the black market. But organized crime rings just want to look for legitimate ways to clean their money. That's why my book with Kate's stamped appraisal would be attractive to them. They use crime money to buy it, putting the dirty money out into the community, where it's spread around in every direction. Then they resell the book to some unsuspecting legitimate collector, get their money back cleaned, leaving a paper trail that isn't linked to having been acquired through ill-gotten gains. The Feds can't touch it."

"Well, then . . . this whole missing book thing just got a lot more interesting, didn't it?" Simon blew out a breath.

"I wonder what Marvin and Patrick were arguing about?" Serena laid her head back on the sofa and stared up at the ceiling. "Just follow me on this for a second. Addie, you said you left the appraisal on the desk in Teresa's office, and it's now missing, along with the book. Would someone, say Marvin or Patrick, see an opportunity to steal the book and the documents and then sell it to an actual collector later? Which would leave them up sixty thousand to maybe pocket for themselves, but they'd still have the original crime-ring money to invest in something else. Their employer would be none the wiser to the theft and the money having been pocketed. The crime bosses would just be happy when their investment was cleaned."

Addie pursed her lips together. "Yeah, that could have happened, but I don't see Patrick as working with organized crime to have been involved in that respect. He was Teresa's assistant for over a year."

"Yeah, and he came from some small town in the Midwest. Not really the crime syndicate hub of the country. But then again, Chicago is in the Midwest, isn't it?" Serena said. "That's something to consider."

"Since we know for sure that Marvin does work with organized crime"—Simon studied the list of names on the board—"we need to find out if he was in town when Teresa fell down the stairs and the book went missing."

Addie studied the board. "He must have been. The highways and airports were closed the day she fell and still are. He would have had to have been here before that, wouldn't he?"

"Yes," Simon nodded, "he would have."

Addie studied the board. "Maybe . . ." She picked up the pen and wrote, *Patrick caught on to Marvin's book theft, confronted him, they argued.*

"Or vice versa," Serena chirped in.

"Yeah, maybe, but I believe Marvin is likely the guilty one in this scenario." Addie scanned the board.

Simon's emergency alarm sounded on his phone. He glanced at the message and frowned. "I have to go. ER is getting slammed. A trauma was just brought in, too." He kissed Addie's cheek and ruffled Serena's hair on his way out. "Let me know later what you two come up with."

Serena tucked her legs up under her and read through clues on the board. "You know, there's an awful lot of strange coincidences, but we still don't know if Teresa's death was accidental or not, or if the book was stolen, or if she put it somewhere else to store it. There's no real proof so far of anything we've written down."

Addie slunk onto a chair. "You're right, but, like my dad used to say, 'One is an incident. Two is a coincidence, and three is a pattern.' This tells me there is more to it than an accidental fall and a misplaced book."

"With Patrick's disappearance, we definitely have the three now."

"Yeah." Addie rested her head in her hands. "And now, with the added information about Marvin, who I know is a scumbag, being in town and—"

"That makes four, and if your dad was right, there must be a pattern emerging."

"We just need to follow the links and get the proof we need." Addie stared out the window, chewing on her lip. "You know. I think this might even be bigger than we first thought."

"You still have Jonathan on there?"

"So?" She glanced at Serena.

"Do you think with all this new information that he's still involved?"

"More than ever." Addie stretched out her shoulders and arms. "He works in the world of antiquities and rare books, too, just like David did. There's no doubt that over the years he had dealings with Marvin at some point. Actually, it all makes me even more suspicious of him."

"Why?"

"Because I could never figure out what side he was on."

They jumped at a banging noise and looked at the front door. Addie snickered. "I wonder what Simon forgot?" She flung the door open. "Marc?"

"Hi." He removed his police cap. "Do you have a few minutes?"

"Sure, come in."

"I see your other overnight guest has left?"

"What do you want, Marc?" Addie huffed out a breath in frustration.

His jaw tensed, and his gaze flicked to the living room, where Serena was busily writing on the board.

"What are you doing, sis?"

"Just making notes." Serena's hand never stilled.

He drilled Addie with a piercing gaze. "I see once again my warnings about you getting involved in investigations have been ignored."

"What can I do for you?"

"I just had a call back from Carolyn," he said, and strolled into the living room. "Do you want to talk about your connection to Marvin Gibson?" He settled into a chair by the window and pulled his notepad out.

"There's not much to tell, other than what I already told Carolyn." She sat on the arm of the sofa. "We weren't friends or anything."

"But you did know him?" He tapped his pen on the coil ring of his notebook. "Is that correct?"

She relayed the information she had shared earlier with Simon and Serena, leaving out the parts about them suspecting him of having links to the missing book and Teresa's death. When she finished, she sat silently waiting for a response, but he continued writing without giving her any acknowledgment.

He picked up his hat from the table. "Thanks for the information. I'll be on my way now."

Addie leapt to her feet. "Wait, that's it? You're not going to tell us what you found out about his connection to Patrick, or even what's happened to Patrick?"

His jaw tensed. "You know I can't share information about an ongoing investigation."

"That's crap, Marc. Give it a rest." Serena glared as she swept past him. "I need a cup of tea. You two get it together while I'm gone. I'm so tired of the quips and snipes." She disappeared out into the foyer; then she reappeared around the doorframe. "Besides, you know full well that you couldn't have solved the other murders without considering her theories." She disappeared again.

"She's right." Addie crossed her arms and scowled at him. "Remember, too, that I was the one who found the body, and it's my book that's missing. I have a vested interest in all this." He let out a deep breath, toying with his cap in his hands. "And frankly, your hostile treatment toward me lately is ridiculous. You're acting like a spoiled child." Her eyes bore into his. "Just remember, you walked out on me."

He took one step closer. "Yes, I did"—he glanced into the hallway and lowered his voice—"and if you remember it was because there were one too many people in the room that night, and now every time I look there's one more added to that mix." His tightened jaw flinched. "It's killing me, Addie. I know I messed up. I know I should have been more understanding about David and what the two of you had, and how much he meant to you, and the fact that he was murdered and taken away from you wasn't the same as a breakup. But to hear you moan his name when I was kissing you, well, it hurt. Damn it, and this . . . this whole thing with Simon now . . ." He scrubbed his hand over his face. "It's tearing me apart. So, yes, hostile, angry, hurt, distant, aloof, whatever you want to call it all, it's the only way I know how to react because I know it's all my fault, and I've practically shoved you into Simon's arms."

Addie whispered, "So where do we go from here?"

"I don't know. I guess you have to make a decision."

"I've told you that I'm not ready." She placed her hand on his arm. "And I've told Simon that, too. But with the way you've been treating me lately, it's making any decision I might make when I am ready easier."

"I know it hasn't helped." He placed his hands on her shoulders, his gaze searching hers. "I can't blame you. I've been a real jerk." He dropped his hands and fumbled with the rim of his hat. "I'll try harder." A slight smile tugged at the corners of his mouth.

"I'd like that." She attempted a smile.

His eyes softened. "After all, why would you choose an ass, anyway?"

"You said it, I didn't."

His hand reached for hers and caressed the back of it with his thumb. "Yeah, I guess I've made it pretty easy lately for you to want to spend time with Simon."

"That you have." Her hand responded to the touch of his fingers laced with hers.

"But I'll tell you right now"—he tugged gently on her hand—"I'll only be civil to him regarding work. I won't be friends with him. That would be just too weird."

"Deal."

"Deal." His eyes crinkled with a smile. "So, now back to your original question."

"Ah yes, Patrick. Have you found any leads as to where he is or what happened?"

"He was found this morning, bound and unconscious, locked in a housekeeping closet in the hospital."

Addie's hand flew up to her mouth. "Jeez, is he okay?"

"We don't know yet. Last I heard he was still unconscious. Your boyfrien—" Addie's brows shot up. "Um—" Marc coughed. "Simon just went in to treat him."

Marc's text alert pinged. "It looks like he's just woken up. I have to go." He slipped his phone back into his pocket. "But in looking at your board, you can add one more thing."

"What's that?"

"Leave police work to the police." Her jaw tensed. "We think it's best to investigate the trail of evidence and not go chasing our tails based on nothing but some half-cocked theories. It's a distraction. We operate on proof." Before she could think of a snappy retort, he pulled her to him and brought his lips centimeters from hers. "And remember, I have first dibs when you've made your decision." His whisper was the only thing to touch her lips before he released her and walked out.

Serena popped her head in the living room. "Sometimes I think my brother is the biggest idiot on the eastern seaboard. The fool didn't kiss you?" She shook her head. "Moron."

The warmth of his breath still on her lips, Addie avoided answering her friend and focused her eyes on Marvin's name. "Want to go on a little adventure?"

Serena eyed her. "What are you thinking?"

"These aren't 'half-cocked' theories. They're actual clues." She surveyed the board, studying the names and links they'd come up with. "If your brother can't see that and take them seriously, then we need to put some of these pieces together for him and find the proof he keeps going on about."

"That'd shut him up, wouldn't it?"

"I certainly hope so. Grab your coat. We're going on a road trip."

Chapter 14

"Okay, Grey Gull Inn, last stop. Marvin's apparently not staying at the hotel or any of the bed and breakfasts on this list. There are no other options in town." Addie lightly nudged Serena. "I think you'd better take this one since the manager knows you. Maybe we can get more than a head shake out of him."

Before Serena could reply, they reached the front desk.

"Serena, how nice to see you, but your boyfriend isn't working today, if that's who you're looking for?"

"Hi, Bruce, no, I'm not. I know Zach's at the clinic today. That is, if they're open. But I see your power's back on?"

"Yup, just a few minutes ago. I couldn't open for lunch, but now the Grey Gull Inn will be back to normal by dinner service. I hope Zach is planning on working his shift."

"As far as I know, he is."

"Good, he's my most dependable employee, and I

hope he plans on sticking around even after he graduates from that naturopathic doctor course he's studying. He's definitely got more brains than some of the others around here." He shuffled a stack of papers in his hand. "What can I do for you today?"

"I'm hoping you can do us a favor," said Serena.

"Sure, if I can."

"You remember my friend, Addie Greyborne?"

"Of course." He smiled at Addie.

"It seems that an old acquaintance of hers is rumored to be in town, and we were wondering if he was staying here." Serena pasted her most award-winning smile across her face.

"I'd love to help, Serena, but you know I shouldn't really give out the names of my guests."

"I'm not asking for his name. I was just wondering if he's staying here."

"Maybe, if you tell me his name and describe the gentleman in question to me, I could tell you if I'd seen him around." Bruce grinned conspiratorially.

Addie stepped forward. "His name is Marvin Gibson, and he's about mid-height, maybe five-ten or -eleven. Dark hair, slight graying around the temples, stocky build, a really sharp dresser. You couldn't miss him. He looks like he just stepped out of *GQ* magazine." She gave a shaky smile. "Does that ring a bell?"

"As a matter of fact, a man matching that description was here. I remember seeing him the day the storm hit." He looked down at the papers in his hands.

"Do you remember seeing him after that?" Serena leaned across the counter.

"Might have?" He looked steadily at her. "Yes, I think I did. Maybe it was just this morning that I saw that same fellow going upstairs, carrying a takeout cup of coffee. As I said, our power's been out, so he must have been up by the highway there to buy that coffee. It looked like he was going to visit someone. Maybe a guest in room . . . 222." He winked at Serena.

Serena slapped her hand on the desk. "Thanks, Bruce, that's all we need to know." She headed for the door, Addie close behind her.

"There's one other thing," Bruce called after them. "I don't know if it's important, but I remember seeing another man, snappy dresser, too, heading up to see that same guest this morning."

"What did he look like?" Addie's tummy started to perk up.

"From what I could see, he was tall, had on a black—"

"Did he have silver hair?"

Bruce nodded. "From what I could tell under his black hat."

"Thank you, thank you." Addie pressed her hands together in gratitude. "You've really been a huge help."

"I told you nothing." He gave a small salute.

They all but ran to the stairs, but Addie hesitated on the bottom step. Serena slammed into her. "You've got to get those brake lights installed." She pushed herself off of Addie. "What's wrong? Don't you want to find out if it's him?"

"What if it is him? He's dangerous. Maybe we should call Marc and tell him we think we found him and let him handle it."

"And get another lecture again? No way. Look, you can just tell Marvin that you heard he was in town, and you've been thinking over the offer he made you about doing some private book appraisals, and you want to talk to him about it."

Addie swallowed the nausea threatening to overwhelm her. "Yeah, that way I might get some information about what he's up to. We might get some proof."

"That's my girl." Serena grinned. "Now, let's go see what he has to say."

Addie marched up the steps and down the open-air hallway to room 222. She knocked before her courage skittered away. No answer, she knocked again.

"Maybe he's in the bathroom?" whispered Serena over her shoulder.

Addie raised her hand to knock again and was thrown to the ground. "Ooffda!" Her breath whooshed out of her lungs.

"Get back," hissed Marc, pushing off of her. "I told you to stay out of this." He yanked her to her feet and firmly put her and Serena several feet from the door. Motioning to Bruce to unlock it, he crouched and slid inside as the door creaked open. Jerry, gun drawn, followed close behind him.

"Clear, Clear, Clear," rang out from the room.

Addie poked her head inside as Marc clipped his revolver back in its holster. "Jerry, get your kit up here. There has to be something."

"Right, Chief." Jerry hustled down the hallway.

Addie hovered in the doorway, studying Marc's body language. Something told her to keep her mouth shut.

Serena, oblivious to Marc's pensive posture, popped her head around Addie's shoulder and waved. "Hi," she chirped.

"You two, get in here now," he barked, the dark blue veins in his neck protruding. "I don't even know where to begin." His glare had Addie snapping her mouth shut. "Don't even start. I don't want to hear your excuses." His jaw clenched so hard, Addie heard his teeth crunch. "I can't even . . . what's the use with you two. Damn it! Do you have any idea how dangerous walking into a situation with Marvin Gibson could have been? You both could have been killed." He spared them a glance and marched into the suite's bedroom.

Serena cleared her throat. "This sure didn't go as planned."

"Nope." Addie let out a deep breath. "It sure didn't. On the other hand, we know now we were on the right track."

Serena chuckled but quickly stifled it when Marc stalked from the bedroom.

"Did you need me for anything else, Chief?" Bruce stepped into the room. "I really should get back downstairs."

"Of course, Bruce. I'll let you know if I have any more questions."

He whispered to Addie, "Sorry if I got you into trouble by what I said."

"Not your fault," Addie whispered back.

"One more thing before you go, Bruce."

"Sure, Chief, what is it?"

"Did Marvin Gibson say anything to you when he checked out, like where he might be going, anything?"

Bruce shook his head. "He didn't check out, but if all my guests left their rooms this spotless, I might not get as upset about being stiffed on the odd bill. It saves on my housekeeping salaries."

"Okay, thanks, that's all."

"He's right. It is spotless." Addie stepped forward and surveyed the room. "It doesn't even look like anyone's been staying in it."

"Too spotless." His gaze flicked to Jerry, who entered with the crime-scene kit. "Jerry, get what you can. Hair, fibers, prints. There must be something left behind. Even professional cleaners can make mistakes."

"Professional cleaners? But Bruce just said that he used his own housekeeping staff." Serena peeked into the suite's bathroom, where Marc was studying the sink. "Maybe I could have them clean my place."

Addie's voice dropped. "Not that kind of cleaner."

"What other kind is there?"

"Criminal organizations," Addie whispered, "and some secret-type government agencies use specialists in making evidence disappear. They send a person or a small team in to scrub a crime scene before the police arrive so there's no evidence left."

Serena's mouth dropped, her voice rising on a squeak. "Do you think that's why Jonathan was here?"

Marc poked his head out of the bathroom. "What do you mean Jonathan was here?"

"Nothing." Serena looked at everything but her brother.

"Addie, what's she talking about?"

"It's just that . . ." She hated narcing somebody out, especially Bruce, but she had no choice. "It's just that Bruce told us Marvin might have had a visitor this morning."

"And he said it was Jonathan? Does he know him?"

"No, but the man he described sounded a lot like Jonathan."

"Jerry," he called.

"Yes, Chief." He popped his head out of the bedroom.

"Find anything so far?" he asked, his eyes never wavering from Addie's.

"No, sir, nothing, not even one print. It's like no one's ever set foot in this room."

"That's what I was afraid of." Marc's eyes seemed to take in every detail. "Okay, we might as well wrap it up. We won't find anything."

"How can there be nothing?" Serena's brow creased. "Hundreds, no, thousands of people must have slept in here over the years. What about all those television shows that use some kind of special light to show viewers the hidden yuck and stuff in hotel rooms?"

Marc ignored her and scribbled in his notepad. He flipped his notebook closed and stuffed it into his shirt pocket. "My suggestion is that both of you go back to minding your own businesses and forget all about this today." He headed for the door and pierced them with a hard look. "And don't tell anyone what happened here. I have to go and talk to Bruce. Jerry," he called, "you know what to do when you leave." The door thudded closed behind him.

Jerry packed up his bag. "You heard the chief, go. What are you waiting for?"

Addie peered through the snowflakes settling on the windshield of Serena's Jeep and spied Jerry as he trudged to his cruiser. He had hung a DO NOT DISTURB sign on the doorknob but hadn't posted crime-scene tape across the door. Why? Was it a secret? Marc had said not to tell anyone about today. What did he know that he didn't tell them?

"Do you remember once when you thought your house had been broken into?" Serena turned the heater defrost on high when the vehicle warmed up enough to blow warm air. "But it hadn't been, and then minutes later Marc got a call saying your shop had been?"

"Yeah, and then he teased me about being the crazy psychic lady."

"Yup, but remember when you said this morning that you thought this whole thing might be bigger than we thought?" Serena backed out of the parking stall. "Well, it looks like you're right."

"Yeah." Addie took one last look at the hotel. "It sure does."

Chapter 15

Addie collapsed into her foyer. Her nightmarish day was finally over, and she wanted to curl up on the sofa, watch some mindless television with a coffee in hand, and forget all about the madness. Serena was right. This whole thing was bigger than she first thought, and her head felt like it was going to explode trying to fit all the pieces together. But enough was enough for one day.

Flipping on the foyer light, she tugged off her boots and wiggled her numb toes into her pink fuzzy house slippers. On her way to the kitchen, there were only two things on her mind: coffee and then sweet, mind-numbing oblivion.

Coffee in hand, she bypassed the wall light switch and the table lamp, snatched the remote from on top of the television, and flipped past documentaries, history shows, and news broadcasts. A Christmas romantic comedy? Perfect. She snuggled into the arm of the sofa and took a sip of coffee. Like magic, the tension seeped from her body. The dimness of the room and soft flickering from the television screen lulled her into a slight doze. Before fully nodding off, she glimpsed a flash of movement out of the corner of her eye. She bolted upright and brandished the remote control above her head. "Who's there?"

The table lamp switched on.

She clutched at the crushing pain through her chest. "Jonathan. What . . . how? What are you doing, scaring me like that?" When her heart quit knocking against her rib cage, she pinned her unwelcome guest with a venomous stare.

"Good evening, Addie." He folded his hands across his lap. "I didn't mean to give you such a start. I really would have announced my presence earlier, but I must have dozed off waiting for your return."

"Get out." He made no move to do so. "How did you even get in here? The alarm was still set when I came in." She struggled to her feet, adrenaline the only force willing her knees to cooperate. "And why are you here . . . like this? You nearly gave me a heart attack. Haven't you heard of a telephone?"

"It wasn't my intent to harm you in any way, and telephones come with"—he arched a sly brow—"some risks, shall we say."

"Risks? What about the risk of breaking into a person's house and scaring them to death?"

"You're made of hardier stock than that." He clucked his tongue. "I've seen you in action."

His persistent monotone needled her nerves at the base of her spine. "Jeez"—she clasped her head—"this is insane."

He paced the room, toying with his hat in his hands. "I only wanted to talk to you away from prying eyes and ears, nothing more."

"What could you possibly have to say to me that requires this, this tactic of intrusion?" She hoped her look of hatred would drop him to the floor, but he still paced, very much alive.

He took a step toward her and his eyes held hers in an unyielding stare. She quickly shuffled backward. A second later, the edge of the coffee table smacked across the back of her knees as her breaths quickened. She stiffened her back and braced her feet.

His brows bumped together in a scowl. "My dear, it's not what you think."

"How do you know what I'm thinking?" Her fist clenched, ready to pop him one at the slightest move toward her.

"The fast breathing, signifying a racing heart, the rapid eye movements, the small beads of perspiration on your brow, your stiffened muscles ready to do battle, those are all indications that you're feeling what a trapped animal does when cornered. How am I doing?"

Her eyes widened in a gaped-mouth stare.

"That's what I thought. Please, sit down, before your knees give away again." He gestured toward the sofa.

She obediently followed his lead. If for no other reason than she would hate to prove him right when the only thing keeping her upright was a high dose of adrenaline.

He took a seat beside her on the sofa and took her hand in his. She pulled away from him, but he didn't release his hold. "I'm only going to say this once; then we never speak of it again. Do you understand?"

Addie had never truly known if she'd ever felt hatred for somebody. Her question was answered. She refused to give him a response and returned his gaze with feral intensity.

He clasped her hand firmer. "I know what happened today at the Grey Gull Inn—" He shook his head when she opened her mouth to speak. "Don't ask me how, but pursuing Marvin Gibson or any of those suspects you have on that"—his head motioned toward her crime board—"has to stop now for your own safety. What you and your friends are doing is too dangerous. Do I make myself clear?"

His eyes remained as impassive as ever. "Are you threatening me?" Addie ground out.

"Not in the least, my dear. I'm just laying the cards on the table for you."

"Who are you, Jonathan . . . really?"

"Just remember, if you go off looking for a problem, you'd better be prepared to deal with the solution."

She recoiled and pulled her hand away.

"Just stay as far away from all this as you can, for your own sake." He stood up, kissed the top of her head, and shuffled toward the door, pausing. "I almost forgot, I guess I'll be seeing you tomorrow for brunch at Catherine's, won't I?"

Her forehead creased, was that tomorrow? It couldn't be Sunday already, could it? Her eyes never wavered from his, but she gave no sign she'd heard him.

"I see why my son adored you so. You have spunk." He smiled. "And don't worry, no security systems were harmed during my entry." He tipped his hat to her and closed the front door with a gentle click.

Addie chucked a throw pillow where her almost-father-in-law had stood. Emotions she had shoved into corners finally broke free and ran rampant through her body. Shivering uncontrollably, she tugged the throw from the back of the sofa and wrapped it around her, willing her body to relax. Her body soon relented, but her mind spiraled like a crazy kaleidoscope. The murder board! Something on it scared him. So the answer had to be there. She studied the names and notes she'd made, closed her eyes to try to see the bigger picture, but it was no use. None of it made sense. Maybe Jonathan and Marc and Simon were right. This was too big for her to handle. Jonathan's name, black and thick against the paper, seemed to taunt her.

What was he so afraid of her discovering that he'd break into her house just to warn her to back off? No, there was no way she was quitting now. She grabbed a pen from the table and began to scribble notes beside the name of her number-one suspect. There was something here he didn't want her to find, and she'd make sure she found it before it found her.

Chapter 16

Addie's foot skated off the bottom porch step. The two travel mugs she clasped in her hands quivered wildly in the air. "Simon, grab the hot chocolate." He skidded around the hood of Carolyn's pickup and seized the mugs from her hands as she stumbled over a snowdrift at the bottom.

"Whoa." He propelled his body in front of hers.

She thudded against his chest and struggled to regain her footing.

"Why didn't you wait for me?" He shook dripping liquid from his gloves. "I was on my way up to get you."

"Where would the adventure be in that?" She laughed and snatched a mug from his hand and knocked back a mouthful. "Ah, there's nothing like adding a shot of chocolate to a morning rush of adrenaline." She wiped a frothy chocolate moustache from her upper lip and grinned up at him. "Thank you for saving me from a face-plant into the snow."

"In hindsight"—he rubbed his chest, grinning—"I think I should have let you fall."

"Yeah, you would have loved that, seeing me kiss a snowbank." She jeered and hiked herself up into the passenger seat. "Remind me to buy some ice melt today."

He climbed into his seat and sipped from his mug. "The least I can do for the hot chocolate. Thanks."

"I thought we'd need it to get into the spirit for this pre-Christmas brunch." She buckled up her seat belt. The truck tossed from side to side on the uneven ruts up the driveway. Addie gripped the dash and held on for her life as Simon pulled hard on the steering wheel and bounced over a deep furrow at the top onto the road. "Are the main streets this bad?"

"Not once we get down the hill, but as you can see the plows haven't made it all the way up here yet. Hang on." They lurched forward. Addie hissed out a breath. Simon sniggered and patted her hand. "Don't worry, they get better farther down. I promise."

"I'll try to take your word for it." She glanced out the side window at the roof-high snowbanks and shivered, exhaling. "Look at this. It's so freaking cold I can see my breath in here. Is the heater even working?"

"Yes, it is," he choked, stifling a laugh. "We don't have to go if you don't want to." Simon turned onto the main road at the bottom of the hill. "If not, tell me now, and we can turn around and go back."

"No, we have to go," she grumbled, swiping at her breath clouds. "I need some answers."

"And you think you're going to find them over brunch?"

"I don't know, maybe." Her lips tightened. "Do you think I'm crazy for pursuing this whole missing book thing and suggesting that Teresa might have been killed because of it?"

"Crazy, no, but determined to solve a mystery? An

emphatic yes. You seem to attract them and have no willpower to resist their enigmatic lure." He reached across the seat and squeezed her hand. "Why all the self-doubt? That's unusual for you."

She relayed the tale of her visitor the evening before. Simon listened attentively, and when she finished, silence filled the pickup. The only thing moving was Simon's chest, which expanded with hard breaths.

"Are you okay?" Addie ran a finger up and down his coat sleeve.

"I'm fine."

"That's what women say." When he didn't raise his brows at her humor, she scooted as close as her seat belt would allow. "Your face doesn't tell me you're fine."

He blew out a noisy breath. "No, really, it sounds like you handled yourself like a pro, better than I would have. I think I'd have taken a swing at him or worse."

"It's not that I didn't think about it but—"

"But what? He broke into your house."

"I know, but he's David's father."

"So?" His voice rose. "He crossed a line. What did he say when you asked him who he really was?"

"Nothing, he ignored it."

Simon said nothing and fixed his eyes on the road ahead.

"Any ideas?"

"Nope, but there is definitely something he's hiding."

"That's what I thought, too, and why I need to go to this brunch even though he's the last person I want to see today."

"I hate to keep echoing these words, but be careful. He sounds like a professional. The way he got into your house? You never know what else he's capable of." He parked behind Serena's Jeep. His hands didn't drop from the steering wheel, instead they constricted around the leather, strangling the surface.

"Simon?" Addie unbuckled and slid over to him, her thigh touching his. She unwrapped his hands from the steering wheel and held them in her hands. When he refused to meet her gaze, she called his name. "Simon? I'm fine. Nothing happened last night. What we need to figure out is, what's his angle, and what exactly he's a professional at. I can't do this without you."

A smile flickered across his face, and he brought her hands up to his lips. "I am honored to be your trusty sidekick. Now, let's go eat."

Catherine opened the door. Her face lit up at the sight of the two of them. Christmas music, laughter, and the smell of fresh gingerbread emanated from inside the house and melted any qualms Addie had about attending the festive occasion. Her friends were not Jonathan, as he was certainly not her friend. She would not and could not take her animosity for one person out on the rest of them. The welcoming scents and decorations took her back to Christmases past, but she flinched at the glimpse of her Christmas present. There stood Jonathan, with a mug in hand, and a smile on his lips that didn't quite reach his eyes. Without acknowledgment of his presence Addie made a wide berth around him and carried on into the living room.

Catherine introduced her and Simon to her sister, Joyce Walker, who was visiting from Long Island for the holidays; her husband, Jack; and their teenage daughter, Adel, who fleetingly raised her eyes up from her cell phone to wave. Catherine pointed out Jack was a physician, and Simon gravitated to his side. The two quickly became immersed in conversation.

"I'm surprised to see you here." Addie smiled, shaking Joyce's outstretched hand. "Did you have any travel troubles?"

"We got lucky and came through just as they were closing the highway's north."

"It was touch and go for the last hundred miles, but we made it," Jack chuckled from his perch on the sofa, "but if it stays like this, we may be stuck here until spring. Got a job for an old doc at that hospital of yours?" He slapped Simon's shoulder.

Serena and Zach emerged from the kitchen, Zach bearing two steaming mugs of spiced punch. He handed one to her and one to Simon, and joined him and Jack on the couch. Addie's skin pricked under Jonathan's unrelenting gaze. Needing escape, she followed Catherine into the kitchen.

"Addie, this is Crystal Parker." Catherine gestured toward the young woman sneaking an hors d'oeuvre from a platter. "We met through my volunteer work at the hospital when she moved here last year."

"We've met." Addie stepped forward, her hand outstretched. "Nice to see you again, Crystal."

"Nice to see you, too." She smiled and shook Addie's hand.

"When I mentioned to Jonathan that her Caribbean holiday plans were changed due to the weather, he suggested I invite her to join us today."

"Jonathan suggested it?" Addie pasted a smile on her face.

"Yes, he has such a big heart and hates to see anyone on their own for the holidays, and I agreed."

"I'm glad you could join us." Addie's throat tightened. *Big heart, my foot.* She remembered a few years that Jonathan couldn't even bother to call David over the holidays, let alone drop in for one of his flyby visits.

"I didn't know that you and Catherine were friends," Crystal said, picking up a covered buffet pan from the counter. "Typical of small towns, though, isn't it?" She shrugged. "I guess everyone knows everyone."

"Yeah, and you can't keep too many secrets, either, if you haven't noticed by now." Addie noted the lack of eye contact from the young woman as she took the serving dish from her. "Do you want this taken into the dining room now, Catherine?"

"Yes, and I think that's it. We're ready to eat. Serena and Zach appear to have taken everything else in. Oh, the appetizers?" She eyed the platter, down by one tasty tidbit. "Could you bring it out with you? I'll round up the rest, and we can start." She swept out of the kitchen, leaving Addie alone with the petite redhead.

"So, if you've only been in town a year, where are you from originally?" Addie reached around the young woman and grabbed a serving spoon.

"The Midwest."

"Any part in particular?"

"No, we moved a lot."

"I see. I heard that Patrick was from the Midwest. He moved here last year, too. Did you know each other before you came here?"

Crystal's shoulders stiffened. "No." She stirred the simmering pot of Christmas punch.

Addie studied the young woman's back. "Not knowing anyone can make it hard moving to a new place. I'm glad you've met Catherine, though. She's one of the nicest women I've met since I moved here not that long ago myself."

Crystal took a carton of orange juice from the refrigerator and poured it into a glass pitcher.

"Have you managed to make many other friends? I

know this town can take a while to accept outsiders, but once they do—"

"Not many." Crystal sidestepped around her. "We should get these in." She disappeared with the juice into the dining room. Addie frowned, grabbed the platter, and followed her out.

Addie set out the last of the buffet dishes as everyone lined up along the side service table. She slipped into last place behind Crystal and heaped her plate with an assortment of hash browns, eggs, sausages, bacon, flapjacks, and chicken and dumplings, which she smothered in gravy. She looked down at her plate and cringed. This was going to force her to do extra stomach crunches tonight for sure. She shrugged. 'Tis the season and all that.

Addie slid into a chair between Crystal and Simon, who was seated beside his new buddy, Jack. Apparently, they were now bound by the brotherhood of stethoscopes. Out of the corner of her eye, Addie noticed Jonathan take a chair at the end of the table on the other side of Crystal. Her senses began buzzing.

Crystal's elbow bumped Addie's as she dug around in her purse. She pulled out her cell phone and laid it beside her on the table. She glanced at Addie. "I'm expecting an important call. I hope you don't mind."

Jonathan laughed, setting Addie's teeth on edge. "Here." He placed his cell on the table as well. "Now everyone has to get mad at both of us."

Crystal's laugh chimed in with Jonathan's, and they turned away from Addie and were soon in quiet discussion. Fine with her, she thought, as she shoved a forkful of chicken and dumplings in her mouth. It was as if she had disappeared. Conversations whirled about her. Instead of feeling lonely, she shifted closer to Crystal and strained to hear what she and Jonathan were discussing. But it was no good. Jonathan and Crystal's soft tones were easy muffled by the overexcited physicians to her right. Within five minutes, she had learned more about the latest medical breakthrough in cellular regeneration than she had ever cared to.

She caught a glimpse of Jonathan's hand clasping Crystal's, his thumb stroking small circles over the back of it. No wonder the poor girl's food was untouched. Jonathan briefly met Addie's stare. His attention flicked away and went back to ogling Crystal, but Addie shivered at the challenge in his eyes. Or had it been a warning?

If only Catherine could see this. But her friend, oblivious to the fondling under the table, laughed with her guests and played the merry hostess. Fearing what she might do, Addie excused herself and took refuge in the kitchen. Addie put a stranglehold on the kitchen counter, her body vibrating with rage. A hand rested on her shoulder, and she jumped.

"Are you feeling ill?" Catherine asked.

"No, I'm fine." She blinked away stinging tears. "It's just . . . never mind. I'm tired and feeling a bit overwhelmed right now." She loosened her death grip on the counter, her whitened knuckles pinking back with life.

"Yes, the holidays can do that, and it all sneaks up on one at the darnedest times."

Addie searched her face. "Catherine"—she sucked in a shallow breath—"there's something I need to talk to you—"

"Ah, here you two are." Jonathan appeared in the doorway. "Is everything okay?"

"Nothing to worry about." Catherine stroked Addie's arm. "She just had a spell of holiday anxiety and needs a few minutes."

"That's too bad." Jonathan's gaze narrowed on Addie's. "Nothing too serious, I hope."

"You tell me, Jonathan. Is everything okay?"

Catherine scoffed. "Why on earth would Jonathan not be okay?"

His smile looked forced. "Perhaps our friend here needs a cup of tea to soothe whatever ails her today."

"Good idea. It's time to put the kettle on and make coffee, anyway." Catherine went to work filling the kettle and switched on the coffeemaker.

Addie swept by Jonathan and returned to the dining room to her seat. Crystal removed her plate to the side table and headed toward the front hall coat closet and retrieved her coat. She called out her thanks to Catherine and waved good-bye to the group at the table. Jonathan appeared in the foyer and whispered something to the young woman before he closed the door.

Addie leaned toward Simon. "Where's she going?"

"She asked me if Patrick could have visitors yet, and I said yes." He shrugged. "I guess that's where she's off to."

Catherine entered the dining room carrying a serving tray laden with hot tea and coffee and set in on the sideboard. Jonathan took his seat at the end of the table, and Catherine served his coffee, measuring out his required five spoonfuls of sugar. Addie wondered how many other women knew how he took his coffee? Did Crystal? That thought sent her imagination into overdrive, and she almost missed Catherine asking her what she would like to drink. Needing something without caffeine, for once, she selected an herbal tea with Serena's business logo on the tag. She studied Jonathan and his eyes flicked to hers.

His cold, unyielding gaze broke off when he glanced at his vibrating cell phone. "I'm sorry, my dear Catherine. I have to go out for a while." He patted his shirt pocket. "I appear to be out of cigarettes and couldn't possibly indulge in gingerbread cake and not top it off without one."

"Do you really need one so badly? You promised me you were quitting." Catherine made her way around the table to him and placed her hand on his arm.

He clasped her hand in his. "Sorry, bad habits. I shouldn't be long." He kissed her forehead.

"Better listen to her," Jack piped in. "After all, you have not one, but two doctors who back her fully on this." He raised a coffee cup in a salute.

Addie glanced at Crystal's empty chair and then at Catherine, her heart aching for her friend.

"We'll save you some cake," Catherine smiled, "but hurry back before Jack tries to teach you a lesson about smoking and finishes all the cake off."

Jonathan chuckled as he made his way to the front door and put on his coat. Before leaving, he pinned Addie with a look, his eyes cold and unreadable. Addie shivered and sought out the warmth of friendly conversation and tea.

Chapter 17

Catherine kissed Addie's cheek. "Thank you both for helping with the cleanup. I'm sorry Jonathan hasn't come back yet." She glanced at her watch. "I can't think what's keeping him this long."

Addie forced a smile. At least, she hoped it came off as a smile and not the teeth-gnashing grimace she was feeling. "And thank you for such a wonderful meal. It was more than you should have done, really."

"Yes, thank you for including me, too," Simon grinned, "but Addie's right. You shouldn't have gone to so much trouble. I think this motley crew would have been happy just to get together over muffins and cold cereal."

"It was no problem." Catherine's eyes lit up. "When Joyce and I get together in the kitchen, we become a regular Julia Child cooking team."

Addie poked her head into the living room. "It was nice to meet you all. I hope we can get together again over the holidays."

Jack waved. "Yes, we definitely have to make a plan.

Simon and I still have a lot of groundbreaking medical discoveries to discuss."

"Yes, we do." Simon pulled on his gloves. "See you soon, Jack. Joyce, it was great to meet you." He waved and stepped outside.

Addie pulled her coat collar up and grabbed the back of Simon's jacket as she skidded down the slick pathway behind him. Simon's laughs chugged out as fog as he sled-dogged her across the street to the truck.

"That was fun." He helped her gain her footing on the ice-covered running board into the truck.

She snorted, buckling up her seat belt. "It seems Catherine decided to invite every stray soul in town."

"Does that mean I was invited because I'm a stray soul?"

"No." She stifled a giggle. "I wasn't talking about you. I think Catherine wishes she was twenty years younger because she has a thing for tall, dark, handsome doctors, as her sister apparently does, too."

That produced a laugh from both of them as she closed her door and Simon slipped his way around the truck and got in. "Phew! Good thing Carolyn didn't need her truck back today. It's getting pretty icy."

"I hope the hill up to my house isn't going to be an issue."

He turned onto Main Street. "Sanding trucks appear to have started. That will help."

Addie arched her back and rubbed her hand over her aching stomach. "I don't ever remember being this full. I can't wait to get home and get into my yoga pants," she moaned.

"I was surprised Serena stayed after us. I thought she'd want to get out of there to spend some alone time with Zach."

"Poor Serena. With Zach's schedule, they hardly see each other." Addie shifted in her seat and groaned. "But staying really wasn't her choice. Apparently, Adel has been bugging her mother to let her dye her hair the same fiery-red shade as Serena's, and Joyce finally gave in, so they're upstairs playing beauty salon this evening." She looked out her side window as they approached the hospital. "Stop," she cried.

"Why?"

"Just pull over, now."

He slid to a stop on the slushy gutter snow. "What is going on?"

"Look"—she pointed—"isn't that Crystal walking out of the hospital toward the parking lot?"

"Yes, so? It appears she did go visit Patrick, and judging by her arms full of folders, he's given her some homework to do while he's laid up. Is that why you made me pull over?" He shook his head as Crystal got into a blue Honda Accord and exited the lot. "Anything else, or can I take you home now? I have to be back here to work at seven to pull an all-nighter in the ER and need to go home and have a nap first."

"Sorry, I was just curious." She batted her lashes at him; then she yelped, "Stop."

"What now?" He slammed on the brakes.

"There. Isn't that Jonathan walking out the main doors around to the back parking lot?"

"It looks like him. I wonder why he's here."

"Pretty sure he didn't find any cigarettes at the hospital gift shop."

"No, he wouldn't have. They're not sold on-site."

"Yeah." She looked sideways at Simon. "That's what I thought." She frowned and glanced back at the parking lot just as a black Land Rover spun around the corner from the back lot, speeding toward the exit in front of them. "Duck." She grabbed Simon's coat collar and pulled him down with her.

Simon, his head under the dash, looked sideways at her. "Is this really necessary?"

"Yes," she whispered. "I don't want him to see us, or he'll know we caught him in his lie to Catherine."

"Why are we whispering?"

"Because—" She jumped at a sharp knock on the window above her ahead. She looked up over her shoulder and swallowed. "Jonathan?" She sat up and rolled down the window. "Hello there."

"Hello, Addie, Simon," he nodded, "is everything okay here?"

"Yes, everything's just fine. Why?"

"No particular reason." His eyes bore into hers. "I'm just wondering why you're hiding here in the truck."

"Hiding?" She looked at Simon, then back at Jonathan. "Us? No, Simon was just driving me home and—"

"And my contact popped out," Simon chimed in.

"Yes, we were just looking for it." Addie pasted a sugary-sweet smile on her lips.

"Glad to hear everything's all right." He drummed his fingers on the lower window casing.

"Found it." Simon poked around his eye. "There, now I can see again."

"See, just fine." Addie pasted her toothy grin back on her face. "Are you heading back to Catherine's now? I know she's wondering where you are. It has been a while since you left for cigarettes."

Jonathan's expression didn't change. There it was again, no tell, just that steel cold gaze.

"Yes, heading back now." He double tapped the side

of the truck. "I just wanted to make sure you both were okay." He hopped back into his Land Rover and skidded out of the lot.

"Can you believe that?" She flipped the window button to close. "The nerve of him questioning us. He lies about everything. Cigarettes? Yeah, and my name is Queen Elizabeth. All he was doing was finding an excuse to chase after a woman half his age." She slammed her palm on the dash. "And look"—she pointed—"he's going the same direction as Crystal did. Catherine's house is the opposite way."

Simon studied her as if she'd sprouted a second head.

"What?" She glared at him. "You have nothing to say? Well, mister, I sure do. I told you what he was like. Now poor Catherine is going to be so hurt, and with Crystal of all people. What is he thinking?"

"Forget Crystal. It's Jonathan's uncanny—"

"I can't forget Crystal," she snapped. "You didn't see the two of them carrying on during brunch, right under Catherine's nose."

"No, I didn't, and I know how much you care for Catherine, but—"

"Of course, I do, and I should have talked to her sooner. He's nothing but a playboy and always has been. He'll never change."

"Addie"—he looked at her from under a raised brow—"do you really think that he met Crystal here for some tryst in a storage room closet?"

"It happens in hospitals every day, doesn't it?"

He choked on a laugh. "Only on medical televisions shows. Take my word for it, not in real life."

"Then what were they doing? Wait, I know!" She snapped her fingers. "With Patrick laid up, they met in his office for their little liaison." She spun toward Simon, her seat belt locking against the sudden force. "That's it, isn't it?"

He grasped her hand. "Stop, and think about it."

"That's all I am doing." She slammed her body against the seat. Who cared if pouting was childish? She didn't. Not about anything anymore.

"But you're thinking about what you know to be true about Jonathan and not what you don't know. Put your non-emotional, rational hat on instead of being so bent on proving to yourself that Jonathan's the snake you think he is. Remember your big-picture thinking. That's what you need here."

"What are you talking about?" She struggled against the tight seat belt, unfastened it, and reclicked it. "I'm being totally rational."

"Are you?" He started to pull out and slammed on the brakes. A taxi skidded to a stop directly in front of them. He glanced at Addie's hand still on the seat belt fastener. "Nice timing." He brushed his hand over hers. "And they wonder why there's so many traffic accidents." Simon growled under his breath at the driver as they pulled out and passed the taxi. "Did you see that? He just flipped me off." Simon's eyes darted between the rearview mirror and the road ahead, uttering words that Addie didn't know he was capable of using.

"What's wrong with you?"

"That idiot taxi driver again. Some guy raced out and jumped in, and he's been right on my tail since the hospital. Hang on." Simon swerved over to the side, his curse words burning in her ears.

The white and blue cab sped by them. Addie clutched her chest.

"You saw that, too?" Simon snarled. "He almost side-swiped us."

"No, it wasn't that. The guy in the passenger seat looked like Marvin Gibson."

"The crooked broker?"

"Yeah." She snapped her mouth shut and clutched at the thoughts buzzing through her head. "Okay, just hear me out. What if Jonathan went to meet with him?" Her gaze followed the taillights as the car disappeared around the corner on Birch Road. "Which means Marvin, Jonathan, and Crystal were all at the hospital at the same time. Aha! And Patrick's there, too." She stroked her chin. "That's all the top suspects on my crime board."

"Crystal isn't really a suspect, though, is she?"

"No." Her forehead puckered. "I think you were right. She just went to see Patrick, not meet up with Jonathan. With the auction coming up, I'm sure he's dumped a lot more work on her now that he's laid up."

"I'm guessing that you were just too blinded by Jonathan's past performances with women to see that when you saw them both coming out of the hospital?" He cocked his head to the side. "Apology accepted."

"Apology for what?"

"Nothing."

Her lips pursed into a pout. "I'm sorry for my rant and shouting at you."

"That's my girl." He ruffled her hair. "Now that your blinders are off concerning Jonathan, what do you think is really going on? The fact that Marvin was also at the hospital puts a whole new spin on it."

"Yeah, this definitely is more than some dalliance with a pretty young woman."

"I don't know what's going on, and it might not mean anything but a coincidence, but now I'm getting worried . . . about you, mostly."

"Me, why?"

"Remember Jonathan's strange visit last night?"

"Of course, I do," she scowled. "I was there, wasn't I?"

"He essentially broke in and then gave you a warning."

"Yeah, he warned me to stay away from what was happening."

"And you saw Jonathan's face just now when he was talking to us? He obviously wasn't happy seeing us there. He wasn't ticked because we caught him having a fling with Crystal. He was there for another reason."

"Yeah, I should have thought about that then. He's never cared about getting caught having an affair before."

They bounced over the ruts at the top of the hill and slid to a halt at her front door. She reached for the door handle. "You're right. I have to stop thinking of Jonathan only as the womanizer and remember he is the number-one suspect on my list, right above Marvin and Patrick."

He leaned across the seat. "Yeah, and from what we just saw, this, whatever this is"—his finger tucked a loose wave of hair behind her ear—"with the book, the death, Jonathan, and Marvin, is more than you should be handling on your own. He's already given you one warning. What's going to happen next?"

"Especially after this afternoon." She deflated into her seat. "How did he know we were in the truck? His ability to see and seem to know everything bothers me."

"I think what I said earlier about him is right on. He is a professional something."

"Exactly. He knew Serena and I went to the Grey Gull Inn looking for Marvin Gibson. He's like a freaking ghost, and it's gotten me thinking."

He groaned. "Please don't do that."

"Why not? I happen to have great thoughts."

He ran a finger down her cheek. "It's been a long day already, and I still have to go to work."

"Just hear me out for a minute. Something interesting happened during lunch, and I think it means more than I first thought. Crystal set her phone on the table, saying that she hoped no one would object during the meal, but that she was waiting for an important call."

"She was probably waiting to hear how Patrick was. He is her boss, and they do have the auction coming up."

"Yeah, yeah, I know all that, but then Jonathan set his phone right beside hers and made a joke that if anyone complained, they'd have to get mad at him, too."

Simon shrugged. "It sounds like he was only being polite."

"Could be." Addie's finger rubbed over her bottom lip. "She kept glancing at her phone, but it didn't ring, and I didn't see her reading any messages."

"Okay, so what?"

"After I went into the kitchen, did you ever see her on it?"

"I was mostly talking to Jack about a new surgical mesh." He rubbed his neck. "Let's see. You left the table, and then she leaned over and asked me how Patrick was doing. I told her he was in good condition and mostly likely going to be released within a day or two. Yes, then she received a text, you came back, and she got up to leave."

"Then Jonathan got a message and left shortly after?" She flopped her head back against the seat. "Go with me on this. I'm just throwing ideas out there. Whatever his attraction to Crystal is might not be in the romance department as I first suspected, but she *must* be connected to the whole thing somehow."

"Maybe," he shrugged, "but how? There's been no proof."

"His partner? What if she has the book and it was her who sent him the text telling him to come get it?"

"But she left the hospital first, and she was the one with an armful of whatever. He was empty-handed."

"You're right. But what if he, because as you said is a professional whatever, used his phone to—"

"What, clone hers?"

Her eyes lit up. "Yes, and maybe she is completely innocent, and Jonathan wanted to be able to clone her texts and calls on his phone, so he always knows what's going on? Patrick was Teresa's assistant. What if Jonathan is working with him, but he's afraid Patrick might be trying to double-cross him?" She frowned. "But how does Marvin fit into all this? Is he a partner, too?"

Simon snorted, grinning. "I don't know, is he?"

"Maybe Marvin's just irked about buying a ticket for a book sale with a disappearing book."

"That sounds more logical to me. I think you've been reading too many Ian Fleming–type novels and making this all more cloak-and-daggery than it really is." He shook his head. "Cloned phones? Major conspiracy plots? What's next?"

"Did Patrick ever identify who it was that struck him and tied him up in the closet."

"Nope, he said whoever it was hit him from behind."

"What if—"

His hand flew up. "Whatever it is you're thinking, just stop. Please just back off from your own personal sleuthing escapades and take whatever it is you're thinking to Marc right away. We have no idea what's really going on, and I am afraid you are the one who will end up getting hurt trying to figure it out."

A shrill, emergency siren ring tone on his phone shrieked. He read the message twice before looking at her.

"What's wrong?"

Simon scratched his head. "I really don't know. It's Dr. Harris. He just administered Naloxone to Patrick."

"What's that?"

"Narcan." His thumbs clicked across the face of his phone. "It reverses narcotic overdoses. I have to go and see what happed."

"I thought he was doing better? Why is he on narcotics?"

"He had a couple of cracked ribs that are still causing a lot of pain, but he's on a minimal dosage, so I don't understand how he could overdose." His lips set in a grim line. "I just don't get it."

Chapter 18

"How did your car get here?" Serena pulled into her spot in the alley behind their shops.

"I have no idea." Addie shrugged. "Last I checked it was still under three feet of snow in the police parking lot." Addie stared in disbelief at her completely snow-free Mini Cooper.

"A guardian angel, maybe?"

"I guess so. I'd better see what Paige knows about it. Thanks for the lift."

"Thanks for my morning coffee." Serena raised her travel mug in a salute.

Addie opened the back door of her store greeted by the sounds of Christmas carols drifting from the front of the shop followed by a round of applause and cheers. "What's going on?" She flung her coat across the desk and headed into the bookstore in time to see a group dressed in classic Dickens period costumes leaving.

Paige hurried toward her. "You just missed the town carolers. They were awesome."

"That's too bad. I could use a bit of Christmas cheer today."

"But before I forget, Marc told me when he dropped off your car that you'll have to get the door lock fixed. He said it broke when they opened it to hot-wire it so they could bring it here."

"He broke into my car?" Her eyes flashed. "Why didn't he just ask for the key? Better yet, just text and ask me to pick it up if they wanted it off the lot."

She winced. "He wanted to surprise you."

"Yeah, nice surprise," Addie spouted, her voice holding a bite. "I returned your car, but it will cost you three hundred dollars."

"He said for me to tell you that he'd pay for it."

Addie's cheeks warmed. "I guess in that case he's off the hook, and I'll appreciate the gesture." She rounded a bookshelf and stopped, blinked, and blinked again. Were her eyes deceiving her, or was the white-haired, full-figured woman seated at the counter sipping a cup of coffee and reading actually Martha. She looked back at Paige, then back at Martha, and then back at Paige.

"I hope you don't mind," Paige whispered. "The furnace in the bakery is on the fritz, and she's waiting for the repair guy to come."

"Of course, I don't mind," she whispered back. "I just can't believe that she's really in my shop."

Paige grinned. "It is a good start, isn't it?"

"It sure is." Addie straightened her shoulders and leisurely walked to the coffeemaker, dropped a pod in, and smiled at her unexpected guest. "Hello, Martha, I see you found something to read."

Martha harrumphed and shoved the book across the counter.

"*The Joy of Cooking* by Irma S. Rombauer." Addie

tapped her finger on the cover. "Now, there's a real classic."

Without looking up, Martha drummed the fingers of her left hand on the counter and sipped her coffee in her right.

"You know. A customer brought in a few more of those last week. I haven't had the time to price them yet or get them on the shelves, but I do remember seeing *The Joy of Cooking: Squares & Cookies* and *The Joy of Cooking Christmas Cookies* in there. You might like those for your bakery." She waited for some sort of acknowledgment from Martha, but there was nothing.

Hovering beside Addie, Paige spun around and disappeared into the back. When she returned, she presented Addie with the two books and a third one she'd found, *The Joy of Cooking Cakes*. Addie's face lit up, and she set the books on the counter. "Here they are, just as I remembered." She pushed them toward Martha and went about her business, just out of Martha's line of sight, occasionally glancing to see if the bait worked.

Martha drained her coffee cup, still drumming her fingers, and then stopped. Her hand inched across the counter and caressed the spine of the *Squares & Cookies* edition. Paige nudged Addie's arm. Addie's hand flew up to her mouth to stifle a giggle.

Martha glanced to either side of her and then pulled the book toward her. A grin spread across Addie's face, but then shriveled when the furnace repair truck pulled into a parking spot out front of the store. Martha pushed the book away and started to head out. Addie grabbed the books and stopped Martha at the door.

"Here, Martha. Merry Christmas." She smiled down at Martha's pudgy, paling cheeks. Martha looked at the books and then back at Addie, surprise in her eyes. "Please, take them as my gift to you." She held them out to her. Martha took the books from her hands and nearly, very nearly smiled, and left.

Addie let out a deep breath, turned to Paige, and grinned. "Fingers crossed that things might start to change between us."

Paige held up crossed fingers. "Yup, let's hope."

Addie returned to the counter and totaled up what she owed her consignment customer for the three Christmas cookbooks, wrote out an IOU, and slipped it into the cash register drawer, then noted the total in her receipt book. Over her head a husky voice cleared his throat. She looked up into Marc's rather sheepish face.

"I suppose Paige told you what happened." He toyed with the rim of his cap.

Addie nodded.

"Sorry." He winced. "It was an accident. Jerry was jimmying the lock open and something inside the doorframe popped, and then we couldn't get the door to lock again."

"If you wanted me to move it off the lot, why didn't you just tell me?"

"I was trying to surprise you." He shifted his weight from one foot to the other. "You know, do something nice for you?"

She let out a deep, slow breath. "Then why didn't you just ask for the key?"

He shuffled his feet again and looked down at the floor.

"Well?"

"I heard you were out with Simon all day yesterday, and I was afraid he'd still be there this morning."

She flipped her head. Her ponytail swung around, slapping her face. She glared at him and marched toward the book cart at the end of the counter.

"Addie, I'm sorry. I'm trying. I really am, but the whole thing with you two makes me crazy."

Her lips tightened. She grabbed two books off the cart and tossed them to the side, sending them skidding across the counter. "I've told you a hundred times before that we don't have that kind of relationship."

He scrubbed his hand through his hair.

"And since you know everything, as you assume to, then you know he worked all night in the ER." She crossed her arms. "As a matter of fact, he got called in early last night because he had to treat Patrick."

"Patrick? What happened?"

She looked at him. "So, you don't know everything."

"Last I heard he was being discharged tomorrow."

"See, I can admit it when I don't know something. I wish you could and would stop making *assumptions*."

"I guess I deserved that." He put his cap on and turned toward the door, the bells giving a merry jingle as he opened it and closed it behind him.

She leaned on the counter, cupping her chin in her hand. Addie pulled out her phone from her boyfriend jacket pocket, her fingers flying across the keypad. **SOS, need to meet for lunch, say noon??? . . . Your pig-headed brother attacks again**. She hoped she'd feel like eating by then, because right now her stomach was full of churning acid.

A woman dropped a stack of books down in front of her. "It looks like you found what you were looking for." Addie laughed and pulled a shopping bag out from under the counter.

"And then some. I think this completes my Christmas shopping list." She eyed the early edition of *The Joy of Cooking* still sitting on the counter and tossed it on top of her other purchases. "My husband's been telling me for years that I need this." She grinned as Addie rang her books through.

"Is that just a suggestion because it's considered by Julia Child to be the bible of all cookbooks, or is he hinting at something else?"

"It means that he's tired of doing all the cooking, and now it's my turn." The customer huffed out an exaggerated breath.

"Maybe you could just pretend you didn't see it today."

The woman laughed, pulling out her wallet. "That's tempting, but after thirty years, I guess it's only fair I take my turn." She wished Addie a Merry Christmas and left, the door chimes jingling over her head, a sound that went nonstop for the remainder of the morning.

Exhaustion gnawed at her bones, and even though Addie loved the fact that books were flying out the door, she struggled with small talk with her customers. She almost wept with joy when the clock struck twelve and Serena's beaming face greeted her across the counter.

"You are punctual today, aren't you?" chuckled Addie. Serena held up four bagged lunches, grinning. "And hungry, or are we expecting company?"

Serena slid onto a stool. "No, I thought if you didn't mind, we could send Paige next door to eat with Elli."

"Good plan. Paige." She called her assistant to the front. "How's it looking back there?"

Paige stretched out her back. "Pretty good right now. We always seem to have a lull around this time of day."

Serena held up two lunch bags. "Why don't you take your break now and go have lunch with Elli?"

Paige's eyes lit up. "Thanks." She grabbed the lunch

bags and her coat from under the counter and dashed off.

Serena opened her paper bag and pulled a sandwich bun out and chomped into it. "Mmm, I needed this. I think everyone in town's been in this morning, finishing off their shopping," she said between mouthfuls.

"I know." Addie bit into her chicken salad sandwich. "It's been the same for me."

"So, what did my idiot brother do now?" Serena took another bite.

Addie relayed how he had returned her car, broken door lock and all, and their following conversation about his assumption that Simon had spent the night. Serena stuffed the last of her roll into her mouth and looked at Addie. "What are you going to do about it?"

"Me? There's nothing I can do. We can't even speak civilly to each other anymore. He's always jumping to conclusions about me and Simon. He's short and snappy about everything."

"He's short and snappy with everyone these days, even Mom and Dad."

"Is he sick or something? Is there anything you need to tell me?" Serena's silence had Addie's hairs standing on end. "What is it? God, he isn't sick, is he?"

"Yeah, he is." Serena leaned closer and whispered, "He's love-sick, he mopes around, doesn't sleep, won't eat. What else would you call it?"

"Love-sick? Over whom?"

"You, silly."

"Me?" She emphatically shook her head. "No, no way."

"How can you be so smart and yet so clueless? He asks about you at least ten times a day."

"I'll admit we've always had some sort of attraction, but love? No, it's too soon."

"For you maybe, as you keep telling him, but obviously not for him. Why do you think he gets so upset when he knows you're with Simon? He's thinking you just didn't want him, and it makes him crazy."

She went cold. "I thought we were just good friends with, you know, a few benefits like the odd kiss." She licked her lips. "He is a very good kisser."

"As Simon must be, too."

"I wouldn't know."

"You've never kissed Simon?"

She shook her head. "Almost once, but no."

"Well, then you have to remedy that before you can make an informed choice. But my BFF advice is to stop flirting with the two of them and decide on one of them."

"I'm not flirting. I'm . . . I'm just being friendly."

"Is that what it's called? I think you've taken a page right out of Marc's ex's book."

Addie's mouth dropped open. "Are you actually comparing me to her?"

"Well, you've been stringing them both along until"— her fingers made quotation marks—"you are ready."

Addie's cheeks puffed out.

"Just saying." She shrugged and tossed her lunch bag in the trash can.

"But Marc's been so nasty lately. He's become hard to even like."

"Just remember he's new at all this and never had to try to win over a woman before. His ex, Lacey, had him cornered since they were in middle school. But I'd better get back. I don't want Elli thinking long lunch breaks are normal. She's kind of a handful about following good business practices, anyway."

Addie stared down at her half-eaten sandwich, barely aware that Serena was still talking. Her mind raced over the past months. Marc, Simon, and her, was she just a flirt? Had she really become one of those girls she detested in college? Worse yet, was she no different than Lacey and her butterfly lashes?

"Did you hear what I said? I'm going now."

Addie looked up at her. "Right. Yeah, I heard she needed to be kept on a short leash."

Serena's brows rose to her cherry-red hairline. "Who told you that? Never mind. Doesn't matter." She patted Addie's shoulder and paused. "I almost forgot. Yesterday after you left Catherine's, did you happen to see Jonathan's Land Rover broken down on the side of the road anywhere?"

"No, why?"

"Because he never got back to Catherine's until Zach and I were leaving at about seven."

"What? He left around two thirty. He was out getting cigarettes till then?"

"Yup."

"What did Catherine say?"

"Nothing, he came in and apologized, said his car broke down, and that he needed a hot shower to warm up, and then said he'd be back down in a few minutes."

"But his Land Rover is brand new."

"That's what I thought, and if he did break down, why didn't he at least call. One of us could have picked him up."

Addie picked at the crust on her sandwich. "And then he went right up and had a shower without taking a minute to visit with anyone first?"

"Yeah, I heard the shower running when we left."

"And Catherine said nothing about it?"

"No, she seemed more relieved than ticked. Which I thought kind of weird, but I'm not her. I would have torn a strip off Zach right in front of everyone, I'll tell you."

Addie worried her bottom lip between her teeth. "Yeah, I think I would have, too. At least ask a lot of questions."

"I got to run. Love you and remember what I said, Miss *Coquette*." Addie groaned. Serena kissed the top of Addie's head. The bells signaled her departure.

What kind of person jumps in the shower immediately after being delayed on what should have been a quick trip to the store? She leaned on her elbow, twisting a strand of loose hair behind her ear. Someone who wants to wash away the scent of another woman's perfume, that's who. Her eyes widened. Maybe she and Simon had overthought the situation yesterday, and her first instinct about Crystal and Jonathan had been right, and it was just as she feared. They had met up for a fling, and it didn't have anything to do with Marvin, Teresa, or the missing book.

Chapter 19

"Can you believe we still have over a week and a half to get through this Christmas shopping frenzy?" Addie leaned her back against the door after seeing their last customer out.

Paige looked up from arranging the bottom shelf of the Children's book section. "On the upside, I am enjoying the full-time hours right now. It really helps this time of year."

Addie glanced at the colorful book Paige held in her hand. It was a cloth-bound, primary-level, board book edition of *A Christmas Carol* by Jennifer Adams. "I wonder if Patrick would take that in place of the missing book for the auction."

Paige looked down at the book in her hand. "Well, it does have a price sticker on it for eight ninety-nine, so maybe." She arched a sly brow.

Addie imagined adding a few zeros behind the paltry number and handing it over to that insufferable man. "I'd need to wrap it first." A chuckle formed low in her belly as she pictured his face melting from surprised appreciation to stunned silence when he tore the wrapping paper off it. The chuckle grew until she felt she would burst. Her eyes watered, and she could barely make out Paige's slightly cocked face, studying her. "Good heavens," she snorted. "I've gone absolutely mad after today." Addie clasped her aching side.

"Are you okay?" Paige grabbed her cell phone. "Should I call somebody? Maybe Serena? Or Simon?"

"I can just picture his face now." Another fit of laughter seized her, and this time Paige joined in. Soon both were sitting on the floor, sprawled next to a pile of unstacked children's books, tears streaking down their faces, and the occasional hiccup making them laugh even harder.

"Looks like I missed a good joke." Simon stood with his hands on his hips, his head tilted to the side.

Addie gasped to catch her breath but snorted instead.

"You snorted. Again!" Paige whipped out a tissue from her pocket and waved it in the air. "I surrender. I'll die unless I quit laughing."

Simon looked from Addie to Paige and then broke out laughing in chorus with them. Addie stared. "Why are you laughing?" she choked out.

He shook his head. "I have no idea. Laughter's contagious, I guess." A deep chuckle rumbled in his chest. And they were off again, tears streaming down their cheeks.

Addie held her aching side, trying to compose herself and put her manager's hat back on. Only barely winning the struggle, she locked the door after Paige stumbled, still giggling, into the street. She pasted a serious look across her face. Simon wiped tears from his eyes. A smirk invaded her lips. Clearing her throat, she managed to speak relatively seriously. "Clearly, there's nothing like a bit of silliness to relieve the stresses of the day."

"I wish I hadn't missed the joke and knew what it was I was laughing at."

She waved her hand. "It was one of those things you had to be here for. Not as funny if I tell you. You'd think us nuts."

"It wouldn't be the first time." He playfully winked.

She flipped her ponytailed head, and closed the cash register without looking at him. Suppressing her giggle wasn't easy, but she managed it. "Did you get any sleep today? And how's Patrick?" She slipped the receipt book into the drawer under the counter. "Did you figure out why he went from good condition to needing emergency treatment?"

"Yeah." Simon slid onto a stool and stretched out his neck. "I managed a few hours, and he's going to be okay now."

"What happened? Did the staff goof and double-dose him?"

"No, but someone did."

"What do you mean?"

"All narcotics taken out of the locked med cupboard have to be witnessed and recorded. When I checked the available stock against all the dosages signed out, it added up. So I started asking questions and came across something interesting." He paused and waited for Addie to take a seat on the stool beside him. "Debra, his nurse, told me that she was in Patrick's room checking his vitals when Crystal came in. Deb knows her from around the hospital. Anyway, she started to leave so they'd have some privacy, but Crystal started right in telling him they need to cancel the auction and then, bam, they were in a heated argument. Patrick's blood pressure shot sky high, and Deb had to stay in the room to keep an eye on it for a few minutes."

"I'm glad to hear that at least Crystal understands that he can't carry on with the live auction portion of the gala as planned."

"Yeah, but Debra said their argument didn't sound like it was just about canceling the live auction. According to her, she said Crystal was insisting they just forget about the whole thing and move on."

"Maybe she's worried about taking on too much of the workload herself with Patrick somewhat out of the picture."

"Maybe, but then Debra mentioned something else."

"What?"

"She said Crystal stormed out, and he settled a bit so she left to check on her other patients, and when she went back to Patrick's room to recheck his BP, she saw a man who she described as a 'drop-dead gorgeous silver fox' getting into the elevator. She never thought anything of it at the time, and the only reason why she remembers him was, in her words, *he looked delicious.*"

"Only one person matching that description comes to my mind."

"Exactly. She went on to say that Patrick was fine then. His blood pressure had stabilized, so she gave him his pain medication and left."

"So, Jonathan paid him a visit. Or at least was on his floor."

Simon nodded. "When I questioned her further, trying to determine how Patrick received more than a double dose of morphine, it got interesting." Addie leaned closer. "She told me a minute or so later there was a code called, a heart attack, on the patient in the room across the hall from Patrick's. She and the rest of the code team went flying into the patient's room with the crash cart and out of the corner of her eye, she thought she saw someone going into Patrick's room."

"Could she describe the person?"

"No, she said it was all a blur in the hustle. When they were finished, she went in to check on Patrick and found him unresponsive and his vital signs bottoming out. She called Dr. Harris, who was still across the hall. He checked Patrick and administered the Narcan and then called me to report the incident."

"So, that means Jonathan and Crystal both paid Patrick a visit. We also know Marvin was at the hospital then, too."

"Yes, but Crystal left, and then she saw Jonathan leaving the unit before Patrick went into distress."

"That means it must have been Marvin she saw going into his room during the code alarm."

"Could have been, unless Jonathan or Crystal came back, knowing the commotion that would be happening on the unit because codes are called over the hospital intercom." Simon's finger tapped the countertop.

"Maybe, but we saw them both leave before Marvin came out later, and remember Patrick and Marvin had an argument before Patrick was attacked that night."

"Yes, and we speculated that Marvin attacked him because he was furious. After all, he'd heard the book he came here to launder money through was missing. But Patrick couldn't identify his attacker."

"Maybe he lied and knows exactly who beat him up and stuffed him in the closet."

Simon ran his hand over his five-o'clock chin stubble. "But why didn't Marvin just kill him then? Why come into the hospital to knock him off?"

"Maybe Marvin is involved in Teresa's death and the missing book, and he's afraid Patrick knows that and the attack was a warning to him not to talk, but his bosses are afraid that Patrick might slip up and say something about Marvin and ordered him to make sure that couldn't happen."

Simon scrubbed his hands over his face. "We still have nothing but what-ifs."

"How do we prove any of this?"

"We don't. The police do. All we can do is take our theories to Marc and let him decide if they're worth looking into or not. That's his job; mine, as far as this case is concerned, is what I find in the lab. Yours is, well, I guess to do what you do best: research and keep your eyes open and report what you find out."

"Boring."

He grabbed her hand and pulled her to her feet. "I know something that's not boring." Her heart did a little flip when his warm breath brushed her cheek. "It's the reason I came here tonight in the first place." He pulled her closer, close enough for his heart to beat against hers. Was he actually going to kiss her? She tilted her chin up. Her lips slightly parted in anticipation. "To take you to the festival."

"The festival?"

"Yes, the tree lighting. The twelve days before Christmas annual town event."

"That's tonight?"

He laughed. "You've lived here longer than I have. Why is it I can remember such a momentous occasion and you can't? Come on. Get your coat, bundle up, and let's go a-caroling." He swept her out the door, helped her navigate over the snow-plowed drifts, and dragged her into the park.

The Victorian gazebo sparkled in Christmas splendor. Twinkling Christmas lights dripped from the roof, and garland swathed each post with festive greenery.

The same Dickens carolers from her shop this morning were center stage as the gathering crowd joined them in chorus. She had thought the displays for the Founder's Day celebrations were spectacular, but this . . . this was Christmas magic come to life. The wonder of it skittered through her, taking her back to her childhood, the lights shimmering off the snow-covered boughs, causing tears of joy to glisten in her eyes. That was until her gaze came to rest on Jonathan and Crystal standing side by side in the crowd.

Addie nudged Simon's shoulder and gestured with her head at the couple. Crystal, her come-hither eyes focused on Jonathan. Her lips curved in a smile, her shoulder just close enough to his that when he moved they would touch. Now, that was a flirt if Addie ever saw one. She wracked her brain to remember when she had ever behaved that way with Marc or Simon.

She looked up and studied the profile of the man standing beside her and noted his chiseled chin, squared jaw, and those long, thick black lashes, but most of all she saw his wit, the way he could make her laugh, and the way he made her feel. So, what was holding her back, or was Serena right? Was she just a tease, a flirt, one of those women who craved attention from all men, not just one? She channeled her inner Scarlett O'Hara. *I'll think about it tomorrow.* Right now, she had to figure out what was going on and find her book.

Chapter 20

Addie squinted and studied the small group on the other side of the gazebo, her fingers trailing over the glassy surface of her phone inside her warm coat pocket. Catherine stood to Jonathan's right, laughing with Joyce and Jack, seemingly oblivious to the performance playing out on her left. Addie fixed her gaze on Crystal, whose head was so far tilted in flirtation that Addie feared it would detach and roll on the ground. Now, that would put the final bow on the celebration. A little too Christmas future for her liking. Addie took tally over how many times Crystal licked her pouting lips. At twenty, Addie gave up counting and snapped a picture. This would say it all and was perhaps enough to convince Catherine of Jonathan's womanizing. She glanced down at the photo. Her chest constricted. Peach color from Crystal's lips glimmered back at her. Although it was a great advertisement for the lipstick's wear and tear.

She tugged on Simon's jacket sleeve. "Did you ever get the DNA results back from the lab?"

"No, probably not till next week. Why?"

"Just curious." She glanced again at Crystal, whose tongue trailed across her upper peach lip. "Do you really want to stay for the main tree-lighting ceremony?"

"Don't you?" He glanced at her. "I thought you liked this sort of thing?"

"I do and thank you for bringing me, but . . ."

"But what?"

She shoved her icy hands back into the warmth of her coat pockets. "There's just something else that I want to check out."

His arm wrapped around her shoulder. "This wouldn't involve some private investigating, would it, Miss Jessica Fletcher?" He squeezed her, his laughter purring in his chest and vibrating her side.

"Just a quick trip, and who knows? Maybe we'll be back in time to see the main tree lighting."

"Okay," he groaned, "where are we off to now?"

"It's not far." A smile dangled at the corners of her lips as she raked her gaze over his face.

"What?" His hand brushed over his mouth. "Do I have something on my face?"

"No," she sighed, "just thinking how lucky I am to have such a tolerant . . . friend."

He cupped her face in his hands and brushed his lips against hers, just a light caress, a whisper-light kiss, and smiled. His arm tightened around her shoulder, and he led her back across the street to Carolyn's truck, which he, apparently, had now claimed as his own. Her mind replayed what had just occurred, her heart and head struggling to come to terms. What exactly had occurred? This wasn't the first time his lips teased hers, but why didn't he want to kiss her, like really kiss her?

She knew what he'd said before, but he didn't even

seem tempted. Was that weird, or was he truly just a good man and waiting for her permission and invitation? Serena was right. She had to make him want to kiss her. It was time to make an informed decision and choose one of them. Why was this all bubbling to the surface now? Was it the time of year? Was she just lonely and missing what she and David had shared? Or was it because Serena couldn't leave well enough alone. She had been perfectly happy to let things just carry on in their merry little way, but now her friend's words were festering inside her.

Simon pulled into his parking stall at the rear of the hospital, fished his keys out of his jean pocket, and opened the staff door. Addie turned to her left and started up the stairwell.

"Wouldn't the elevator be faster?" Simon called when she hit the fifth step.

"No, I don't want anyone who might be lurking around to see us."

"By *anyone*, do you mean Marc?"

She ignored his last statement. They approached the third-floor exit door. "Do we need a key?"

"After hours yes, because it's only the executive offices on this wing." He inserted a key in the lock. "But my staff key won't open any of the private offices, if that's what you have in mind."

"Too bad. I sure would like to have another look around Patrick's to see if the book is hidden anywhere."

"I thought you did that right before you found Teresa's body."

"Yeah, but I didn't know she was dead at the time and didn't do a thorough search." She plopped down onto Crystal's chair at the reception desk. "Does it open desk drawers by chance?"

"Nope, sorry."

"I got it, then." She pulled a bobby pin from under her ponytail, straightened it, and jimmied with the top drawer. It clicked open.

"Where did you learn how to do that?"

"A misspent youth." She dug around in the drawer.

"That's a story I want to hear one day."

"There it is." She pulled a tissue from the box on the desk and wrapped it around the tube of lipstick she'd seen Crystal applying the day after Teresa's fall. She folded it and handed it to him. "You said you needed an actual sample of the lipstick on the cup."

"And you think this is it?"

"I'm not sure"—she closed the drawer—"but it's worth checking out."

"Let's go to my office, and I'll get it ready to send to the DNA lab tomorrow."

Back at the gazebo, Addie slid in beside Serena, giving her a quick hip-check, laughed, and joined in the final countdown to the tree lighting. ". . . three . . . two . . . one . . . Merry Christmas." Cheers rang in the crisp night air amongst shrieks of laughter and applause.

Serena threw her arms around Addie's neck, tears of joy glistening in her eyes. "Zach wants us to live together."

"What?" Addie held her out to arm's length. "Are you ready for that?"

"I've never been so ready for anything in my entire life." Tears trickled down her glowing cheeks. "Are you happy for me?"

"Of course, I am. If that's what you want?"

"Well"—she leaned closer to Addie—"what I really want is a ring, but I guess this is the first step."

"You want to marry him?"

"Yes," she squealed, hugging her arms tight around herself, her feet dancing beneath her. "I do. I do."

Zach appeared over Serena's shoulder. "I take it she's told you the news." The corners of his amber-brown eyes crinkled when he smiled and looked down at Serena. "I thought we were keeping this a secret until after the holidays?"

"Not from Addie." She looked up at the dark-haired, lanky man towering over her. "No secrets from my bestie, ever."

He kissed the top of her head.

"I'm thrilled for the two of you, but where will you live? Neither of your apartments are really big enough for two people."

"We haven't gotten that far yet," Serena said.

Zach placed his arm around Serena's shoulders, "No, but we'll figure it out. We'll start looking after the holidays."

"I'm thrilled for you." Addie kissed Serena's cheek.

"Are you really?"

"Of course, I am." She gave her friend a hug. "Congratulations."

Serena squealed. "Come on, Zach. Let's get a hot chocolate to celebrate. I'm freezing." She grabbed his hand.

Addie tittered, watching the two of them disappear into the crowd.

"I missed another joke, didn't I?" Simon placed a hand on the small of her back.

"I hope it's not. Serena and Zach are moving in together, but shhh"—her finger covered his lip—"it's a secret for now."

His fingers tucked a strand of windblown hair behind her ear. "So, besides the cold, there's romance in the air tonight, is there?" His finger lingered on her cheek, his thumb stroking the outline of her jaw. Was this it? Was this finally the moment? His fingertip lifted her chin. She smiled, but her gaze went not to his eyes, but to his lips so close to hers.

"There you are." A husky voice filled the closing space between them.

Addie groaned. Not again. "Marc?"

"Addie, Simon." He nodded, a mischievous look dancing in his eyes. "I hate to tear you away from . . . the festivities . . . but I want to talk to you for a minute, Simon."

"Okay." Simon placed his hand on the small of her back again. Addie leaned into it.

"Alone, if you don't mind. It's official business."

A growl rumbled from the back of her throat. She glared at them as they conversed over by the gazebo stairs, just out of earshot. She spun on her heel and headed for the bake table. Gingerbread. She needed gingerbread to calm her down or else . . . well. She wasn't sure, but she needed to stuff something in her mouth to stifle the words she wanted to scream at Marc. What an incorrigible . . . insufferable man. She slapped a dollar on the table, picked up a gingerbread man, and bit its head off.

Martha looked at her from behind the table. Her pencil-sketched eyebrow cocked. "Having a bad day, are we?"

"Men," was all Addie could get out of her stuffed mouth.

"Here"—Martha held up another gingerbread man— "I've killed a few of these myself over the years." She gave Addie a conspiratorial wink.

Addie sputtered, a few bits of gingerbread shrapnel escaping her lips. Martha grinned and handed her a napkin. "Thanks." Addie wiped the remnants of gingerbread off her lips.

Martha moved away to assist another customer, leaving Addie flabbergasted. She glanced back at the baker. But if Ebenezer Scrooge could change his surly ways, why couldn't Martha? A Christmas miracle? Spotting Catherine and her group over by the hot chocolate table, Addie headed toward them. An arm slipped through hers, the comforting familiarity of it causing her heart to expand even further. "So, Simon, what did our friend want to talk about that was so hush-hush?"

"Nothing, actually, at least nothing you couldn't have overheard."

"Really?"

"Yeah, he just told me he's getting a lot of pressure from the DA and asked me if I had heard anything back from the major crimes lab yet."

"Have you?"

"No"—Simon's eyes narrowed—"and he knows full well that I would have given him the report as soon as I received it." He bit the words out.

"So, what's the delay? Have they said?"

"Just that they're still working on it. It's an organic compound they haven't been able to identify conclusively yet."

"At least you know you weren't the only one puzzled by the findings."

"Whatever it is that's causing the anomalies, it must be rare if they have to go to an international database for a match. But I think Marc's interruption had more to do with breaking up what he thought was about to occur between us."

"And"—she swallowed—"what was going to occur?" Her eyes locked with his.

"Something I want more than anything in the world right now." His fingers trailed down her cheek.

"You do?" She rose onto her tippy toes, her lips parted. His head dipped. She drew in a slow, unsteady breath. She paused and looked at the group by the hot chocolate table. Her eyes met Jonathan's. She shivered when the reflection of David looked back at her. She glanced beside him and saw the pained expression on Marc's face as he looked at her and Simon. She rested back on the soles of her feet.

Simon's eyes followed the direction of her gaze and then locked on Addie. "Funny thing about ghosts from the past, isn't it?" Her lip quivered. "They disappear and reappear at the darnedest times." He shoved his hands into his pockets and turned toward the street.

"Simon, no." She chased after him. "Let me explain."

He stopped. "You know what? What I'm feeling, and started to believe you were, too, doesn't require any explanation. It just happens." He clasped her shoulders. "The way you make me feel doesn't come along every day. It happens once, maybe twice in a lifetime if you're lucky, at least for me, but apparently, that's not true for you, and you've just made that very clear."

"What are you talking about?"

"I'm just saying that what I'm feeling, it hits you when you're not looking or when you think you're not ready. You can't fight it, you can only go with it, no matter what's happening around you."

"But, it was just—"

He shook his head and pulled away. "I do understand loss and grieving, and I was willing to wait to give you all the time in the world after David to be ready. Now, I don't think that's what you really want, and I'm not sure I can wait anymore."

She struggled to find words, tears threatening to overtake her.

"I guess that tells me everything I need to know." He turned on his boot heel.

She grabbed his sleeve. "Can we at least talk, so I can explain what just happened?"

"Maybe another time." He waved his hand in the air over his head. "I'm not in the mood now." He marched toward the truck and pulled away.

Chapter 21

Addie scrunched her clothes in a ball, flung them at the laundry basket, and missed. "Men," she roared, stomping on them and kicking them aside, scattering her undies, jeans, and blouse across the bedroom. She yanked open her middle dresser drawer, looked at her spaghetti-strapped sleeping top and cropped leggings, shivered, slammed it shut, and flung open the bottom drawer. She plucked out a pair of flannel pajamas, shoved her arms and legs into the appropriate holes, snatched her pink plush robe from the hook on the back of the closet door, thrust her toes into matching fuzzy slippers, and padded down the stairs into the kitchen. She picked up the tea canister, slammed it on the counter, withdrew a bag, dropped it in her cup, plugged in the kettle, and waited for it to boil.

The steam coming from the kettle mirrored her rage. Her brewed tea in hand, she nestled onto her couch and took a sip. "Well, Nighty-Night tea, I sure hope you do what Serena said you would." She took another sip. "Ah, yes, much better now." She rested her head against the deep throw pillow propped up behind her and stared at the makeshift crime board. "Okay, talk to me. No one else wants to tonight. First, Marc excludes me, and then Simon stomps off."

Her gaze trailed across the clues she'd written down. What was she missing? Was it in plain sight and she just didn't see it? She set her cup on the table, picked up the pen, and stood in front of the brown paper. But it was no use. Nothing fit together, except . . . she drew a curved line from Jonathan's name to Crystal's and stabbed the pen for exclamation when she wrote the word *peach*. She stepped back and looked at her number two suspect. "Marvin, Marvin, Marvin." She tried to remember everything she knew about him, but nothing more came to light. Her focus went to Patrick, but she still had nothing new to add and her hand dropped to her side. She wrote *victim*, her hand unsteady, or was he really? "What's missing?" Well, aside from a full autopsy report and not knowing if a murder had actually been committed and the fact that her book was still MIA, she had nothing. Maybe that's what all the clues were telling her. Nothing unusual had happened. A woman fell down the stairs, and her book was just lost because Teresa couldn't tell anyone now where she had moved it.

She grabbed a corner of the paper, ripped it off the wall, folded it, and stuffed it into her tote bag on the table. Addie took a gulp of her cold tea, wishing it was something stronger, flipped off the lights, and made her way up to bed, hoping the so-called calming effects of the tea hadn't started to wear off yet. All this other stuff would have to wait until tomorrow. She grinned, cocooning herself in the blankets, and snuggled into bed. She had become a very good Scarlett

O'Hara lately. Margaret Mitchell would have been proud of her.

The bees swarmed at her again. She batted at the air with her parasol screaming for Rhett Butler to shoo them away. One landed on her cheek. She slapped at it and bolted up in bed. The incessant buzzing didn't stop. Where's Rhett? She ran her fingers over her face, finding no stings. With a groan, she slammed her hand on the buzzing alarm clock. It was only a dream. She wasn't Scarlett and sadly would have to face the music today. Rhett had waited for her, too, but in the end he'd had enough and walked away. She couldn't. No, wouldn't let Simon do the same.

She fumbled for her robe at the foot of the bed and, one eye open, stumbled down the stairs. When she reached the bottom, a bang on the front door jerked her fully awake. She tightened her robe belt and peered out the peephole and moaned. "It's too early to do perky."

Serena swept past her and went directly into the living room, making herself at home on the sofa.

"And to what do I owe this early morning visit?"

"I've been thinking." Serena took her coat off and drew her legs up under her. "You know that two-bedroom apartment over your garage?"

"Yes." Addie flopped down on the arm of the sofa. "And you had to come here at seven a.m. to remind me of it?"

"I guess it could have waited until later, but—"

"Do you think?"

"It's just that I haven't been able to sleep all night thinking about it."

"Why on earth would that keep you up all night?"

"It's just that I remembered at one time you had offered to rent it out to Paige and her little girl, but since Paige is enjoying"—she coughed—"living with her mother now. I was wondering if it's still available."

"Why, what are you thinking?"

"That it would be perfect for me and Zach." She jumped to her feet. "Wouldn't it, and we'd be next-door neighbors so to speak."

Addie's hand ran through her tangled, bed-head hair. "Well, that would also make me your landlord. Can you live with that?"

"I swear"—Serena crossed her heart—"that we'd be the best tenants ever. You wouldn't even know we were there."

"Knowing you, I don't see that happening." Addie grinned. "But seriously, I hadn't thought about renting it out since I offered it to Paige last year."

"But it's just sitting there, so, could we take a look at it?"

"It does need clearing out. I have no idea what's all up there. It hasn't been used as anything but storage for years by my understanding."

"Zach has some time off now from the clinic for term break. He could clear it out, and then it would be ready for us to move into after the holidays."

"I'm sure it needs repairs and painting, though, and—"

"Can we please, please, please take a look? Maybe some of it we could do after we move in, like the painting."

"Really, all this before I even have my morning coffee?" She shook her head. "Okay, what the heck, if you really want to."

"I want," giggled Serena. "How much?"

"I have no idea." She looked around her comfortably decorated living room. "I don't need the money.

Let me think on it, *after* coffee." Addie gave up counting how many times Serena's head bobbed up and down. "If"—Addie's gaze narrowed—"you and Zach promise to do the work to fix it up. I still haven't gotten to half of what needs doing in this house yet."

"You're the best." Serena flung her arms around her.

Addie grinned and pried her off. "I was just going to make breakfast. Want some eggs and toast?"

"Have you ever known me to refuse food?" Serena followed her into the kitchen.

Addie glanced back at her. "Somehow, I get the feeling that in the future this might become a regular occurrence."

"What?" Serena patted her chest, feigning innocence. "I'd never impose myself on you."

"Yes, you would."

Serena retrieved a carton of eggs from the refrigerator. "So, what happened to Simon last night? Did he get called into the hospital early?"

"I don't want to talk about him, or Marc, ever again. So, you can stop worrying about me being a flirt. Juggling more than one man at a time is a skill I don't seem to possess." She banged the frying pan on the counter.

"Okay, if you say so." Serena set a mixing bowl on the counter. "But—"

Addie's hand flew up in front of Serena's face. "Shhh!" She smacked an egg on the side of the bowl rim, sending innards and shell debris flying across the counter.

"Is that someone knocking on the front door?"

"I didn't hear anything except this." Addie cracked another one against the rim.

The pounding continued.

"Are you expecting anyone? Maybe one of those names I'm not allowed to mention." Serena glanced out of the kitchen entrance and down to hall.

"No, definitely not, but would you mind seeing who else besides you dares to disturb me before my morning coffee."

Serena ruffled her hair on her way by. "But you look so cute first thing in the morning. You should really go. Especially if you are serious about having nothing more to do with either of them. It might scare them off." She ducked the dishtowel Addie threw at her and escaped into the hallway, giggling.

Serena's voice drifted down the hall. "What are you doing here at this time of the morning?"

"I could ask you the same."

Addie flinched and dropped an eggshell into the bowl at the sound of Marc's voice.

"I assure you it's police business. Can I come in?"

"Now what have I done?" Addie muttered, rinsing her hands.

"Morning, Addie, sorry to interrupt your breakfast, but I need to ask you something."

She dried her hands on a kitchen towel and flung it on the counter. "Okay, what have I done now?"

"Nothing. I want to pick your researcher's brain is all."

"I see." She placed her hands on the edge of the island countertop. "Last night, everything is all secret, don't let Addie hear, but today you need my help?"

He ignored her, his gaze darkening for only a moment. "What do you know about tetrodotoxin?"

"That sounds like a medical term. You're probably better off asking *Dr. Emerson*, not me."

"Dr. Emerson now, is it?" He didn't flinch at her glare. "I would expect he's in surgery right now. There was a bad traffic accident up on the highway last night."

She dropped her glare and studied the broken eggs in the bowl.

"I was just wondering if you'd come across it in any of those books you read?"

"Tetrodotoxin," she repeated. "It kind of sounds like something I've heard of before, but it's not something my kind of research generally comes across except . . . maybe in fiction reading." She snapped her fingers. "That's it. I have read the word before. There was something mentioned about it in a book I read a few years ago."

"Marc, my dear Stone Age brother"—Serena rolled her eyes and sighed—"have you thought of checking on the Internet like the rest of the world would?"

"I was just hoping . . ."

Serena glanced sideways at him. "Yeah, I can imagine what you were hoping for by this poor dumb me, I don't know how to do an Internet search routine." She gave him an exaggerated wink.

Addie willed herself not to laugh, but it was hard given the expression on Serena's face. "Come on, let's go. I'll teach you how it's done." She stalked from the kitchen, Serena's bubbling laughter following them down the hall into the living room. Addie sank onto the sofa, adjusted her gaping robe closed, and flipped her laptop open.

Marc motioned to the crime board. "Looks like you've been doing some of your own research lately?"

"Yeah, so? It hasn't gotten me anywhere." She typed in "tetrodotoxin" and a full page of results rolled down her screen. "Okay, here's one by the Centers for Disease Control and Prevention."

Marc sat down, leaned into her, and read aloud.

"Appearance: Colorless. Description: Tetrodotoxin is an extremely potent poison (toxin) found mainly in the liver and sex organs (gonads) of some fish, such as puffer fish, globefish, and toadfish and in some amphibian, octopus, and shellfish species. Human poisonings occur when the flesh and/or organs of the fish are improperly prepared and eaten."

"Found in some fish, hmm." Serena leaned her chin in her hand on the sofa back and poked her head between them. "Zach loves fish, I should tell him about this."

"I'm sure as a naturopath he knows already." Addie cleared her throat. "Just like a trained police officer would know how to conduct his own research," she mumbled under her breath, and looked over her shoulder at Serena. "So don't worry"—she noted Marc's ears had turned a fire-engine red—"it's none of the fish we commonly eat even at our little House of Sushi. Maybe in some fancy restaurant, and even then, the chef would have to be a highly trained and licensed professional to prepare it." She tapped her finger on the edge of her laptop. "So, how did Teresa manage to eat some if all she had was sushi?"

"And how exactly do you know what came back in the initial autopsy report?" Marc questioned, but then sighed. "Never mind, I know."

She crossed her eyes and poked her tongue out at him, then refocused on the keyboard. "Yes, here it is, the book I read. *State of Fear* by Michael Crichton. Look"—she pointed to the screen—"it's about a terrorist that utilized the blue-ringed octopus's deadly venom as a favored murder weapon." Her fingers flashed over the keys, typing in "blue-ringed octopus."

Marc leaned over her shoulder. "This I wouldn't have been able to find on my own as I've never read the book." He spun the laptop toward him and read.

"*They are recognized as one of the world's most venomous marine animals. Although generally the size of a golf ball, they carry enough venom to kill twenty-six adult humans within minutes—*"

"It's so cute and look at those pretty colors." Serena pointed at the screen. "How could it be so dangerous?"

Marc continued on reading as if not hearing her. "*The venom can result in nausea, numbness of the mouth and tongue, paralysis, blurred vision, difficulty in speaking, blindness, respiratory arrest, heart failure, total paralysis, and can lead to death within minutes. No antivenom is available, making it one of the deadliest reef inhabitants in the ocean.*" He spared his sister a glance. "Yeah, really cute, it would make the perfect pet, wouldn't it?"

Addie rubbed her throat. "If this, or something like it, was the mysterious chemical in Teresa's blood work, then the crime lab should have been able to figure that out. Toxic fish poisonings aren't that rare. Surely in New York City they'd come across accidental poisonings in seafood restaurants from time to time?"

"You'd think, but it sounds like the holdup was because they were trying to narrow it down to exactly what kind of fish, but I'll ask Simon more about that later. All I can tell from this"—he waved his hand at the screen—"is that blue-ringed octopuses, or none of the others for that matter, are found in this part of the world."

Addie read farther down the page. "No, they're not; it says here that they're found in tide pools and coral reefs in the Pacific and Indian oceans from Japan to Australia." She sat back and stared at the screen. "The question is. How did it get into Teresa's food and blood samples?"

Chapter 22

"Has he gone?"

Serena snapped the blind closed. "Yup, just pulled out. What's up with all the cloak-'n'-dagger surveillance?"

Addie's fingers flew over her cell screen. "There, I've just let Paige know I'll be late. You should probably tell Elli, too."

"What? Where are we going?"

Addie tossed Serena her coat and dragged her out the door. "On an adventure." She hopped into Serena's Jeep. "I hope you don't mind driving?"

"Looks like I don't have a choice," Serena mumbled, putting the vehicle in drive. She obeyed Addie's orders until the House of Sushi came into view.

"Okay, just pull up here." Addie pointed to the nearest parking spot to the restaurant. Through the side mirror she studied the hospital across the street.

"A sushi restaurant open for breakfast?" Serena shuddered. "Maybe they serve those one-hundred-year-old eggs or something."

"I think those are Chinese cuisine." Addie opened the door and was greeted by a smiling young woman. "Good morning." Addie returned the smile. "Is Mr. Yamada here by chance?" The woman nodded and disappeared in the back room.

Colorful lanterns hung from the ceiling, and delicate, water-colored paintings covered the walls around the cozy room. Her eyes came to rest on a framed certificate above one of the seating booths. She moved closer and smiled. "Well, this answers one of my questions."

"What's that?" Serena came to her side.

"Mr. Yamada is a specially trained and certified fish cutter in the city of Shimonoseki, Japan." She pointed. "That certificate is issued by the Japanese government."

"What does that mean?"

"It means Mr. Yamada knows his stuff and would never serve toxic fish to his customers. Not every fish cutter or chef can get this. It's a very specialized training program."

"So, I don't have to worry about Zach eating here anymore?"

"No, you don't."

Mr. Yamada approached her. "Miss Greyborne"—he bowed from the waist—"my daughter said you wished to speak with me?"

"Good morning. Yes, if you have a few minutes, I have a couple of questions."

"Of course, how may I be of help?"

Addie opened her mouth but then snapped it shut again, not sure where to begin.

Serena leaned across the counter and looked at the assorted sizes of food take-out containers. "Hey, I saw one of those on a table for the hospital charity auction, didn't I? Yeah, and it had a gift certificate beside it."

"Yes, I make a donation every year to Miss Lang's charity." He looked down reverently.

"Then you knew her?" Addie smile sympathetically.

"Yes, sad news about her. Very sad."

"Was she a regular customer?"

"Yes, well, sometimes. Why?"

"I'm just wondering if she came in for lunch on the day of her accident."

He shook his head.

Addie pulled her phone out of her pocket, flipped to her photos. "Do you remember if this woman came in?" She showed him the picture she'd taken of Crystal.

"No, I've never seen her, but Mr. Patrick was in that day. About once a week, he picked up their lunch."

"Patrick? Are you sure it was the day of her accident?"

"Yes, I remember because he came in early that day."

"What time was that?"

"Ten thirty, maybe, I remember it because we weren't finished setting up for lunch, and then he wanted three orders to go, not the usual two."

"And did he say anything about who the third meal was for?"

He shook his head. "I don't ask. I just serve."

"I understand." She glanced behind her at the wall certificate. "I see you have the very coveted license for serving things like puffer fish."

He grinned and nodded.

"Have you ever served it here?"

"No, too dangerous in America to find. Only one

approved importer of puffer fish in New York and only two, maybe three times a year. Very expensive."

"I see. What about blue-ringed octopus?"

"More dangerous. In Japan, some fish handlers on the docks die if they touch them when sorting. Very bad when they get caught in the nets or traps."

"I wasn't aware you couldn't touch them, either. Well, thank you, Mr. Yamada, you've been a big help today." She smiled and bowed her head in respect.

"Come back for lunch. Pretty ladies have to eat, too." He grinned.

"We will," she said, and flashed him a broad smile and waved. "Thanks again." When they walked out, Addie asked, "Did you hear all that? Patrick bought three lunches that day. Who was the other one for? And why was there no sign of the take-out boxes in the office?"

"Whomever she had lunch with was tidy?" Serena shrugged and hopped in the driver's seat.

"But not tidy enough to take out the lipstick-stained coffee cups, so that doesn't make sense." Addie jumped up and down in her seat. "I got it! It's because one of the boxes had something in it that would have pointed to murder. The reason the cup with alcohol was left behind was to throw the investigation off—"

"And make everyone think Teresa was drinking and fell down the stairs."

Addie grinned at her. "You catch on quick. That's exactly what I'm thinking. Okay, now drive to the industrial Dumpsters behind the hospital."

Serena's mouth tightened. "I don't think I like what you're thinking anymore."

"Come on, how bad can it be?"

* * *

"I'm not joining you in there." Serena pulled up in front of the Dumpster and clutched the steering wheel. "No, nope, no way I'm climbing in one of those."

"Chicken," Addie scowled.

Serena tucked her hands into her armpits and flapped them. "Bak bak bak."

"Well"—Addie hopped out—"at least give me a boost up." She leaned her hand on Serena's shoulder, stepped up on the front bumper, and peered over the edge of the trash bin. She gagged and jumped down, wiping her hands on her pants. "Yeah, not my best plan. Yuck." She shuddered and eyed the back of the police station. "The police have hazmat suits just for this kind of thing."

"Even with one of those on, there's no way you'll get me in there."

Addie arched a sly brow. "I wasn't thinking of us going in. Come on, let's go talk to Marc."

Serena slid her phone into her jean pocket. "I can't. I just had a frantic text from Elli. Apparently, there are four customers in the store at the same time, and she's run off her poor little feet."

"Four whole customers, you say?"

"Did I mention her work ethic before?" Serena scowled at her phone screen, which lit up again.

"You go rescue her, and I'll see you later. Thanks for everything. But don't forget that I'll need a ride home tonight, if you don't mind?"

"Then it's a good thing we're going to be neighbors then, isn't it?" Serena laughed and waved as she pulled away.

* * *

"Hi, Addie," Carolyn greeted her when she skidded to a stop in front of her desk. Concern laced her question. "Are you okay?"

"Yes, why?"

"Simon called me last night and told me that you had a sudden change of plans for Christmas dinner and wouldn't be able to make it."

"Really?" Addie's cheeks stung as if she'd been slapped. "He said that?"

"Yes." Carolyn came around the desk. "I've been so worried that something happened. But if it's Jonathan being here, he's welcome, too."

Addie struggled not to show the emotions waging war on her senses. "No, it's not that." She swallowed hard. "Something just came up, and I'm not sure I can—"

"Good, I'm just happy to hear that you're okay."

Addie forced herself to breathe. "Yes, I'm fine, thanks." Her smile hurt her face. She flicked a look toward Marc's office. "Any chance I could see him for a minute?"

"Sure, I think he's just catching up on his filing, or he was just before you arrived."

Addie sank into Marc's visiting chair, blinking back tears. So, that was it. Simon had sent her a message loud and clear. He was done. Her head ached from stemming the dam of tears threatening to burst.

Marc paused in his rifling through one of his many file cabinets. "I thought I heard your voice out there. What can I do for you?"

She stared at the floor, afraid that if she opened her mouth, a deluge of emotion would pour out instead of words.

"Addie? Is everything okay?"

"Yes." It hurt. To think. To breathe. To speak.

"So, what brings you in?"

Breath, damn it. Just breathe. She took a breath and recounted her and Serena's morning adventure.

When she finished, he looked down at her from across the desk. "What makes you think the boxes were deliberately removed from the office?"

"Because according to my . . . sources, the office trash cans are emptied every night. The two cups were in there, but no sign of a sushi lunch from Mr. Yamada's restaurant. The boxes have to be somewhere."

"Have you ever been inside a Dumpster, especially one from a hospital?"

"No, but you're the one who always says leave no stone unturned."

He blew out a deep breath. "You're right, and . . . you might be on to something."

"Then, you'll check it out and ask Patrick about the three lunch boxes?" He nodded, his eyes fixed on hers. "Good, because after what I found out, he has to be behind it or at least know who is? That third box was for someone."

"I guess, but all the witnesses we talked to said he was downstairs all morning."

"Well, someone got it wrong, because Mr. Yamada can place him in his restaurant at ten thirty."

"Okay, I'll check out the timeline with him."

"You do that. There might be something else he can remember now that I stirred up his memories."

"I know how to do my job, and now that the reports point to Teresa's death as suspicious, I'm obligated to follow every lead, regardless of the source."

"Suspicious? Not murder?"

"Not yet. It could still be an accident." He shrugged.

"It could be a matter of consuming tainted fish and not a deliberate poisoning."

"But I just told you what Mr. Yamada said. When you talk to him, he'll tell you the same thing."

"The DA needs more proof to call it a murder. We have to be certain."

She rose to her feet, grinning. "And maybe you'll find that in the Dumpster."

"You seem pretty sure of yourself. I noticed Patrick's name on your crime board."

"I am, and as far as I can tell, he had the most to gain by killing her and getting his hands on the book. It's worth more than he probably makes in a year."

She flipped her ponytailed head and got as far as the door before he spoke again. "You're not a very good liar."

She pinned him with a glare. "I didn't lie to you."

He dropped a handful of folders on his desk, walked across the room to her, and placed his hands on her shoulders, his gaze searching her face. "I know when something's bothering you."

His eyes, those deep pools of warm chocolate brown got to her every time, but they couldn't now. She couldn't allow him in. Not this time. What would she say? Your competition apparently isn't competition anymore? He'd hardly give her any sympathy, and right now she needed a hug, not mocking laughter. "I'm just tired."

"Are you sure? My instincts tell me different."

She pulled away. "Then let your instincts lead you to the Dumpster and hopefully to my missing book and a murderer." She scooted past Carolyn's desk, her pent-up tears streaming down her cheeks.

Chapter 23

Addie stopped short. Out of the corner of her eye, she saw exactly what she needed right now. There it was in the front window of Martha's Bakery, not the candy-decorated gingerbread house, but the two gingerbread men beside it with their stupid, grinning faces. She glared at them, certain they were mocking her. Moments later, she returned to the street, clasping a man in each hand and proceeded to bite the head off of each. A smile of satisfaction tugged at the corners of her lips. Revenge had never been so sweet.

The door chimes rang out over her head. Paige looked up from reshelving a book on the sales rack by the door. "Was one of those meant for me?" She looked from one decapitated gingerbread man to the other.

Addie looked down at them, melted icing dripping from her fingers. "Sure"—she held one out—"here."

"Thanks"—Paige winced—"but I think I'll pass."

"Yeah, sorry about that. They were therapy. I'll buy you one later, if you want."

"Don't worry about it. Mom's enlisted me as her taste-tester ever since she got those new cookbooks from you." She patted her stomach. "I think it's her plan to make me just like her by Christmas."

"As long as you have her sense of humor, too. There could be far worse things to become."

"Excuse me. You have met my mother, haven't you?"

Addie snorted.

"Don't you dare start that laughy-snorty thing again," Paige snickered.

"Then I'd better go wash." She licked her gooey fingers and headed for the back room. "Why don't you grab lunch while it's quiet?" The door chimes rang seconds later. "No telling her twice anymore," Addie chuckled.

Washed up and icing free, Addie removed the drop cloth from her blackboard and pulled the makeshift crime list from her tote bag. After copying the information, she glared at the chalky words. "It's useless. All we have are some silly suspicions. Where's the actual proof of a crime?" She stabbed the chalk into her final sentence on the board, bits flying in all directions.

"What's wrong?"

"Serena." Addie patted her pounding chest. "I didn't hear you come in."

"I don't doubt it. Looks like you got your head back into that again." She nodded toward the crime board. "But just so you know, since you're off in another world, Nancy Drew, three boys just did a grab-'n'-dash out your front door."

"What?" Addie's face whitened, and she started toward the shop door.

Serena's cackles of laughter stopped her in her tracks.

"You're kidding, right?"

"You should have seen your face." Serena grabbed her side and hunched over with a fit of laughter.

"Not funny." Addie threw the piece of chalk at her.

Serena ducked. "Yes, it was, and a good reminder that you are trying to run a successful business here. So, may I suggest that when Paige is out, you keep your head in the game of shopkeeper, not sleuth?"

"Yes, Mother." Addie wiped the chalk from her hands and stalked to the front counter. Serena followed her. "Go away, I'm mad at you." Addie shifted a stack of books from one side of the counter to the other.

"How can you be mad at this face?" Serena fluttered her eyelashes, grinning like a Cheshire cat.

"Speaking of running successful businesses, who's in charge of yours right now? Miss Flighty-pants?"

"I prefer to call her Miss Scaredy-pants, but whatever." She shrugged. Addie choked in an attempt to suppress the laughter threatening to escape from her rumbling chest.

Serena howled and slipped off the edge of her stool. Caught herself before she hit the floor, and pulled herself upright, a serious look glued across her face. She straightened her shoulders, cleared her throat, locked her fingers together on the countertop, and looked up at Addie. "In all seriousness, though, are you going to the meeting?"

"What meeting?"

"The auction donator's meeting. Didn't you get the e-mail?"

Addie scrolled through the e-mails on her phone. "No, when was it sent?"

"About an hour ago. Apparently, Patrick was re-

leased this morning and has asked all the local dona-
tors to attend a meeting in the event room at two
o'clock."

"Why wouldn't he invite me?" She shoved her
phone back into her pocket.

Serena's lips pursed. "Maybe because he doesn't
want to have to say in front of you, and all the other
merchants, that he still hasn't found the sixty-thousand-
dollar missing book you entrusted to him for safekeep-
ing."

"Yeah, and I might start asking questions that would
embarrass him in front of half the town." Addie
smiled. "So, it's settled. I'm going with you."

They stepped off the elevator on the lower level.
Serena scurried to the event room, and Addie took
a detour to Simon's office, clenched her fist, and
knocked on the door.

"If you're looking for Simon"—a pretty dark-haired
nurse paused, a flush rising up her neck—"I mean, Dr.
Emerson, I think he just got called up to the emergency department."

Addie thanked her and followed the woman down
the hall, noting how her nursing scrubs clung just
enough around her trim frame to show off her flawless
figure, and when she walked, her long dark braid
swung across her back in perfect rhythm with her
shapely hips. Addie sighed with envy and turned down
the corridor toward the meeting room. She slipped
through the door and took a place along the sidewall
beside two smartly dressed men in suits and ties.

Patrick was beginning to make an announcement
to the large group, and Addie's attention was diverted

from the two men when Patrick's high-pitched voice cracked over the loudspeaker attempting to be heard over the murmurings of the crowd.

"If I could have your attention, please." He thudded a gavel on the surface of the podium, bringing a hush to the room. "As foundation representative, I have called this meeting to inform you that I plan to go ahead with the silent auction and dinner." Mixed whispers of approval and discontent spread through the crowd. "Despite the foundation's recent loss of our beloved Teresa Lang and the woman I came to know and care for deeply." He bowed his head and crossed his heart, sucked in a deep breath, and continued. "She would have wanted her work to carry on despite the tragedy and setbacks that have plagued this worthwhile event. However"—his arms rose to quiet the increasing murmurs—"due to conditions out of my control, the live auction planned for *A Christmas Carol* will not be proceeding. In addition, because of the recent weather resulting in road closures, the date of the gala will be changed to December thirty-first."

His quivering voice rose over the rumblings that rippled through the crowed room. His hands rose in another attempt to regain control, and he went on to explain that this minor modification was necessary as any other date chosen in the future would make the Christmas decorations, already purchased, a useless expense, which would impact the community work the foundation would be able to conduct in the following year.

The room quieted, and he proceeded to explain that the event would now be promoted as the New Year's Eve Gala and Silent Auction, which allowed more time for marketing and would perhaps draw in a larger crowd because it was after Christmas, and people were likely to be less busy with family and holiday commitments. Addie snickered to herself at the adoption of an all-too-familiar plan. Serena, seated in the back row, twisted her head to look around, caught sight of Addie, and grinned.

A man Addie didn't recognize leapt to his feet. "I sold tickets to friends who are planning a New Year's Eve cruise. What happens to them?" he shouted. "Are they just out of luck with the money they spent for tickets?"

Whispers and jeers of support crept through the crowded room. Patrick held up his hand, regaining their attention. "Not at all, please be assured that anyone who purchased tickets who cannot attend on the new date due to conflicts with time or because of the discontinuation of the book auction will have all their money refunded." This was met with murmurs of approval from the group. "The hospital board has guaranteed to inject the foundation with the money needed to refund those ticket holders in full."

"You promised him that?" the gray-haired man beside Addie snapped at his companion.

"We really didn't have any choice, Walter. He showed me the foundation books. It's broke."

Addie took a deep breath and inched her way along the wall closer to the two men when their voices dropped.

"I'll tell you, Dan, that doesn't make sense to me. As chairman of the hospital board, I have been in every monthly budget meeting with Teresa. Her books have always shown a surplus, so what happened between last month and this?"

"I know. When the finance department did the last quarterly review of her department, the ledgers showed there should be more than enough to cover the costs of this year's gala and then some."

"So, then why does Patrick need an emergency budget increase for these tickets he has to refund?" His face reddened. "I have to get to a board of directors meeting, but I want you and your department to go through those books with a fine-tooth comb."

The man he'd called Dan nodded. "Look—" Walter leaned toward him and glanced at Addie, who quickly refocused on the crowd in the room. His voice turned to a hushed whisper. "I'm not accusing him of anything, but something's not adding up."

"But, Walter, Patrick is a pretty stand-up guy. Teresa was more than happy with his work this past year, and I know her accident shook him up pretty bad."

"As it did all of us." Walter's nostrils flared. "You should never have approved that event budgetary increase without going through my office first."

Dan, the stocky, dark-haired man, nodded.

"Just get back to me as soon as you can." He turned and started toward the door.

"Sure thing." Dan blew out a deep breath. Addie looked at him and smiled. His jaw tightened and on rather shaky-looking legs, he also turned and left the event room.

Addie let out a breath she didn't even know she'd been holding.

Serena waved her hand in front of Addie's face. "Hello, anyone home in there?"

Addie stared at her. "Sorry, just thinking."

"Pretty cool. He finally did what we suggested."

"I'm not sure everyone else agreed, but what else could he do? The roads are only starting to reopen, and he still doesn't have the book."

"They'll come around when it sinks in that they just have to mark a different date on their calendars, and no one is going to lose anything."

Addie caught sight of Patrick chatting with a group of merchants by the door, her eyes narrowing. "Yeah, I guess it's a win-win for everyone, isn't it?"

Serena linked her arm through Addie's as they headed for the elevator. The door opened and Simon darted out, slamming right into Addie. He grabbed her shoulders, bracing them both.

"We really do have to stop meeting like this." She gave a hesitant smile.

His eyes darkened to a shade of tidal-wave blue. "Yes, we do." He released her as if burned.

She twisted her purse strap around her clammy hand. "Funny, me running into you like this. A little while ago I went to your office and—"

"Look, Addie"—he backed away—"I really have to go. I've got . . . got a thing." He pointed down the hall toward his office. "Have to run."

"But I just wanted to talk for a minute, you know about—"

"If it's about the case, then talk to Marc." He turned his back on her. "I've just sent him over the final findings. I'm sure he'll be very happy to help you with whatever it is you want."

Stunned by the sting that his words left behind, Addie could only watch him walk away.

Chapter 24

Addie sat in Serena's Jeep, staring out the windshield, seeing nothing.

"Okay, spill." Serena turned on the vehicle but kept it in park.

Addie shook her head, fighting the tears that burned at the back of her eyes.

"I mean it. We're not moving from this spot until you tell me exactly what happened between you and Simon." Serena reached over and pressed her fingers to the side of Addie's jaw, forcing Addie to look at her. "Whatever happened seems a bit more serious than you let on."

"That's the thing. I really don't know what happened." Through tears and the occasional hiccup, Addie explained her recent dealings with Simon, from the tree lighting to her uninvited Christmas dinner guest status.

Serena squeezed her hand. "Well, you certainly aren't going to be alone for Christmas, that I can guarantee. You'll spend it with us." She slammed the Jeep into drive and pulled onto Main Street.

"Don't be silly. I can't. Your mom and dad, and Marc?" Her voice faltered on Marc's name.

Serena gave her a side glance, her eyes twinkling. "Mom and Dad are going to my aunt's in New Hampshire, and Marc is working extra shifts so that more of the crew can have Christmas off, you have no excuses." She pulled into her parking spot in the alley. "It'll be just Zach and me, and now you."

"But do you want me to intrude on your first Christmas together."

"To be honest, yes, I'm used to having a houseful around and well—"

"It's a deal, then. We'll be the Three Musketeers."

Serena drummed her fingers on the steering wheel. "Can we have dinner at your house, then?"

Addie eyed the delicious-looking snowbank outside the back door of the shop. "Ah, yeah"—she bent over, grabbed a handful of snow, and formed a perfect ball—"that should work."

"What a relief. Otherwise, we'd have to eat at House of Sushi, and, well, I don't think—" A snowball to Serena's chest cut her off. "Two can play that game."

A few seconds later, a snowball landed on Addie's jacket hood, sending snow down her back. "That's it. War!" Addie gave a war whoop and descended upon Serena, throwing snowballs and dodging behind Dumpsters.

When Serena cornered her, Addie held her hands up. "I surrender."

Even though Serena's smile resembled that of a Cheshire cat, Addie allowed her to hoist her to her feet. "First rule of snowball fights? Don't trust the enemy." With a laugh, Serena playfully shoved Addie into a snowbank.

Addie landed face first in the snow, sputtering out a mouthful just as Martha's back door opened. Her flour-covered face peered out. She harrumphed and slammed the door. Addie snorted, brushing snow off herself. She stumbled to her feet and kicked snow in Serena's direction. Serena gathered another snowball and aimed.

Addie threw her hands up. "Stop, I give up, uncle. Not fair. You grew up with a brother."

"Feel better?" Serena panted and dropped the snowball.

Addie swept snow from under her jacket collar. "What was this, therapy?"

Serena giggled, trying to catch her breath. "The best kind ever."

In the back room of her shop, Addie glanced in the mirror as she passed and stopped short. "Yeesh!" She fluffed at the stringy wet hair strands stuck to the sides of her face like honey-blond octopus tentacles, but it was no use. The pouf she worked so hard to achieve in her bangs every morning was definitely done for the day. She took out her workday ponytail, wrapped her hair, and pinned it up in a tight topknot, giving her the appearance of a stern librarian. Act like a crazy book lady, look like a crazy book lady. She shrugged and headed to the storefront.

Paige looked at her, did a double take, and went back to assisting a customer. Addie glanced over her shoulder, but there was no mistaking the smirk on Paige's face. Addie stopped when a woman, whose eye contact flitted between Addie's eyes and her instant face-lift hairdo, inquired about a children's version of *A Christmas Carol*, one that would be suitable for her eight-year-old grandson. Addie took her to the Young

Reader's section and pulled out an illustrated copy. The woman added it to her armful of books and followed Addie to the sales counter. She ignored the snickers and curious glances from customers as she passed by them. Jonathan appeared from around the corner of a book-shelf, slid onto a counter stool, and flipped open the newspaper.

When the woman left, a faint snigger could be heard from behind his paper shield. "Love the new look. It has that vintage schoolmarm-librarian thing going on."

Her nostrils flared. "Did you just come in here to in-sult me?"

"Not at all. Catherine's in here somewhere finishing her shopping," he said without looking up from the newspaper. "Me, I'm just passing time."

"Then I'll go and assist *her*. At least she won't in-sult me."

"I wouldn't count on that," he chuckled from be-hind his paper barrier.

Addie didn't get far. Catherine dropped an arm-load of books down in front of her. "There, I think I'm finally finished." She fished around in her large tote bag for her wallet. "Paige was such a great help. She is a wonder, isn't she? There it is." She pulled her wallet out and stared at Addie, a smirk fighting for space on her befuddled face.

Addie smiled sweetly and rang up Catherine's pur-chases, aware that Catherine's eyes never left her hair. Addie, without looking at her, explained the perils of a snowball fight.

Catherine's lips pulled back into a grin. "Sorry I missed it. Sounds and looks like fun. It's been ages since I've thrown a snowball."

Jonathan laid his paper on the counter and patted

Addie's hand. "Whatever the reason for the change in appearance today, you look lovely, my dear."

"Liar." She snatched her hand away from his, and for the first time noted a momentary tic in his cheek.

"It's nothing that can't be fixed." Was he talking about her hair or their relationship, which had imploded? Answering that question, he stood up and reached around the back of her head, undid her topknot, fluffed her hair, and scrunched her bangs. "Now, give it good shake, and you'll just look like someone who had fun playing in the snow."

Addie scooted away from him. "Don't. Touch. Me," she bit out. Thankful Catherine's attention had been diverted by a screaming toddler who insisted upon having a cookie *right now.*

"You know, my dear"—he ignored Addie's bared teeth and clasped Catherine's hand, bringing it to his lips to kiss the tips of her fingers—"a romp in the snow is exactly what we should do before we go home today."

Addie gripped the edge of the counter. Did he just call Catherine's house home?

"After all, I did miss out on all this fun when I was in Australia last year for Christmas, and what better way to celebrate the season than having a good, old-fashioned snowball fight."

Catherine's eyes sparkled with delight. "Could we? At our age?"

"We won't know if we don't try." He grinned. "Thanks for the coffee, Addie. We'll be back to pick up the books, and by then, I'm sure both of us will look far worse than you thought you did."

Addie's eyes remained fixed on the two as they giggled like school kids all the way out the door. Australia? Her face scrunched up in concentration. She snapped her fingers and headed for the back room. "Paige, call me if you need help," she said as she passed her in the Mystery book aisle.

Addie whisked the cover from the board and wrote furiously, the chalk spitting and sputtering with: *Tetrodotoxin. Puffer fish? Blue-ringed octopus? Pacific and Indian oceans, from Japan to Australia.* Circling the last word, she read back what she'd written beside Jonathan's name. She tossed the cover back over the blackboard and headed to the front to find Paige. Searching the aisles, she finally located her assisting a customer in the Poetry section in the far back corner of the shop. "Are you okay here for a few minutes?"

"Yup." Page looked at the young man she was serving. "We're fine."

Addie couldn't miss the sidelong glances between the two hunched over, head-to-head in the corner with a copy of *The Major Works of John Keats.*

"Good, I'll be back soon, just have a quick errand to run."

A slow smile tugged at the corners of Paige's lips. Addie turned away. Her little Paige appeared to be falling for a very eye-catching young gentleman, who she hoped wouldn't distract her from her other duties. One-to-one customer service was great, but not at the expense of the rest. She made a mental note to discuss this with Paige later, but right now she was on a mission.

Addie drummed her fingers at the vacated police reception counter. Even Marc's office was empty. Where was everybody? Five minutes of sheer boredom later found Addie in Marc's office, again. He needed a makeover team in here, stat. The garbage wasn't anywhere near

his desk, the scrunched-up balls of paper on the floor
proof of that. Coffee rings on the wood spoke of a lack
of cleaning, and a file folder . . . her eyes paused in
their perusal. DNA report. She glanced over her
shoulder and pulled it toward her. She flipped it open
and scanned down the page, trying to make sense out
of all the medical and legal mumbo-jumbo. She finally
determined that the lipstick sample on the cup sent
for DNA testing came back as a match to someone
named Amy Miller, wanted in Florida on charges of
ecoterrorism.

What? She must have read that wrong. Addie's nose
scrunched up. Her eyes narrowed in concentration,
and she reread the page. "Why on earth would Teresa
be having a drink with an ecoterrorist from Florida?"

"I asked myself the same question." Marc slammed
the door behind him.

Addie jumped and scooted the file folder away from
her. "I was . . . was just—"

"Yeah"—his eyes bored into hers—"I can see what
you were *just* doing. What are you doing in here in the
first place?"

"Waiting for you," she squeaked. "I didn't mean to
be nosy, but—"

"But you're very good at it, aren't you?" He reached
around her, snatched the folder, and snapped it shut
with a growl.

She wagged a finger in the air. "Just one question."

"What is it?"

She slumped down in her chair. "Why isn't there a
photo of this Amy Miller in the report?"

A deep sigh escaped his chest. "Because the DNA
lab doesn't have access to those records, and they only
show a match if someone is already in the system ei-

ther from criminal charges being levied or because of employment reasons like with some government agencies."

"So that means what?"

"Their information is designed to show if a match exists, not to judge what the match relates to. They send the info about the match, and then it's up to the receiving authority to decide if an investigation is warranted."

"And?"

He shuffled a stack of papers. "We will be proceeding with an investigation with the assistance of the FBI because this woman is wanted on Federal and Florida State charges."

"So, why do you think this Amy was here to see Teresa?"

He shrugged. "An old friend maybe?"

"But Jonathan was an old friend, too, and Teresa blew him off for a meeting with this Amy person."

"Who knows, then? All I can do, just like you are"—his eyes narrowed at her—"is guess."

"But—"

"Now tell me what made you sneak into my office." He leaned forward, his shoulder muscles bunching under this uniform.

She shifted in her seat and tried to remember what was so important that she had to talk to him. "I didn't sneak. There was no one at the front counter, and so I just came in." She raised her chin.

"I'm waiting." He tapped his pen on the desk.

"I remember now. Jonathan."

"What about him?"

"He was in Australia last Christmas."

"How nice for him." A soft laugh escaped his throat.

She rose to her feet and leaned across the desk. "Don't you see? Tetrodotoxin is found in puffer fish and blue-ringed octopus that live in the Australian reefs."

"And, if I remember, also Japan and the Indian oceans. His being in Australia last year isn't a connection to or proof of anything."

"I think it is. There's too many coincidences around Jonathan being here for my liking."

"Like what?"

"Like him knowing that snake Marvin for one. And everything else. Him dropping into town, Teresa being murdered—"

"Ah, ah, ah."

"What do you mean, ah, ah, ah. If it wasn't murder, what is it?"

"Her death is just suspicious at this point."

"But you have proof otherwise now."

"Not enough for the DA. He needs absolute proof it was intentionally put in her food and wasn't an accidental ingestion due to contaminated fish."

"Okay, whatever, but now we know Jonathan was in a place he could get his hands on whatever it was."

"Blue-ringed octopus venom."

"It's that for sure?"

He nodded. "Simon explained what the report said in easy-to-understand layman terms. So, yes, and that's why it took so long. The lab was narrowing down the actual source, just as I thought."

"Okay, but can't you see how this all points to Jonathan and the fact he has such a sketchy past?"

Marc shook his head. "I think you're on the wrong path here, and if you continue, you're only going to get hurt"—his fingers interlocked—"and in the best-case scenario, you will end up damaging your relationship with Jonathan."

"I don't have a relationship with Jonathan."

"I think you do and a far deeper one than you realize." Her eyes widened. "Is that all for today?" Marc stood up and adjusted his police utility belt.

"I guess." She pushed herself to her feet. "But explain to me why you are so bent on the fact that Jonathan isn't behind it?"

"Because I think you are too focused on finding something wrong with him and trying to ignore what your real issue is with him."

"And what's that?"

"The fact that every time you look at him you see the ghost of David."

She swallowed hard to release the lump in the back of her throat. "Who . . . who told you that?"

His brown eyes softened. "Serena."

"Of course, she did." Addie crossed her arms, hoping to hide her trembling.

"It's not her fault. She knows how torn up you've been since he arrived."

"Have not." She shook her head.

"Yes, you are. Even Simon referred to you today as Miss Greyborne and not Addie." His brow rose in question. "I'm guessing that things aren't going well—"

She spun on her heel and all but ran to the door.

"One more thing."

She stopped but didn't look back at him.

"You can take Marvin Gibson off your crime board."

"Why?" She swung around.

"That highway accident the other night? He was the driver who was killed when his brakes failed. Plowed into the back of a semi."

Her eyes widened. "Faulty brakes or cut?"

Marc shrugged. "Not sure yet. His rental car's in the

Chapter 25

"Hello, Miss Greyborne."

Addie whirled around. Jerry stared at her from behind the desk, a look of concern on his face. "Hi, Jerry, how are you?"

"Doing well. I had no idea you were in there. I thought the chief was talking on the phone."

"Nope, just me. When I came in, there was no one at the desk."

"We were planning the office Christmas party, sorry about that."

"No problem. I got what I came for, so I'll be off now." Her gaze settled on a thick five-inch binder on a shelf behind Jerry. The words "Most Wanted" glared back at her. "What's that?" She pointed.

Jerry looked over his shoulder. "What?"

"That Most Wanted binder."

"It's a weekly updated list of all the new bad guys to be on the lookout for."

"Is the public allowed to look at it?"

"Sure, the more eyes on some of those posters the better. You never know when one of them might stop in town." He grabbed it off the shelf and dropped it down on the countertop. "You looking for someone in particular?"

"No, I'm just curious. I've never seen one of these before."

"We even post the ones who were last seen in Massachusetts on the wall over there." He pointed to a corkboard.

She glanced at it and then started to thumb through the book. "Is there a system to this, like sections for the crimes they committed or the states that have a warrant out for them?"

"No, we just do alphabetical listings."

"That's easy." Addie flipped to the *m*s, hoping to get a glimpse of a photo of this Amy Miller, scanned through the pages, and closed the binder. "Are all the Most Wanted in the country in here?"

"No, that's just the Most Wanted on the east coast, but not if there's a Federal warrant out on them."

"Is there a separate book for those ones?"

"We don't keep those in an actual binder, but they're listed on the FBI database."

"I see. Thanks for your help. Catch you later."

"Take care out there, Miss Greyborne. The temperatures plummeted, and the roads are starting to slick over now."

"Thanks, I'll be careful." She turned toward the door.

"And watch out for a few downed power lines," Jerry called behind her. "Some branches snapped off with the cold and snow buildup, and they're blocking some of the roads."

She smiled her gratitude and braced herself against the blustery wind when the door flew open in her hand.

Addie tossed her coat on the end of the counter and briskly rubbed her hands up and down her arms in an attempt to ward off Mother Nature's latest glacial assault and scanned the shop for Paige. She spotted her shelving books in the Romance section and headed toward her. "You seem to be attracted to this type of thing today."

Paige looked up at her. "What, books?"

"No, romance. I saw what was going on between you and that dreamy blond guy who was in here."

Paige stood up. "Grant? He's just an old friend."

"Okay, if you say so."

Paige's cheeks flushed with a rosy glow. "Well, he did ask me to go to the gala with him." A smile crept across her lips.

"Good going." Addie grinned and rubbed her still-icy hands together. "Did I miss anything?"

"No." Paige picked up another book from the book cart. "But Jonathan and Catherine came back to pick up her books. You should have seen their bright-red cheeks. They looked so happy. Catherine said she had the most fun she's had in years." Paige sighed. "Someday I want to fall in love just like they did."

"Love?" Addie choked.

Paige nodded, grinning. A low growl escaped from the back of Addie's throat as she headed back to the counter. "Love, my foot. What game are you playing now, Jonathan?" She stabbed at the cash key. The drawer flung open. She glanced down at the bill dividers and gasped. "Paige, can you come here for a minute, please?"

Paige popped her head around a bookshelf. "Is there a problem?"

Addie's hands waved over the cash. "Did you bring all this in today?"

"And the credit card receipts and the daily tally from online sales are under the tray."

"It looks like there might be a little something extra in your stocking this year." Addie grinned.

"We just had a good day."

"No, it's more than that. I can't thank you enough for the extra effort you have to put in when I'm out of the shop." She pulled a stack of bills from the drawer.

"Just doing what I love to do."

"Sales?"

"No, talking."

Addie howled and continued counting the cash. The door chimes rang, heralding the appearance of a redhead with flushed freckled cheeks.

Addie's eyes narrowed to crinkled slits. "You are aware that your freckles pop out whenever you feel flustered or embarrassed or excited and maybe even"—Addie tapped her finger on her jaw—"guilty?" Addie felt only a slight stab of pity when her friend paled. "I know what you did."

"Yup, I heard."

Paige looked from one to the other and backed away. Addie glanced sideways at her. "Can you give us a minute, please?" Paige nodded, grabbed the book cart, and headed for the back room.

Addie returned her focus to a twitchy Serena, shifting her weight from one foot to the other. "Do you tell Marc everything about me and what we talk about?"

"No, of course not." Serena slunk onto a stool. "But I

told you he asks about you all the time, and today he said he had a meeting with Simon and things seemed . . . well, he asked if everything was still good with the two of you."

"So, you felt that was an opening to tell him what I said about looking at Jonathan and seeing David?"

"Well, no"—she twisted her fingers together—"but yes, kind of." She winced. "I didn't give him any details. I just said you were struggling because he stirred up so many memories."

"Yeah, some days they hit me like a punch in the stomach and take my breath away, kind of like when Marc told me what you said to him."

"I know"—Serena reached across the counter and clasped her hand—"and I'm sorry, but can I give you a little bit of friendly advice, and only because I care about you?"

"Something tells me that even if I say no, you will, anyway."

"You're right, because I'm your friend. But you really do need to stop being such a Scrooge about everything right now. You don't even have a Christmas tree at home or lights or anything yet."

"What are you talking about? I'm not a Scrooge." Addie looked down. "And as far as the decorations at home, well . . . I've been busy is all." She scuffed her foot over a scratch on a wooden floorboard.

"Look, something horrible happened to David, and it hurt you, that I get. But since then Marc kisses you, and you call him David, which pushes him away. Jonathan comes to town and reminds you of David, and you look for ways to push him away, too. Then Simon is just about to do exactly what you thought you wanted him to do, and . . . your attention suddenly was on Marc instead of the man about to kiss you." She squeezed Addie's hand. "Can't you see that you're pushing people away from you who care about you? I think Scrooge did the same, didn't he?"

"I don't do that. It's just that my past was perfect, and then it wasn't. Now my present sucks, and my future looks bleak." She scrubbed her hands over her face. "Argh! I am Scrooge."

"Then change it before it's too late, like he did."

"But he had spirits to help him see his ways."

"As you do."

Addie scoffed. "I think you're on a Christmas sugar cookie high."

"Just listen to me." She tightened her hold on Addie's hand. "This whole thing with Jonathan and how you feel like David is staring back at you."

"Yeah, so?"

"Maybe he is, and he's trying to tell you something."

"Like what?"

"Like maybe it's time to change the present because you can't do anything about the past, and the best way is to start by fixing things with his father. You can leave some of those memories where they belong, in the past, and you can start moving forward with your life, so it doesn't turn out so bleak."

Addie snorted.

"Jonathan seems like a good guy to me because Catherine appears to be head over heels, and she's a pretty good judge of character. In fact, they popped into my shop after their *frolic* in the park, and I've never seen her or him grin like that before."

Addie crossed her arms. "Don't forget his dallying with Crystal. He looked pretty happy then, too."

"Whatever it was that you think you saw happening with her, it didn't bother Catherine, so don't let it bother you."

"I just can't get past the feeling that something is off with him. I've always felt that. Come on. Take a look at what I'm talking about." She directed Serena to the back room.

Paige looked up from pricing the books on the back desk. Addie motioned with her head to the door, and she nodded, grabbed a load of books, tossed them on the book trolley, and headed for the front of the store.

Addie pulled the cover off the blackboard, a tic of smugness in her eyes as she held Serena's gaze. "See what I mean? Now, you read that and then tell me there's nothing to suspect Jonathan of?"

"Umm, Addie, I . . ." Serena's face drained of color.

Addie spun around. Her breath caught in her throat. She forced down the acid rising up from the pit of her stomach as she read the message written across the otherwise blank blackboard. *This is your last warning!!!* She leaned against the desk, her knees giving way under her.

Serena collapsed on a wooden book crate. "Who would have done this?"

"Paige." Addie's voice rose to a shrill shriek. "Come here."

She appeared around the corner of the door. "What's wrong?"

"Who . . . who?" She pointed to the blackboard.

Wide-eyed, Paige read the words on the board, her face, too, draining of color.

"When Jonathan and Catherine came in, did he come back here?" Addie questioned.

"I don't think so, but I'm not sure. I was looking for a book Catherine wanted to add to her earlier purchase, and we were talking. He could have. I really wasn't paying attention to him."

"Have you ever told him or anyone else about this board being back here?"

Paige shook her head, blinking back tears.

Serena shifted on the box. "Your store was busy today, and if Paige was busy out front, it could have been anyone that slipped back."

"Was anyone in the store today that you recognized from the names that were on here?"

"I've only ever glanced at it when I happened to come back here and you were writing on it." She fumbled with a book in her hand. "I've never taken a close look."

"I'm not accusing you of spying, but when you did take a look, did you happen to remember seeing anyone else's name that was listed on it come into the store today?"

"I didn't know any of the people you had written down, so maybe. I don't really know."

"My money's on Jonathan." Addie's lips twitched as she reread the message.

"Why are you so sure it was him?"

"Because there were a lot of incriminating clues against him pointing to the fact that he's not such a squeaky-clean, upstanding person as you might think." She pinned Serena with a scowl. "That combined with something else he did recently is how I know this was his doing. This means"—her face screwed up in concentration—"he somehow found out about this board and now knows every clue we had written down regarding him and anyone else he might be working with. I don't believe what's happened was a one-person job."

Serena's face was grim. "And if it wasn't him, then someone else has that information now, too."

"I know it was him"—she drummed her fingers on the edge of the desk—"because he broke into my house the other night and was waiting for me when I got home."

Serena and Paige gasped.

"He . . . he did what?" Serena leapt to her feet. "Why? What did he want?"

"He warned me then to leave all this alone when he saw the makeshift board on my wall in the living room or, as he said, I'd end up getting hurt."

"He threatened you before?" Serena looked back at the warning on the board and shuddered.

Addie shook her head. "He denied then that it was a threat. He said he was just laying the cards on the table for me."

"What does that mean?"

"I think"—she waved her hand at the board—"he's just played his ace."

Chapter 26

Serena sat on the book crate, her head in her hands. "This is all getting to be more like a James Bond movie than something that would happen in Greyborne Harbor."

"That's for sure. Ian Fleming wouldn't even believe this was happening outside of one of his novels." Addie slouched back in her chair, feet up on her desk, staring at the message on the board. She pulled her phone out of her jacket pocket and snapped a picture of it, then got up and started erasing the cryptic warning.

"What are you doing?" Serena shot to her feet. "You have to call Marc and show him this." Her hand covered the eraser brush clutched in Addie's.

"I took a picture of it." She struggled with her friend for control over the brush.

"What about prints and all that?"

"I doubt highly they can get anything off this eraser or a piece of chalk." Addie jerked the brush from Serena's hand.

"You never know. Technology has come a long way." Serena lunged forward, trying to wrestle the brush from Addie's grasp. Addie laughed and held it over her head out of Serena's reach.

"I give up. If you don't care, then neither do I." Serena flopped back down on the box.

Addie finished wiping the board. "It's not that I don't care. It's just that I'm ninety-nine percent sure it was Jonathan, anyway."

"What if you're wrong, though? You heard Paige. She doesn't know any of the other people we had on the board, like Patrick or Crystal or Marvin, and any one of them could have been in the store today."

"Well, if it were Marvin, he's a ghost of Christmas present, because he was the fatality in the highway accident the other night."

Serena stood up. "You're kidding. I heard someone died, but I had no idea it was him."

Addie reread the message on the photo. *This is your last warning!!!* "His brakes failed, did you hear that? Marc doesn't know yet if it was faulty brakes, or if they were cut."

"Are you saying he could have been murdered, too?" Serena scowled when Addie just shrugged. She grabbed Addie's phone and stuck the picture of the threatening message in her face. "What do you think is going to happen to you if the same person who cut Marvin's brakes left this for you?"

"I just don't know." Addie pushed the phone away from her face. "There's still a few other suspects on the list, but I'm—"

"I know. You still think it was Jonathan, but what if Marvin's accident was a revenge killing. Maybe he *was* working with Patrick like you suspected before and found out that Patrick double-crossed him. After all, we still think he was the one who beat Patrick up and stuffed him in the closet, even though he won't say who it was. Maybe he's known all along and then discovered Marvin was the one who tried to overdose him, too."

"Or . . . he was working with Jonathan, and that's why they met at the Grey Gull Inn. Jonathan didn't want to split the sixty thousand dollars two ways because half wouldn't be much of a score, would it?"

Serena threw her hands up in the air. "Look, Ian Fleming had to stop sometimes, too, and I'm starving. I need to eat before my head explodes with all of this theorizing. Ever since you said Grey Gull Inn, that's all I can focus on now. Come on, my treat."

Addie looked at the board and then at the pleading expression in her friend's eyes. "You're right. It is only speculation," she said, pulling on her coat. "But your offer to treat sounds more like you know Zach is working so you're counting on getting a big discount." She playfully nudged Serena and locked the back door behind them.

"Serena, Miss Greyborne, how wonderful to see you. Do you have a reservation?" Bruce glanced down at the list in front of him.

"No, sorry." Serena sucked her bottom lip between her teeth. "We were just hoping."

"Humm." He reviewed the table diagram. "You're in luck. I have one table for two in the back, and . . . it's in Zach's section." He grinned at Serena, grabbed two menus, and led them into the dining room.

Addie paused. Her eyes couldn't skim the large room fast enough to take in all of the Christmas splendor. Twinkling white fairy lights covered the entire ceiling and hung down like dripping icicles. The lighted wall of windows facing the harbor created the same breathtaking effect. Serena bumped into her, sending her stumbling against a chair. She quickly apologized to the startled diner and, red-faced, slid onto a chair at a table Bruce indicated as theirs.

Serena thanked him for the table as he filled their water glasses, but as soon as he left, she glared at Addie. "Just once I'd like the chair facing the dining room instead of . . ." She waved her hand at the wall. "Just once." She pouted.

Addie picked up her napkin and placed it on her lap. "Haven't I ever told you about my aversion to sitting with my back to the door?"

"Why?"

Addie leaned across the table. "Because when I was little I watched too many old westerns."

"So? What does that have to do with always taking the best seat for people watching and leaving me nothing to look at except . . . *you?*"

Addie preened her hair and then lowered her voice. "Because you never know who's going to come through the saloon doors with their guns blazing."

"What?" Serena grabbed her napkin off the table and threw it at Addie. "That's the silliest thing I've ever heard."

Addie snatched it up and threw it back. "It's true. In every movie, the good guy sits facing the door."

"Does that make me the *bad guy?*"

"Of course not. You're just the poor, unsuspecting sidekick."

"You're using me as a shield. Is that what you're saying?"

"Pfftt, just figure out what you want," Addie scoffed. "I thought you were starving."

"I guess in your Wild West scenario, I'd better. This could be my last meal."

Addie chuckled, shaking her head, and glanced down at her menu, but a sideward glimpse of the twelve-foot Christmas tree in the far corner stole her attention. It was decked out in soft whites and shades of blues and touched the spirit of the little girl inside her. It made her heart dance in step with the elves she envisioned skipping around the lower tree boughs. This room tonight reminded her that Christmas was pure magic.

"Addie, earth to Addie."

She jerked and looked up. "Zach, hi."

"Are you ready to order?" His smile was contagious and Addie beamed back at him.

"He's been standing here talking to me for at least five minutes. Where have you been?" Serena whispered across the table.

Addie glanced back over at the tree. "I was just dancing."

Zach cleared his throat, glanced sideways at Serena, wrote down Addie's order, and left, shaking his head.

Serena studied Addie. "That is water you're drinking, right?"

"Yes."

"You're sure?"

"I am not drunk or crazy, if that's what you're implying."

"Just making sure." Serena's eyes didn't waver off Addie's as she drummed her fingers on the tabletop.

Addie spread her hands out over the table. "Okay, when I was little I used to pretend that elves danced around my Christmas tree and I'd join them. It was just a silly childhood memory that came back when I saw the tree, that's all."

"Now it makes sense," Serena said, and looked in the direction of the tree, her smile quickly changing to an openmouthed stare. "Will you look at who's here?"

"Who? Where?" Addie craned her neck to see around another patron.

"There, directly across from us by the window. Isn't that Crystal and Patrick?"

Addie rose slightly in her seat and nodded. "It sure is, and they do look kind of cozy for coworkers, don't they?"

"I'd say." Serena leaned forward, looking sideways at their table. "From where I sit, it looks like her hand is clasping his on the table."

"I can't see from here." Addie turned her chair a touch. "Nope, still can't see."

"They look happy together, and not in a boss-subordinate kind of way, either." Serena took a sip of water, her eyes still on Patrick's table.

"I wonder what's up?" Addie stared in the same direction.

"Maybe since they started working together, they just developed an attraction for each other." Serena shrugged. "Workplace romances happen all the time."

The diners who had been blocking Addie's view left, giving her a clear line of sight. "Did I tell you what I overheard at the meeting today?"

Serena shook her head. "We kind of got distracted by the message on the board, remember?"

Addie repeated the conversation she'd heard between the hospital chairman and the fellow she assumed was from the accounts department.

"So, Patrick wasn't lying, then?"

Addie shrugged. "He showed them the books, and they're in the red apparently, but Walter, the chairman, said it didn't make sense because all the books

Teresa showed him previously indicated that there was a surplus in the foundation account."

"What happened? He just overspent on the bills?"

"Or maybe she did." Addie gestured with her head toward Crystal and Patrick's table. "Some girlfriends can be high maintenance, and she strikes me as being that."

Serena toyed with her napkin on the table. "I hope Zach doesn't think I'm like that."

"You? Hardly." She grinned as Zach set their salads in front of them. "Tell me something, Zach—"

"Don't you dare ask him." Serena slapped at her wrist.

"Relax, will you?" Addie arched a brow and looked up at him. "See that couple over by the window, the girl with the kind of reddish hair and the mid-thirties, balding guy she's with?" Zach looked over at the tables by the window. "Any chance that's your section?"

"No, sorry, it's Maria's. Why?"

"Does Maria need any help with bussing the tables around theirs by chance?" Addie feigned innocence.

Obviously not impressed with her acting skills, he peered at her. "What are you two up to?"

"I think what she's asking you to do," Serena's voiced dropped, "is be a spy."

A smile dangled at the corners of his mouth. "What do you want me to find out?"

"Just whatever it is they're talking about." Addie crossed her heart. "That's all."

"Okay, let me get an order out, and I'll play 007 for you."

Addie picked at her salad. "You really have found a great guy there."

"I know," Serena sighed, her eyes fixed on him as he made his way to the kitchen. "He is pretty dreamy."

Her freckles seemed to grow and brighten. For a second, Addie wished she had freckles prominently displayed across her cheeks.

A few minutes later, Zach returned to their table and whipped out his notepad. "You don't need that." Serena looked up at him. "We don't want to order anything else."

"I know, let me play my role, in case they see me talking to you."

"Right, then carry on, 007." Addie pressed her lips tight to stifle a smile.

His voice lowered. "They're talking about a trip to the Cayman Islands"—he pretended to write on his pad—"and meeting her sister from Australia."

"I remember her telling me that one day." Addie placed her fork down. "Is that all they talked about?"

"Yeah"—he glanced over to them—"give me a minute and I'll see if I can get anything else."

Addie slapped the palm of her hand on the table. "That's what I wanted to show you on the board tonight."

"What was?"

"I was telling you why I suspect Jonathan of not being the guy you all think he is. It was because I found out today that he was in Australia last year."

"And that makes him bad? You do know that good people are from and go to Australia, don't you?"

"I know that," Addie huffed in frustration. "It's just because Marc told me the toxin Teresa ingested was definitely from the blue-ringed octopus."

"Okay?"

Addie sighed. "It's found in the reefs off the coast of Australia."

"But Teresa and he were friends. Why would he kill her?"

"Ah, he *said* they were friends, but she blew him off to have drinks and maybe lunch with someone named Amy Miller, according to the DNA results on the lipstick cup." Her voice lowered. "I'm thinking they weren't the best of friends, and maybe he planted something in her food before Amy took it in to her."

"That means that Jonathan would have been working with this Amy person?"

Addie nodded smugly. "And the most interesting thing is, Amy Miller is wanted by the FBI on ecoterrorism charges."

Serena sputtered her water across the table. "What does that have to do with Teresa and your missing book?"

"Who knows? Like we said before, it's all turned rather James Bondish." She plucked her napkin from her lap and tossed it on the table. "You know it's funny. Crystal's sister living in Australia and Jonathan having been there recently, too, could explain why Crystal and he are so friendly with each other."

"Do you think he knows her sister, and that's why they act all chummy with each other?"

"I'm thinking exactly that"—Addie tapped her fork on the table—"and this Amy Miller could possibly be Crystal's sister."

Serena frowned. "That's a long shot, but maybe, I guess."

"Think about it. He and Crystal have something going on. I thought they might be involved, but when I say it now, it could be the sister he's actually involved with."

"Do you know anything else about the sister?"

Addie stared down at her half-eaten meal. "No, nothing that stands out except she had just finished her doctorate."

"What in?"

"Crystal didn't really know. All she said was some nerdy science stuff."

"I'd say the sister got the brains in that family." Serena snickered. "You weren't kidding when you told me she was self-absorbed. I can't imagine not knowing what my own sister was studying at university."

"I know, weird, right?"

Serena glanced at the object of their discussion. "Yeah, by the sounds of it, she's not too bright or worldly, either. I don't know. I think that theory about her knowing Jonathan through her sister is really a stretch." She screwed up her face. "Personally, I still think you're just so bent on finding fault with Jonathan that you'll grasp at any straws to make him look guilty of something." Serena pushed her plate away. "Importing toxic fish, in league with ecoterrorists, to knock off what? Some small-town charity coordinator and steal a book that's not worth all that trouble for. What will you make up about him next?" She leaned forward. "Just face it, Addie. Those facts aren't connected to what happened here, so look at what we do really know."

"Maybe you're right." Addie pursed her lips. "This is Greyborne Harbor and not some spy novel."

A flush-faced Zach appeared at their table. "I think there may have been a problem between them, but I missed hearing what started it. Now I feel too conspicuous lingering to listen. They look pretty upset with each other."

"That's fine," Addie smiled, "thanks for trying."

"Okay, since I'm now retired from the secret service, I'll see you later." He squeezed Serena's shoulder.

Addie and Serena both snuck glances at Patrick and Crystal's table. Her face was the shade of her hair, and

Patrick's usually waxy skin now glistened with beads of perspiration. Their body language didn't quite look as cozy as it had earlier. Her arms were crossed, and his hand thudded on the table. She stood up, grabbed her handbag, and stormed toward the door. Patrick flung his napkin on the table and stomped after her.

"Wow," Addie mouthed. "I wish Zach had heard what caused that scene."

Serena's shoulders tensed. "Remember he is supposed to be working, not playing spy. He tried his best."

"I know. I wasn't suggesting he shouldn't do his job, it's just too bad he missed what led up to that. But never mind. Are you done? We should head out."

"Hey, wait up," Addie called. "You got those huggy things on your feet. My heeled boots don't do as well on this icy pavement."

"I can't wait. I'm freezing. Grab the back of my coat and skate behind me to the Jeep."

Addie reached for Serena's jacket. Her foot skidded, her arms flailed in the air. Hands grasped her from behind and steadied her upright. "Thanks," Addie gasped, and turned toward her savior. "Simon?"

"Are you okay?"

"Yes, thanks to you." She straightened herself, trying to catch her breath. "What are you doing here besides saving me from slamming into you again?" She brushed hair from her eyes.

"I'm just going to have dinner with a friend from work."

"I see. How nice." She smiled, hoping it was as demure as she intended it to be and not the needy, aching one hidden beneath. "Well, have a good evening. I hope to see you . . . soon." A lump rose in the back of her throat. The pretty dark-haired nurse from the hospital appeared at Simon's side.

A look of regret flickered through his eyes before he introduced them. "Addie, this is Courtney"—he shoved his hands into his coat pockets—"a friend of mine." Addie's eyes went immediately to Courtney's arm looped through his.

"Hi, Addie, it's nice to finally meet you. I've seen you a few times around the hospital, haven't I?"

"Yeah, that's me. Just hopping all over the place." She fought the tears coming. "Look, I . . . ah . . . have to go and . . . buy a Christmas tree. Ho, ho, ho, and all that jazz." She didn't, couldn't wait for any response and hustled to the Jeep.

Chapter 27

Addie pulled into her parking spot in the alleyway behind her shop. She glanced in the rearview mirror and groaned. The black circles etched around her eyes definitely spotlighted her red puffy eyelids. How could she go in looking as bad as she did? Still, it was no excuse to call in sick. Or tired. She slammed her hand against the steering wheel, her Mini Cooper beeping in protest. Sick and tired. That's what she was. Sick of the tears, the men, the mystery. Dipping her head, she inhaled deeply for four counts and exhaled through her nose for four more. Despite looking as wretched as she felt, she trudged into her shop and shuffled to the front.

"Good morning." Paige smiled, looking up from reading the newspaper on the counter. Her grin faded as she searched Addie's face. "Or is it?"

Addie's lips made a lame attempt at a smile. "Not really, it was a long night." She shuffled some books on the counter. Stacking them first by size and then alphabetically. Before long, she swooshed them along the counter like fallen dominoes.

"Want some coffee?"

Addie nodded but didn't look up from the books.

"Okay, one strong, hot coffee coming up." Paige dropped a pod into the coffeemaker, and when it finished brewing the single cup, she stirred in some cream. She passed it over the counter to her. "If there's anything I can do to help, let me know."

Addie held on to the cup for dear life, its warmth seeping into her. "Thanks, I will, but I'm fine, really."

"Just know I'm here if you need anything," Paige reminded her as she folded the newspaper. "Ah, first fish of the day." She grinned and, with a winning smile, approached a customer.

Addie shoved the paper under the counter, sipped her coffee, and ran the receipt totals from the previous day. The morning flew by. It appeared half the town was shopping. By lunchtime, the books left to be sold on consignment mounted into three stacks behind the counter. Paige retrieved a bin from the back to store them in until they could be priced. As Addie loaded them, one title caught her eye. *State of Fear* by Michael Crichton. She glanced over the dust jacket blurb on the back. "Do you remember who brought this in?"

"Yeah, it was Marjorie, one of our regulars. She said she found it in her garbage can when she took her trash out. She couldn't understand why someone would throw it away because it's in such good condition, so she thought why not try to sell it. Why, is it important?"

"No, I've just been looking for my copy and couldn't find it. I think I'll buy this one." She set it beside the cash register. "That is weird, though. I never could understand why people would throw away a perfectly good book." Addie shrugged. "Oh well, my gain. Look, it's past lunch, and there's a lull. Why don't you go grab something to eat?"

"I can pick something up for you, too?"

"No, that's fine. I'm not really hungry right now."

"Okay, be back in a minute." Paige grabbed her purse from under the counter and headed out the door.

"Put your coat on," Addie called after her, but it was too late. Addie shook her head, chuckling, and lifted the book bin, struggling to balance it on the top rack of the cart. One hand holding it steady, she attempted to steer it with the other to the back room. The door chimes jingled behind her. She spun around and the bin slid off, crashing to the floor. "Hi, Serena, I'll be with you in a minute. Just let me deal with this." She hoisted it up onto one knee, balanced it, and Serena arrived just in time to help steady it on the top shelf. "Thanks," she puffed. "Are we going to have lunch?" She looked at Serena's pinched face and stopped short. "What's wrong? Did something happen?"

Serena plucked a tissue out of her coat pocket. "Don't worry, it's clean. I stocked up in case you needed them after I tell you what I found out this morning."

"What are you talking about?" They steered the cart off to the side in the back room. "What's going on?"

Serena took a deep breath, fidgeting with the costume rings she wore on her fingers. "I'll start at the beginning," she said, dropping onto a crate.

"That's always the best place." Addie slid onto the crate beside her.

"I dropped in to see Patrick this morning, just to ask

if there were any more updates about the gala. He never sent anyone the confirmation e-mail about what he'd said at the meeting." Serena heaved a sigh. "Well, he wasn't in his office, and Crystal wasn't at her desk, so I went to see if they were downstairs. . . ."

"And?"

"Not there, either. I thought they must be around somewhere, maybe in a meeting or something. . . ."

"Okay," Addie prodded, "and were they?"

"I'll get to that. Just let me say what I have to first, please?"

"Sorry, by all means continue."

Serena shifted on the box and turned slightly toward her. "I decided to go to the cafeteria and grab a coffee and wait awhile and then try to find him again." She glanced at Addie's tapping foot and rolled her eyes. "I saw that nurse, Courtney, the one with Simon last night, having coffee with some nursing friends." Addie swallowed hard. "She didn't see me last night in the Jeep, so I knew she wouldn't recognize me, and I sat at the table beside theirs, just curious, you know." She pulled on one of her gaudy rings. "They were talking about her date with Simon, asking her how it went and if his lips were as delicious as they looked."

"What did she say?"

Serena pressed her lips tight and looked at Addie. "She told them she wasn't the type to kiss and tell, and then giggled and said, 'I can only confirm that the rumors *might* be true.'"

Addie let out a deep breath and leaned back on her hands.

"But that's not all."

"It's enough, isn't it?"

"No. Then one of the others said, 'I heard he had a

girlfriend.' Courtney waved her off and said something like Simon and this chick were just friends. Apparently, she had meant nothing to him."

Addie paced the back room. She fought for control. It was as if Simon himself had punched her in the stomach.

Serena came up behind her and rubbed her shoulders. "I'm afraid it doesn't end there."

Addie hung her head, fighting the urge to spew out the acrid taste rising in the back of her throat.

"According to Courtney, she even got to ride in Simon's Tesla Roadster." Serena rolled her eyes. "Little Miss Fancy-pants now loves the high life and has no intention of letting Simon off her little grubby, infected, skanky—"

Addie grabbed Serena's shoulders. "She really said that?" A smile twisted at the corners of her lips.

Serena drew back. "Well, a variation of that. She certainly made it quite clear that she only wanted him for his money. Why, what does it mean?"

"It means she's one of *those*, the ones that Simon can't stand and goes out of his way to avoid. He told me about her kind the first time we met." She kissed Serena's cheek. "Thank you, thank you. You've made my day."

Serena stepped back, her mouth hanging open.

Addie handed her back the tissue. "I won't need this."

"Not exactly the reaction I expected, but"—Serena shrugged her shoulders—"I'll take it." She peered at Addie. "What do you mean you talked about it the first time you met? I was there, and I don't remember him saying that?"

Addie waved her off. "It was later, after we all left the Grey Gull. He was waiting for me at my house when I got home, and we talked and actually had an argument about it."

"What? You never told me that."

"I'm sure I did."

Serena crossed her arms, and if looks could kill, Marc would be trying to solve her murder right about now. "Well, maybe . . ." Addie bit the side of her lip. "You're right. I didn't tell you because the argument was about you."

"Me? What did I do?" Serena's eyes flashed.

Addie sat on the edge of her desk. "If you remember that day, then you have to also remember your very failed attempt at playing the seductress. You were convinced he was the man of your dreams, just like this Courtney, I might add, and you even got mad at me for talking to him at dinner."

Serena relaxed her arms and crinkled up her nose. "I remember."

"Okay, well, I thought he was being rude to you when he ignored you and only spoke to me, and I let him know it when he showed up at my place later. He explained why, and I guess it made sense, but at the time I thought it was just an excuse and not a heartfelt apology for him having caused friction between you and me."

"What did he say? What did you say?"

"He said he was tired of meeting women who were only interested in him because he was a doctor and knew he could give them a, well . . . a certain lifestyle, and he thought you came across as one of those."

"Me?" Her eyes bulged. "Me?" She stabbed her finger into her chest. "Well, that conceited—"

"I know, I know." Addie waved both hands. "That's exactly what I said, but then he pointed out that you appeared to be more focused on the fact that he was a doctor, and that was clear right from the start when you introduced me to him." Her shoulders sagged. "I couldn't say much after that because it was true."

"I did no such thing."

"Yes, you did. The first thing you said when you introduced me to him was this is *Dr.* Emerson"—her fingers wagged quotation marks in the air—"and then your eyelashes did that crazed butterfly thingy."

Serena slumped down on her crate. "Zach's going to be a doctor, too." She leaned her elbow on her knee and cupped her chin in her hands. "Maybe I do have an issue, like this Courtney."

"No, sweetie." Addie sat down beside her. "You never introduced Zach as a doctor and barely talk about him like that. To you, he's just your Zach, and you love him for who he is, not what he is." She squeezed Serena's shoulder. "Simon just wasn't the one for you, and it didn't take you long to figure that out because then you met Zach."

"Now, I get your reaction. Are you going to tell him what I overheard?"

"I'd love to, but no." Addie gnawed on her lip. "If I do, then I come across as being jealous, and he might just dig his heels in with her, so I have no choice but for him to figure her out on his own."

"And if he doesn't?"

"Then it was meant to be. Not much I can do about it. I already pushed him away, so he is bound to find someone else . . . sometime. I just didn't think it would be this soon."

"But if you had it to do all over again, would you still push him away? Look what just seeing him with her did to you last night. It must mean that you care more than you're letting on."

Addie stood up and stretched out her neck and shoulders.

"You do, don't you?" Serena spun Addie toward her. "Look me in the eye and tell me you don't."

Addie closed her eyes. "I can't because I don't know yet. I feel the same about Marc when I see him talking to another woman."

"Did I hear my name?"

Addie spun around and shrank under Marc's gaze. "How long have you been standing there?"

Addie noted something that she'd never seen from him before, color creeping from under his collar to his cheeks. "I . . . ah . . ."

Both her hands raked over her forehead. "You heard every word, didn't you?"

Marc adjusted his police belt and looked at the covered crime board. "Nice to see for once that you guys aren't back here playing detective."

Serena raised her hands in a helpless gesture. Addie just shook her head. "What brings you in today?" She studied the tips of her boots, not certain she would ever be able to look him in the eye again. She was mortified. Her mind replayed over and over the conversation they'd just had, but it all blurred together, and now she couldn't remember a word she or Serena had said. God, she just wanted the ground to open under her feet and swallow her.

"I was in the neighborhood—"

"Like you are most every day." Serena gave him an exaggerated eye roll.

"Yes, but I was just speaking with Catherine and her sister. Joyce, isn't it?" He rocked back on his heels. "She asked me an interesting question, so I thought I'd drop in and see if either of you knew the answer."

"Riddle me that?" Addie asked her cuticles, which were sadly in a state of disrepair.

A beat of silence, then an exasperated breath from Marc. "She asked me if I'd seen Jonathan today."

"Why?" Her cuticles really needed some work.

"Because when she got up this morning, he wasn't there. She went into his room—"

"They don't share a room?" Addie dropped her hand to her side and met Marc's gaze. "But I thought—"

"See"—Serena poked her elbow in Addie's ribs—"you don't know everything, Sherlock."

Addie's face screwed up, and she responded with a playful elbow jab of her own.

Marc fidgeted with his cap in his hands. "Anyway, he didn't come back and hasn't called, and she just wondered if I'd seen him. I haven't and thought maybe he'd been in here or your place, Serena?"

"Nope, but we'll let you know if he does," Addie said.

"That's interesting," Serena piped up.

"What do you know, Serena?" Marc perched one hip on the edge of the desk.

"This was the part of my story that I didn't have a chance to tell you yet, Addie. When I found Patrick this morning, he was running around like a crazy person. Apparently, Crystal hadn't shown up for work this morning, leaving him all the legwork." She crossed her arms, a smug expression on her face as she rocked back on her heels, displaying a perfect impersonation of her brother.

Any other time Addie would have busted out laughing, but Serena's information reminded her of what she had written on the board before the message appeared. "And now Crystal is MIA, too." She whipped the cover off the board.

"No, no, no, don't disappoint me now." Marc's fingers raked through his hair. "You two were doing so well at minding your own business and not meddling in police matters."

"Not really," Serena giggled. "Before yesterday, this board looked exactly like the one at Addie's house."

"It sounds like yesterday you came to your senses, so don't start back up now."

"Too late." Addie grabbed the chalk and wrote, *Crystal—Jonathan.*

"What are you doing?"

"Helping you with your job," Serena said from her perch on the crate.

Addie joined her and grinned. "We have a theory."

Marc groaned. "Of course, you do."

Chapter 28

While Serena distracted her brother with a narration of past events that took on the flavor of an amateur stand-up comedy night routine, Addie copied the brown paper notes from home to the chalk crime board. She dusted off her hands and then settled onto a crate and enjoyed the remainder of her friend's show.

Serena's song and dance routine about Jonathan and Crystal and their nebulous relationship morphed into a Broadway production displaying Amy Miller, ecoterrorist, aka Crystal's maybe doctorate-educated sister from Australia. During the jazz hand scene, Serena explained that Jonathan, because he was suspicious and had been to Australia as well, could be in on it all. When all the information had been regaled, she flopped breathless onto the crate.

Addie gave her a standing ovation. "Bravo! Encore!"

Marc simply stared, blinked, and then blinked again. "Those are honestly the most outlandish theories that you two have ever come up with. This isn't a spy movie.

It's a simple, old-fashioned case of murder. We now know the where and when, so my job is to find out the who and why, now that we have the what and how figured out. It's standard police procedure, not a freaking stage production."

"But that's what we've done, and it makes perfect sense. Just look." Serena pointed to the board.

His gaze turned to Addie, his eyes twinkling with a hint of amusement, but they darkened when he glanced past her to the board. "I should have known." He gestured over his shoulder. "*She* was just the front man for the real show going on behind my back." He tucked his thumbs in his belt and scanned the board. "You really can't be serious with all this, this . . ." He waved his hand across the blackboard. "Did you think me seeing it in black and white would convince me to believe it and take action on any part of these hare-brained ideas the two of you have come up with while playing back-room detective?"

Addie's eyes flashed. "Yes, look at the names and the connections, and don't try and tell me this all doesn't mean something." She stabbed her finger at the words *murder weapon—blue-ringed octopus toxin, Amy Miller, Teresa falls to death.* "How else do you explain it showing up in a sushi roll when it is far from being considered a delicacy in any culture except maybe a murderer's?"

"That's not the point I'm disputing." His voice quivered with pent-up frustration. "It's this"—his finger pointed to the line linking Crystal, Jonathan, and Amy Miller—"you have implicated your own father-in-law in—"

"He's not actually . . ." Addie's chin jutted out.

"My apologies"—he pursed his lips—"almost father-in-law, and what for? There is no motive listed here for him to be involved in some great conspiracy. You're better off looking closer at what you have written about the connection between Patrick and Marvin and the still-missing book because we do know, *for a fact*"—he stressed those last words, pinning her with a glare—"that Marvin, the known shady book broker, was seen arguing with Patrick the night before he was found in the closet. After getting the results back on Marvin's rental car, the break lines were in fact cut, making Patrick the number-one suspect there." The side of his fist struck the board.

Addie tapped the chalk stick on the board and then wrote *Marvin murdered* and drew a line with a question mark to *Patrick*. "I guess maybe one of our theories might be right. Maybe it was a crime of revenge because of a business deal for the book gone wrong. Marvin was also at the hospital the afternoon Patrick was overdosed."

Marc frowned at her last words. "How do you know that?"

"Because I saw him leaving in a taxi, and Simon got called in soon after to treat Patrick."

Marc's jaw flinched. "Well, I, as a trained officer of the law, will continue to follow the trail of *actual* facts as I uncover them—"

"You uncover them?" Addie crossed her arms and stared at him wide-eyed. "Obviously, I just told you something you didn't know."

Marc's nostrils flared. "Me? My money's on Patrick being behind all of this. Jerry and the crime team are tearing his office apart as we speak, searching for any clues we may have overlooked before. We'll find the evidence and the missing book, since it wasn't with Marvin, and we'll do it using traditional police work"—his eyes flashed—"by following the *evidence*. It certainly won't be based on some fantasy, crime league theories."

Addie's mouth dropped. She looked at Serena, whose face was much like hers, except covered in flaring freckled spots.

He continued on. "The rest of what you have on here about Jonathan and Crystal is nothing but speculative crap."

"It's not crap." Serena shot to her feet. "I didn't want to believe what Addie came up with, either, about Jonathan because I like him, but from what we've seen lately, she might be right. At first, I thought she was just trying to push him out of her life because he reminded her of David, the same reason she's pushed you and now Simon away."

Addie hissed, "Serena, how dare you?"

"Sorry," she mumbled. "I wasn't thinking."

Marc's gaze caressed Addie's face, and it took all her willpower to stay standing.

Serena's eyes implored Addie. "But now you have to tell him about the message on the board and what Jonathan said to you the night he broke into your house."

Marc's head jerked, breaking their moment. "What message? And explain break in." He looked from one to the other.

When Addie refused to speak, Serena explained, "Yesterday, Addie brought me back here to show me the new information she'd come across about Jonathan having been in Australia, and when she took the cover off the board, it was wiped clean except for—"

"This." Addie shoved her phone under Marc's nose. *"This is your last warning!!!* What the . . . ? This was written on the blackboard?" At her shrug, he shook her gently. "Why didn't you call me?"

"I told her to, but she said she knew it was from Jonathan so there was no point involving you."

"Snitch." Addie scowled at her friend.

"I'm glad she did *snitch*. This is serious, Addie. Someone, and it may or may not have been Jonathan, knew about your board and obviously felt something on here was getting too close to the truth. What does this mean"—his finger stabbed the photo—"*your last warning*?" He clutched her shoulders this time. "Have there been others? How long has this been going on?"

"Including the night Jonathan broke into her house and threatened her? Something she only told me about yesterday, too." Serena pouted and ignored Addie's glare.

"He actually broke into your house? Like in smashed a window, jimmied the lock, what?"

"No, it was more like hot-wired the security system or something?"

"Are you sure you didn't just leave the door unlocked or the system off?"

"No, I did not. He was waiting there when I got home, and everything was locked up tight when I went in."

"What did he want?"

Addie relayed the story of her surprise visit, and when she was finished, Marc just nodded his head.

"That's it? You have nothing to say." Serena moved to his side and glared at him. "He broke into her house and threatened her."

Marc crossed his arms and stroked the stubble on his chin. "Actually, if there's no evidence that he broke in, I can't really investigate anything. There's no proof of a crime having been committed." Addie knew by the burning on her face that she was turning the same shade of red as Serena's hair. "And I'd say that anything he said to you wasn't much different than I've been telling you. Stay out of it, you could get hurt. This warning"—he tapped on her phone screen—"is a good indicator of that. So, if you're half as smart as I think you are, you'll listen to at least one of us."

"And you wonder why I don't tell you when things like that happen." She grabbed the piece of chalk from the desk and threw it at him. "You condescending—"

He ducked. "But assaulting an officer of the law is a crime, and I do have a witness."

"Think again, bro." Serena locked her arm through Addie's in solidarity.

"So, that's how it's going to be?"

Serena stuck out her chin.

"You guys win." He shook his head. "I'm definitely no match for the two of you when you're united." His phone alarm screeched. "Sorry, it's Jerry. I have to get this." He stepped out of the back room, leaving Addie and Serena staring at the empty spot where he'd been.

"You know. Your brother is kind of a—twit? Loser?"

"All the above . . . ?"

Marc's reappearance cut Serena off mid-word. "You can erase that line between Patrick and Marvin."

"Why, what did Jerry say?"

"We managed to get a partial print off the break line, and it came back as a match to a Nicky Santoro, a well-known enforcer for the mob."

"What"—Serena grabbed his arm—"the mob here in Greyborne Harbor?"

Addie erased the connecting line and wrote *mob hit*. "So, now we have this and an ecoterrorist known to have been in town. Maybe Teresa wasn't just a small-town charity coordinator." She looked over her shoulder at Marc. "Have you ever done a background check on her?"

He shook his head. "But I'm starting to see that this might be bigger than we first thought."

"That's exactly what I've been saying and trying to prove." Her hand swept across the board. "Will you listen to me now?"

He shook his head and tucked his thumbs in his belt. "I think if you won't listen to me, then you'd better listen to Jonathan. He cares about you as much as I do. So back off, and stay out of this. I think now you can see we're not dealing with amateurs here. Whatever this is all about. Someone means business."

"Wow." Serena's mouth hung open. "Wait till I tell Zach about this."

"No," Marc's voiced barked. "This is confidential, and this information getting out could jeopardize the case and put both of you at more risk."

She shrank back at his tone and words and nodded. "But I do have to go and meet him now. We planned on grabbing a quick bite." Serena made a zipper gesture across her lips. He rolled his eyes. She latched on to Addie's hand. "When is a good time to come and see the apartment?"

"Umm, I'd forgotten. How about tomorrow before work?"

"Perfect," Serena grinned. "See you then." With a little finger wave, Serena waltzed out the door.

"What's wrong?" Marc moved toward Addie. "You're pale all of a sudden. Did all this just sink in?" His hand cupped the side of her face.

Her skin burned. "That's not it at all."

"Then what is it?"

"When you said Jonathan cares about me as much

as you do, did you really mean that?"

"Of course, I do." His thumb traced the outline of her jaw, as his lips brushed across her forehead and lingered with his head pressed against hers. She closed her eyes remembering the taste of his salty-sweet lips on hers and unwittingly sighed. "I've cared since the day we met," he whispered, "but I see now and from what I heard you say earlier this afternoon, you're not ready. Just like you've been trying to tell me all along, but now I think I finally understand." His finger tilted her chin up, and his eyes caressed hers. "But you will be one day"—he kissed the tip of her nose—"and I'll be here."

Her cell rang, and she stiffened.

"Go ahead." His hand dropped to his side.

She checked the caller ID and frowned. "Hello? . . . Hi, Kate . . . no, it's not a bad time." She glanced at Marc, apologizing with her eyes. "What was that? . . . No, I haven't sold the book yet, actually it's gone— What? . . . When?" She looked back at Marc. "Say what? . . . Thanks for letting me know. I'll be in touch soon. . . . Okay . . . thanks again, bye."

"Was that about the book?"

Addie sank onto the edge of the desk. "*A Christmas Carol* just showed up for auction on an online auction, black-market website. What caught Kate's eye and how she knew it was mine was because the authentication certificate had her association membership number posted with the book details."

"So it *was* stolen." Marc softly whistled as he scanned the board.

Chapter 29

"What are you thinking?" Addie followed Marc's gaze to the board.

"Now that we know the book was, in fact, stolen. It gives us the motive we've been missing, and a better idea of who we are looking at in all of these jigsaw puzzle pieces."

"I guess whoever advertised the book, with a picture of the appraisal certificate, knew enough that it would give credibility to the reserved bid price, but not enough to know that the number on it could be traced back to the appraiser."

"Making them an amateur and not a professional book dealer like Marvin was."

"That would be my guess." Addie looked back at the board. "So, who do we have on here who would be smart enough to know about the uses and handling of one of the deadliest sea creatures on earth but knows nothing about unloading a stolen book? Or are we missing someone who should be on here?"

Marc sat on one of the book crates. "Maybe it's more than one person."

"You might be right. What if Teresa was killed for some other reason than we've even considered. You said a complete background check was never run on her because she was the victim and all."

"We did run a routine check, and no red flags popped up, but maybe we need to dig deeper."

Addie sat down beside him. "Let's just pretend it was her past coming back to haunt her and someone, a professional, killed her for whatever reason. Jonathan even said she was an old friend of his. Who knows what she was in a previous life? After all, a known ecoterrorist paid her a visit, too."

"I'm following your thinking. I think."

"What if someone else saw her unrelated death as an opportunity to snatch the book and make some money?"

"Could be a possibility."

"Which means"—she picked the chalk up off the floor and drew one large circle around the information on the board—"we're back to square one." She stabbed at the board, chalk bits flying. "Dang it! That means every name on here is a possible suspect, in one or both of the crimes, again."

Marc came up beside her, his eyes fixed on the names. "If we look at it as two separate crimes, then you're right." He plucked the chalk stick from her fingers. "But if we look at them as related, then we have to find the one person who could have pulled off both of them."

"How are we going to eliminate any of them?"

"By using good, old-fashioned police work and following the evidence on what we know about each one of them."

"I have that there already."

"But is it," he grinned, a twinkle in his eyes, "enough for the process of exclusion?"

"What have I missed?"

"Be patient, and let's run through what we know about each of these people."

"I've done that a hundred times already, here"—she tapped her finger on Jonathan's name—"and here"—pointing to Patrick's—"and here . . ." Marc clasped his hand over hers.

"Okay, I get the picture, but going back to Jonathan's name—" He ignored the low growl escaping the back of her throat. "Look, I know you want to believe he's guilty of something, but think about it now that we have more evidence."

Addie folded her arms and glowered at him.

"Jonathan is smart, and as you have on here, he was recently in Australia. He may very well have heard about the blue-ringed octopus and maybe even read a book where the toxin was used as a murder weapon—"

"*State of Fear.*"

"What?"

"*State of Fear* by Michael Crichton. A terrorist used it as a weapon."

"Okay, maybe he even read that sometime, but"—he looked at her—"and this is a big but . . . Jonathan knows books and works in the same insurance retrieval field as your father and David did, right? So, he would know how to unload a stolen book on the black market, eliminating him."

Her eyes widened. "But only of the book theft, not of the murder if we're considering that they aren't related or carried out by one person."

"Yup, we're back to square one. We need more hard evidence."

Addie let out a deep breath and sat on the desk. "There's Patrick, who I consider to be a buffoon and the last person who should handle a deadly toxin because he'd poison himself, but right from the beginning it bothered me that he was so certain the book wouldn't be found."

"Did he say why he was convinced it was gone?"

"Nope, he avoided my questions about it completely."

"Yeah, but based on what we're thinking right now, he couldn't be guilty of poisoning Teresa because witness reports place him downstairs at the time the toxin would have been ingested."

"However, his run-ins with Marvin do suggest that he could well have been the one to see her death as an opportunity to get his hands on a rare book and make some extra money."

"That would explain the clumsy posting for the book on the Internet. With Marvin dead, he had no idea how to sell it."

Addie shifted on the hard desktop. "And there's also the fact that he picked up three lunches that day, so he must have known Teresa was expecting company." Her brow creased. "Maybe he knew a murder was going to be committed but wasn't actually part of that, and his job was just to get his hands on the book after she was out of the way."

Marc's eyes darted from one name to the next. "Then he would be in conspiracy to commit murder and not have simply acted as an opportunist. He could be charged with both crimes."

"But that still leaves us with no proof of who actually fed her the poison or who he was working with. It wasn't

Marvin or Jonathan. She had a drink with a woman because of the lipstick on the cup." Addie groaned. "Did
your friend at the FBI ever get back to you with information on this Amy Miller person? Is there a link to
Patrick?"

"Not as far as I know and nothing new yet from the
FBI." He rubbed the back of his neck. "They lost track
of her last year and are trying to figure out how she got
by their surveillance and ended up in Greyborne Harbor without them being aware she was even in the
country."

"What if Serena and my theories about Crystal
being Amy Miller's sister and Jonathan being involved
with one or both of them are right? It makes sense
when you look at the big picture and break it down
into possibly two crimes that are only connected by opportunity, allowing for the second one to occur."

"But we've only just discovered that the second was
actually a crime, and not a case of Teresa having hidden the book somewhere."

She threw her hands up in the air. "This is getting
us nowhere. We're just rehashing the same old information."

"Maybe you are, but some of this is new to me."

"Really?"

"You haven't actually been doing what I asked you
to, have you?"

"What are you talking about?"

"Bringing the information you come across directly
to me, so I can investigate it?"

She opened her mouth to retort but snapped it
shut.

He studied the board, his hands on his hips. "What
does that mean?" He pointed to *lipstick tube, Simon to
have analyzed.*

"I'm sure I told you about that, didn't I?"

He folded his arms. "What else haven't you told me?"

"Nothing, I swear." She held her fingers up in a scout salute.

"Addie?" His steely eyes fixed on hers. "What lipstick tube is Simon testing, and why did no one make me aware of this?"

"I discovered what the shade of lipstick on one of the coffee cups was, and one day at the hospital I saw Crystal applying it and . . ." her voice trailed off.

"And what?"

"And then her lipstick tube just kind of fell into my hands, and I gave it to—"

"Fell how?"

"Just fell"—she shrugged—"that's all, just fell."

"Well, now that your partner in evidence concealment doesn't appear to be part of your life anymore." She flinched under the bite of his words. "You'll become more forthright with me again and bring all evidence that happens to *fall* into your hands to me immediately and not bypass channels. Besides, evidence obtained without a search warrant isn't admissible in court. I thought you knew that?" he snapped. "I can't stress enough that I cannot conduct a *thorough* investigation if there's another show being played out behind my back."

As much as she hated to admit it, he was correct. Just this once, though. "I'm sorry. Really, I am."

"Good, but I need to get back to the station and start looking at what evidence I do have. But"—he glanced at the board—"some of this may have been helpful." A smile crept across his lips.

"See, I can be useful." She scrunched up her nose and grinned.

Marc rolled his eyes. "Don't get too big for your britches."

"Why? What interest do you have in my britches?" She enjoyed the second blush she'd ever seen on him creep up his neck.

Her phone chirped at her with a text from Paige. **Is Marc still here?**

Addie sent back a quick, **Yes, but you can go if you're done up there.**

She glanced at the time. "It's almost five. Where did the time go?"

He picked his cap up from the desk. "Yeah, I guess working with you like this brought back good memories, and I didn't want to leave."

Paige's head popped around the doorframe. "Marc, Catherine's here. She's pretty upset and asking for you?"

Marc headed for the front. Addie was close on his heels, where a distraught Catherine greeted them. "He hasn't come back yet, and no word. I'm getting worried, Marc," Catherine sobbed.

Addie plucked a tissue from the box on the counter and handed it to her. "I'm sure he's fine." She squeezed her hand. "He does this sometimes. He says it's part of his work."

"I know. He told me that when he gets a call from his insurance company he can often disappear for a few hours doing research and what-not for them, but it's been over ten hours, and I'm worried now that something has happened."

Addie looked helplessly at Marc. Nothing from him, so she wiped a tear from Catherine's cheek. "Did he take anything with him this morning?"

"What do you mean by anything?"

"Suitcase, his toothbrush, anything?"

She shook her head, wiping her eyes with the tissue.

"That's good news, then." Addie took the damp tissue from her hand and gave her a fresh one. "That means he's planning on coming back. Maybe he just got waylaid somewhere, and the time's gotten away from him." As Addie held her weeping friend, she cursed Jonathan's very name. That man and his destructive wake. Like a tsunami, he'd come crashing into Catherine's life and left nothing but debris of love and affection. If she ever saw him again . . .

Marc's calm voice cut into her reverie. "I can't file a missing person report until he's been gone for at least forty-eight hours."

"I know, I was just hoping that someone had seen him." Catherine squirmed out of Addie's hold and clutched her purse in front of her. "I've called everyone that I know in town that he's met. Joyce and Jack are out searching ditches and snowbanks, but there's no sign of him anywhere." Fresh tears seeped from her swollen eyes.

"Did you call the hospital?" Addie handed her another tissue.

"Five times already. I even spoke with Simon and then tried Crystal, thinking the more eyes on the lookout for him the better."

"What do you mean tried Crystal?"

"I never got a hold of her." Catherine shrugged. "The switchboard said she hadn't been in to work today." She blew her nose.

"It sounds like you have lots of eyes looking for him. Someone will know where he is, and it'll all be fine." So, both Jonathan and Crystal were still MIA. She patted her friend's shoulder and glanced at Marc, her eyes flashing *I told you so.*

Chapter 30

Addie darted back and forth between the bedroom and the bathroom, washing, applying her makeup, and digging through her neglected laundry basket in a desperate attempt to find something clean enough to wear one more day. She pulled out a pair of black skinny slacks, checked for stains, and threw them on, then grabbed a fresh-enough-smelling gray tunic sweater and yanked it over her head. Twisting her hair in a ponytail, she dashed down the stairs when she heard the knock at the door. "Come on in. Just give me a second." She sat on the hall bench and tugged on her boots.

"You really should get a pair of these." Serena stomped snow off her, as Addie called them, huggy things. "They have better traction and must definitely be warmer than those." She pointed to Addie's heeled knee-high boots. Serena peered around the corner into the living room and laughed. "Is that what you're calling a Christmas tree this year? What did you do? Steal it from Charlie Brown?"

"How dare you insult my poor baby. If I hadn't rescued it from the tree lot, who knows what kind of future it would have had."

"After the gorgeous tree you had last year." Serena shook her head. "You must admit it does look a little pathetic with its sparse branches and the what, six ornaments you threw on it?"

"A dozen, and at least you can't call me Scrooge anymore."

Zach snickered. "I can't believe you repeated that to her? I thought you were friends?"

Addie's hands flew to her hips. "You guys have been calling me Scrooge behind my back?"

"Come on, Ebenezer." Serena tugged at Addie's coat sleeve. "Let's go see this apartment. We still have to get to work this morning."

They trudged through the fresh snow and made their way up the side steps to the suite above the triple garage. Addie opened the door and let Serena and Zach enter first. "What do you think?"

Zach whistled. "Wow, you have a lot of stuff in here."

"I warned Serena that it had only been used as storage for years, and she promised that in exchange for free rent, you'd be more than willing to clear it out and do any repairs."

Zach's brows rose as he looked down at Serena. "She did, did she?" He kissed the top of her head. "Thanks for volunteering me."

"Come on, Zach, it's exactly what we've been hoping to find." Serena made her way around a stack of boxes and between piled-high furniture. "It's perfect. Look at that sweet little kitchen, and the size of this room, minus the junk, of course, and it's surprisingly warm in here."

"The garage's heated so it's piped in up here, too.

Good thing or some of this stuff would have been ruined by humidity and temperature changes."

"Like these books." Serena peered into an open box.

"Not more books to sort?" Addie moaned.

Serena laughed and headed for the first bedroom off the living room, popped her head out. "Zach, you have to see the size of this one. It's huge, and I call it. It'll be perfect for me."

Addie peeked inside some of the boxes, cursing how much there was to sort, and she still had half the attic left to get through. She tugged the top off of an old wooden crate and picked up the top book. "I can't believe it." She searched through the other books in the box. "Serena, come here," she called. "There must be at least nineteen Charles Dickens books in here." She flopped down on the sofa and pulled one after another from the crate, scanning the title pages.

"My God, *The Pickwick Papers*, 1837, the original three-volume set of *Oliver Twist*, 1838, *David Copperfield*, 1850, *A Tale of Two Cities*, 1859, and they're all first editions." She clasped a hand over her mouth to stifle a squeal.

"Did you call me? I was just measuring my bedroom to make sure my furniture would fit." Serena grinned down at her and then froze. "What's wrong?" She glanced around the room. "There's not a rat in here, is there?" she squeaked, and danced in a circle on her tippy toes.

Addie held out a copy of *Nicholas Nickleby*. "It's an 1839 first edition." Her hand waved over the box. "These all are. *The Old Curiosity Shop, Bleak House, Great Expectations*. This collection is worth a fortune." The color drained from her face as she thumbed through the other titles.

Serena studied the book she held in her hand. "Wow, and these are all yours, just like all the books in the attic?"

Addie swallowed hard and nodded. "I had no idea this was out here. *A Christmas Carol*, which must have been in here at one time, was in the house. I wonder why these weren't taken in, too."

"Maybe your aunt was trying to hide them or make sure no one sold them or stole them after she passed. After all, she was afraid somebody was stealing from her, right?"

Addie nodded. "And keeping them out here makes sense. Imagine if they'd gotten their hands on these?" She looked at the books stacked beside her.

Serena scrunched up her nose. "But it's funny that she kept *A Christmas Carol* hidden in the box of ornaments. That's where you found it, wasn't it?"

"Yes, but I do vaguely remember when I was little, there was one Christmas that my dad and I were visiting her. I saw it on her desk and asked her to read it to me. She said I was too young, and said she would when I got older." A smile crept across Addie's lips. "She must have tucked it away for that day, but it never came." Her shoulders sagged. "After the feud she had with my grandmother, I wasn't allowed to visit again, and then it was too late." Addie absently stroked the red cloth cover of *A Tale of Two Cities* on her lap.

Zach poked his head out of the second bedroom and looked at Serena. "Well, what do you think?"

"I think it's perfect. When can you have it ready for us to move in?" She gave him a sly wink.

He responded with a playful scowl. "I guess I get stuck with the smaller bedroom, then?" He feigned a pout.

"I told you before." Serena tapped her finger. "No ring, no . . ." she giggled.

"It's also a three-car garage. I have a space, but you two will have to fight over one, do you think you can share that?" She winked at Serena. "When you move in, you can just move all this into the third space." She dusted her hands on her pants. "What do you think?"

"Great," Zach beamed, "I didn't even consider that garage parking would be part of the deal."

Addie checked the time on her phone. "Whoa, we'd better get moving." She looked at Zach. "Any chance I could get you to carry this box into the house for me?"

"No problem."

"Okay, let's go." She locked the door behind them and handed Serena the key. "Welcome to your new home."

"You're the best." Serena locked her in a bear hug. "Thank you so much."

"Just don't make me regret this," Addie laughed.

She opened the front door, letting Zach with his heavy load pass by her. He dropped it on the bench and stretched out his back. "Thanks, I'll take them from there and decide what to do with them after the holidays." She paused at the sight of Marc's patrol car pulling up.

Serena peered around her arm. "What's he doing here?"

Addie shrugged. "Knowing how he looks out for his baby sister, probably coming to make sure I'm not going to gouge you on the rent."

Marc kicked the snow to the sides as he plodded up the steps. "Better get those shoveled soon before you have a lawsuit on your hands."

"Thank you, I'll keep that in mind, *officer*." She

leaned her hip against the doorframe. "What brings you by? Am I under arrest or suspicion this time?"

"Just looking out for these two here." Marc peered inside, nodded at Serena and Zach. "One can't be too careful with all the shifty landlords around these days." The twinkle in his eye had Addie biting back her retort. "But in reality"—the corner of his mouth twitched—"I was hoping to talk privately for a few minutes."

Her heart vibrated in her chest. Business or pleasure? She didn't know anymore after the way things had been between them, but right now it didn't matter. She missed him more than she cared to admit, and she'd be willing to take a scolding from him.

Serena grabbed Zach's sleeve. "Well, we have to go. See you later." She glanced at Addie, a mischievous glint in her eyes.

Addie wanted to hate Marc's velvety-brown eyes and that stupid twitch thingy his lips did, but she couldn't. She had caused the rift between them, not him. She pulled her gaze from his and checked the time on her phone. "I'd better let Paige know I'm going to be running later than I thought." Her phone slipped from her fidgeting fingers and spiraled toward the floor.

In one sweeping motion, Marc nipped it out of midair and placed it back in her hand. "I was just in the shop looking for you. It's not busy yet, and she seems fine. A few more minutes won't hurt." His eyes searched her face.

She looked at his hand, then her phone, and then back at his hands. "How did you do—?"

"Kensuke Miyagi, my Sensei." He bowed from the waist.

"What?"

"When I was a kid, I practiced all the moves he

taught Daniel LaRusso, you know, like catching the fly, and wax on, wax off?" For the third time, a blush blossomed up his neck. "*The Karate Kid*? Didn't you ever see that movie?"

Addie clasped a hand over her mouth and stifled a laugh. "Sorry to say, I haven't."

"You're missing out. It's a classic."

"So, there is meaning to the gibberish you just spouted, and it's an actual thing?"

"Yes, I haven't gone over the deep end yet, although this case is shoving me closer to the edge."

"Sounds like you need some coffee?"

"And a miracle. Got any of those lying around?" He followed her into the kitchen. "I know this isn't by the book but—"

"Whose book, or is this part of the movie again?" She dropped a pod into the machine as Marc slid onto a counter stool.

"My book. The police book."

"Good, now maybe I can keep up." Her eyes locked with his, a smile flittering over her lips, as she handed him a coffee and then made one for herself. "Explain this book. Is it an actual book or something that just goes by Chief Marc Chandler's rules?"

His hand scoured through his hair. "You're not going to make this easy on me, are you?"

She emphatically shook her head.

"I was just trying to be considerate and thought I would share a bit of information with you. But if you're not interested?" He shrugged his shoulders and began to dismount the stool.

"Of course, I am." She pressed him back down. "You said you needed a miracle, and here I am." She grinned. "Or are you going to tell me this was all a setup to get a free coffee?"

"You are good, aren't you?" He saluted her with his coffee cup. "How did you figure out my devious ploy?"

"I can read you like a book, your book." She plopped down onto the stool beside him.

"You think so, do you?" His fingertip stroked the back of her hand from her knuckles to wrist, as his gaze melted with hers. She sucked in a little breath when he laced his fingers through hers. "Okay." He released her hand. "In all seriousness, since you are so invested in this case, and . . . knowing you and your penchant for amateur sleuthing the way I do. I have decided it best to share this with you, otherwise you'll just go out and try to dig it up on your own despite my *warnings* and those of others, and I don't want you to get mixed up with these particular people in your search for answers."

"How cavalier of you."

"Nothing cavalier about it." His eyes held steady on hers. "You have no idea what the people I am going to tell you about are capable of." He cleared his throat. "Broken rule number one. I heard from my friend at the FBI, and since Nicky Santoro, the guy they linked to Marvin's *accident,* is known to work for an organized crime family, his arrest fell under FBI jurisdiction."

"So, the mob is involved."

Marc nodded. "And . . . since he left his fingerprints at the scene, they now have him dead to rights on Marvin's murder, *and* he knows it."

"I don't get it. How could a mob enforcer be so stupid to leave his prints behind?"

"No one ever said Nicky was the sharpest tool in the shed. Apparently, when they asked him, he said his gloves were too bulky, so he took them off."

"Did he say why he killed Marvin?"

"It sounds like it was about the book, and Nicky apparently killed him because he didn't have it and didn't know who did. He said Marvin owed the syndicate a lot of money from a couple of previous failed transactions and promised that he'd pay it back as soon as he scored this book."

"Then his bosses don't have it, either?"

"Nope, and apparently he's singing like a songbird. Names, dates, everything. His arrest on this charge is a jackpot for the FBI because they finally have enough evidence to move on a mob boss they've been after for years."

"This all must have started when Teresa advertised the book online and posted that it also had the certificate, which naturally makes it more valuable. Or was Marvin's intent not to bid on it at all but to steal it himself?"

"My friend just said that when Nicky arrived in town he gave Marvin a warning from the syndicate, and that Marvin explained what had been going on with the book and the delay in getting the money. So maybe you're right, and initially he did plan on stealing it because it sounds like he'd been given a deadline to pay up, but then someone beat him to it."

"Then what happened? Marvin approached Patrick about the book, and what?"

"According to Santoro, when Marvin found out the book and the certificate were gone, he went after Patrick to find out who had it. Patrick wouldn't talk so he beat him up, hoping to loosen his tongue, and when that didn't work, he went to the hospital for another try, threatening him with a syringe of morphine. When Patrick still wouldn't tell him where the book was, I guess he gave him the injection anyway. Nicky was tailing Marvin and figured out that he was planning on making a run for it, so his boss gave the word to take him out."

Addie tapped her fingernail on the counter. "So, we know the book was stolen and not misplaced, and even to save his own life Patrick still wouldn't talk. That means Patrick was protecting someone . . . someone he cared about and was afraid to tell Marvin because he knew he'd go after that person. Or Patrick was more afraid of the person who had it than he was of Marvin." Her finger scratched at a spot on the counter. "Jonathan."

"Nicky was pretty plugged into the family, and he never mentioned anything about a Jonathan Hemingway, so I doubt he's involved."

"But we know for a fact that he was at the Grey Gull Inn when Marvin was staying there. That must mean he has something to do with all this."

"I'd say that was just a coincidence. He had been looking for a room in town, so he didn't impose on Catherine when her guests arrived." Marc shrugged. "Other than that, your theories are good, but we still don't know how Patrick was or if he's involved. We need proof. But I must say, if you're right and we can prove it, the whole case could be solved." His hand slapped the counter. "I'd love to solve this and shove it in my FBI buddy's face," he laughed.

"That's your actual devious ploy? The coffee was a ruse?"

"What?"

She crossed her arms. "You telling me about Nicky Santoro and breaking your own rule about sharing police business with me was just a front to pick my brain so I would help you win a game of mine is bigger than yours with your friend?"

Marc sputtered his mouthful of coffee across the counter.

Chapter 31

"Look at you." Paige eyed the stool Addie was perched on behind the counter. "There're a few days when I've been stuck back here but never thought of doing that."

"Feel free to anytime. I know it doesn't look too professional for customers to see us sitting down on the job"—Addie winced—"but my feet gave out hours ago. How are yours holding up?"

"Well"—Paige looked down at her feet—"they are a few years younger than yours, so . . ." She giggled and dodged a swat from Addie.

The door chimes jingled. Addie's shoulders slumped. "Good, then you can help what I hope is our last customer of the day, because I'm done." She stretched out her legs and tapped her boot toes together. "They're so numb, I may never walk again."

"Addie?"

She spun around. "Hi, Joyce, Jack. Normally, I'd ask what I can help you find, but judging by the looks on your faces, something tells me you aren't here to shop."

Joyce leaned across the counter, her voice muted. "I came to talk to you about Jonathan."

"Why? What happened? Is he okay?" A mixture of fear and dread churned in Addie's stomach.

"That's the trouble." Joyce pursed her lips. "We still don't know."

"You mean he still hasn't shown up?" She flicked a gaze to Jack. He shook his head. "Has he at least called Catherine?"

Jack's scowl deepened. "Not a word."

Addie winced and shifted her weight from one foot to the other. "Well, he does have a long history of disappearing. I wouldn't worry too much."

"Catherine is beside herself." Joyce braced her hands on the counter. "She thinks he's lying in a ditch somewhere, and I'm starting to think she might be right." *More like another woman's bed.* Addie wanted to scream but bit her tongue.

She had convinced herself that Jonathan and Crystal were meeting at the Grey Gull Inn after she witnessed that little sideshow under the table at brunch, and then there was the whole flirty thing at the tree-lighting ceremony. Marc said it was all harmless and every other connection she'd made between the two of them was merely a coincidence, but could it be chalked up to happenstance when they were both still MIA today?

She swallowed hard. This was one of those odd-shaped puzzle pieces that had haunted her for too long now. It was time to shove it into the big picture and see how it fit. Either they were having an affair or they were partners in this whole murder and book theft thing, and it was time to find out if one or both of her hunches were right.

"Are you okay, Addie? You suddenly don't look so good." Jack peered owlishly at her. She was surprised that he didn't pull a stethoscope out of his back pocket and begin examining her right there.

"No, I'm fine." She waved him off. "I was just thinking about other times Jonathan has done this."

Jack's brow creased. "Anything we should know?"

"No, but he does have a tendency to get lost in his pet projects at times." She patted Joyce's hand. "Tell Catherine not to worry. He's bound to show up again. Look, I know Serena had some errands to run today. I'll text her to see if she ran into him while she was out and about."

Joyce gave her a weak smile and nodded.

Addie picked up her cell phone and turned away from prying eyes.

Text Zach and ask him if a blue Honda and a black Land Rover with New York plates are in the Grey Gull parking lot.

"There, we'll see what she says." Addie slipped her phone into her pocket. "Can I get you a coffee or a hot spiced punch while we wait?"

Joyce shook her head and slumped onto a counter stool. It didn't take long for Serena's short and sweet reply, but it wasn't what Addie expected to hear.

He said no cars like that in the lot. Why?

Addie's thumbs flew across the keypad.

Thanks, I'll head over to the hospital and look there. I have a couple of hunches I want to check out. Fill you in later.

Addie snatched her purse from under the counter and tossed in her phone. "Unfortunately, Serena said no, she hasn't seen him today, but she did remind me that I have an appointment. I'm afraid I'll have to run. I'll call you if I hear anything, promise." She patted Joyce's hand and hobbled toward the back room. "Paige," Addie called as she passed her assistant in the Cookbook aisle. "I have to go. You can lock up whenever you're ready, thanks."

Addie cringed when the deep alley snow spilt over the top of her knee-high boots lodging between her toes, but sighed with relief. Standing in the icy slosh immediately eased the burning on the balls of her feet. She brushed the snow off her car and headed toward the hospital. As luck would have it and her throbbing feet, she found a spot in the visitor's parking area close to the main entrance. After today, she was finally convinced that it was time to ditch the heels and buy some of those huggy-snuggy things, whatever they're called, that Serena wore and raved about. She grabbed her bag, opened the door, and then slammed it shut, remaining in her seat.

Carolyn's truck was idling in the drop-off zone by the front doors. She craned her neck to see who was driving. Her chest constricted when Simon walked out of the hospital, arm in arm with Courtney. Addie slumped back in her seat. She had no right to be jealous. She had held him at arm's length, but darn. It hurt. She rubbed the spot over her heart.

"I can do this." She sucked in a deep breath and counted. ". . . eight, nine, and ten." No one was going to stop her from her mission. Not Simon. Not Courtney and not Marc, no matter what he'd said about her staying out of this. If it was facts and evidence that he wanted, she was going to darn well get it for him. How dare he call her theories harebrained? She got out of the car, thrust her head high, and marched, as best her aching feet could march, toward the main doors.

Her keen peripheral vision came in handy as she studied the couple talking beside the truck. As she drew closer, their raised voices pricked her ears. So, this wasn't a lover's tête-à-tête. Courtney was, in fact, refusing to get into the truck.

"I agree completely that the Tesla is a nicer vehicle to ride in, but be realistic, Courtney. The truck is safer in this deep snow. I don't want to get high centered on that road out to The Smuggler's Den restaurant."

"I am not going to be seen driving around in that . . . that farmer's truck." Courtney crossed her arms and glared at Simon.

Simon clasped her shoulders and drew her close. "Come on, Court. Wouldn't you rather be safe than . . ."

Addie couldn't bear to watch or hear any more. She darted through the front door. "Wow," was all she could manage as she wobbled across the lobby toward the elevators. As it whisked to the third floor, she wondered if Simon would give in and drive her ladyship in a chariot she deemed worthy of her, or would he leave her on the curbside? Stay tuned for the next installment of *As Greyborne Harbor Turns.* She crossed her fingers that his decision was the latter. Otherwise, she would have to admit that she had misread him. And she rarely misread people.

With heavy strides, she made her way to the reception desk in the north wing. No one. She glanced at the wall clock, past five. She'd missed her. If Crystal did happen to show up to work today, she was obviously gone now along with everyone else on the floor. She shivered at the empty eeriness.

She started to turn back to the elevators. Out of the corner of her eye, a dim light escaping through a partially opened office door caught her attention. She checked over her shoulder and tiptoed toward it. Patrick's old office? Filled with a combination of stomach-knotting fear and relief that she wasn't alone up here, she knocked on the doorframe and poked her head inside. His winter jacket hung from the coat rack, and his keys and a file box on the desk indicated he planned to return. She glanced back down the hall, went in, and seated herself on a chair.

Addie clutched her purse in her lap, studying the cramped room. If the third key on Teresa's key ring didn't fit anything in her office, maybe it opened something in here? After a quick check of the hall again, she rounded the desk to the file cabinet behind it and caught sight of two red journals previously hidden from view by the file box. She slid one of the ledgers toward her. It appeared to be this year's foundation financial records. The ones Walter, the board chair, had referred to when he was talking to Dan at the meeting. She scanned through the journal entries and frowned. It seemed the foundation was, in fact, broke, just as Patrick claimed. She pushed it aside and opened the second one, skimming through it. Her eyes fixed on the last entry, and her mouth dropped.

"What are you doing here?" Patrick's raspy voice barked. The door banged shut behind him.

Chapter 32

"That's a question I should be asking you." Addie slammed the ledger closed. "You're keeping two sets of financial records, aren't you?" Tiny pearls of perspiration glistened on his brow. "And by my guess, I'd say you've been embezzling money from the foundation ever since you started here."

Without taking his eyes off her, he snatched the account book from her hand, tossed it in the box on the desk, and grabbed his keys from beside it. She shrank under the gleam of malice in his eyes as he laced them between his fingers. She swallowed hard. Maybe poking the bear hadn't been such a good idea. Because what he was doing with the keys was exactly what she'd been trained to do in a woman's self-defense class. Create a weapon to use during an attack. However, in this case, she knew his weapon wasn't one for defense.

A low growl escaped his throat as he inched his way toward her around the side of the desk, his eyes locked with hers. "I asked you what you're doing in here."

"I was looking for Crystal."

"And you assumed she was in my office?"

"Well . . . she wasn't at the front desk and being your assistant . . ."

"Was my assistant." His circling paused. "Crystal doesn't work here anymore, and she's long gone."

"That's too bad, I just thought—"

"What, what did you just think?" The fine hairs on her arms quivered at the glint of deviltry in his eyes. She braced her trembling knees. "I wanted to ask her if she had any idea where Jonathan was."

"Why would she know where he is?"

"You know, since they seemed to be on rather *friendly* terms."

"Huh," he grunted. "She's not with him, that I can guarantee." His lips twisted into a sardonic smile. "She could never resist the attention of an older guy, and would usually only hang around long enough to see if they'd pamper her with expensive gifts."

"Is that what he did, and now she's taken off with him. Is that why you're so angry?" She didn't miss the tic in his cheek.

"I'm angry because as usual you're sticking your nose where it doesn't belong."

Not being one who could ever drop the bear-poking stick once she'd picked it up, Addie thought, why not give him another jab and see what happens? "By the look of what's going on in here"—her hand gestured to the box—"I'd say it's more than that. You and she were business partners in the whole fraud thing, right? What happened, did they run off with all your embezzled money? Leaving you to clean up the mess and take the fall, is that why you're on the run tonight?"

He snorted. "You think you've got it all figured out, don't you?"

Addie continued to work her way around the opposite side of the desk from him. "What did he do, move in on your woman, and then they robbed you just like you'd robbed the foundation?"

"He's just some old fool she liked to toy with and lead on. It amused her. I have no idea where the guy is, but I can assure you that he's not off with Crystal."

"How can you be so sure?" His dark blue neck veins bulged, visibly pulsating as his heart rate accelerated. Addie glanced at the chair and her key chain dangling out of the side pocket of her purse and inched toward it.

His gaze flashed to where she'd looked. "You really shouldn't have telegraphed your next move." He smirked and backed toward the chair. His eyes held fast on hers. He reached behind him, dropped her purse to the floor, and kicked it underneath the chair. His eyes unwavering, he shuffled to the door, leaned against it, and waved his knuckle-bound keys in the air. "There's no way out." His crooked smile made her sick.

She met his gaze head on and slid her hand into her jacket pocket. Her fingers fished for her phone. Empty. Her chest tightened. She glanced at her purse, took in a slow breath unscrambling her thoughts, and leaned forward on the edge of the desk. "So, tell me, Patrick." Her eyes held steadfast on his. "Did Teresa discover you were keeping two sets of books? Is that why you killed her?"

"It's not my fault that she fell down the stairs and broke her neck."

"Really?" She forced the rising bile back down her throat and sucked in another steadying breath. *Breathe, just keep breathing.* You have to breathe to think, and she needed to think fast right now. There was no way she could afford to lose in this the cat-and-mouse game that she'd been thrust into. Reassured by the continued rise and fall of her chest, all the clues and theories she'd come up with flashed through her mind. She pasted on her most confident grin. "But I'm guessing you know whose fault it is? After all, the day she died, you picked up three lunches. Who was the third one for?"

"You always did ask too many questions." The hatred burning behind his eyes reflected on his face. He took a step toward her. "Yes, Teresa found out I was taking money out of the account even though I had the other books to show her everything was in great shape. Then after she was, well . . . gone, the board started asking questions when it looked like I was going to have to refund the ticket money. I knew then that I'd have to show them the real books, the ones Teresa found in my locked drawer one day."

"So, that's what the third key was for?" She studied his ruddy face beaded with perspiration. "I'm surprised that when you took the keys off her dead body, you didn't remove that one."

"I should have." Her cheek twitched. Was that a confession? Too bad she couldn't get her hands on her phone to record it. "It might have stopped you from sniffing around so much," he spat, glaring at her as he moved closer.

"Then you don't know me very well, do you?" She forced a laugh.

"To be honest, I didn't know she had a copy of my key until Crystal overheard her on the phone with someone. She told her caller that she came across a second set of books while in my office looking for the donor's list and said she had no choice but to go to the police."

"Then why didn't she? Right then?" So far, he was ticking off most of the unchecked boxes on her crime

board, but why was he telling her all this? Was he brag-
ging, feeling cocky about what he did? Or . . . as the
callous look in his beady little eyes suggested, did he
plan to kill her, too? Well, she had a plan of her own.
What it was she wasn't certain, but she knew she had to
keep him talking until she figured one out. "I said why
didn't she report the fixed books to the police?"

"I guess whoever she was on the phone with convinced her to wait. That bought me a little more time
to get the real account ledger out of here. That's why I
wasn't worried about anyone discovering what the
third key was for until you showed up. But you were
too late anyway with all your questions because the
proof was already gone."

"So why kill her then? Why not just take the money
and run?" A slow grin spread across Addie's lips. "Unless,
of course, she'd made a copy of the ledgers. Is that when
you decided to get rid of her permanently, just in case
she had her own set of books? She wouldn't be able to go
to the police."

"Yeah," his voice hoarsened. "The original plan was
just as you said, to get out of town before she turned
over the cooked books, but Crystal, my partner, as
you've already guessed, was afraid Teresa *had* made a
copy, which was why Teresa wasn't in a hurry to call the
police. Crystal got nervous, so she hatched the scheme
to kill her. Then she thought, why not steal the book,
too, and make even more money selling it than we had
already gotten out of this deal." He licked his lips, his
eyes showing a glimmer of pride. "And it worked even
better than we thought it would. After she was dead, I
just brought back the other set of books, proved the
foundation was broke, and the hospital committee
gave me another nice, fat check on top of it all to save
the gala and then . . . you walked in tonight as I was

packing to leave." He toyed with the keys, his jaw set. "And now I seem to have one last detail to look after before I go, and then I'll be off to meet Amy, err Crystal—"

"Amy? You mean Amy Miller?"

His face turned ashen. "How do you know that name?"

God, it felt so good to watch him sweat. A sly smile crossed Addie's lips. The puzzle pieces were finally beginning to slide into place, and one more box on her board could be checked off. "Because you got sloppy when you cleaned up Teresa's office after you killed her and forgot about the garbage can. A lipstick sample on one of the cups found in it was tested for DNA, and it came back from the lab as belonging to one Amy Miller, and you've more or less just confirmed that Crystal is none other than her."

"Damn it!" he hissed, spraying spittle in the air and glaring at her. The hold on Addie's chest twisted. She inched backward. A humorless laugh ripped out of him, but the mocking glint in his eye grated on every nerve ending in her body.

"You are such an annoyance." He waved his key-wrapped knuckles in the air. "I guess it's time to follow through with my earlier warnings, the ones you chose to ignore."

She bolted toward the door, but like a cat after a mouse, he sprang at her over the desk, grabbed her ponytail, and pulled her back against him. His key-bound hand seized her throat. Her hands clutched at his, trying to loosen his grasp, but the more she struggled, the harder he pressed a key tip into her neck.

"How did Crystal," she wheezed, "I mean, Amy Miller, the ecoterrorist, come up with the idea to use something as toxic as blue-ringed octopus venom as a weapon?" Addie wedged two fingers under his, fighting to breathe. "Was it from the sister she told me about, the nerdy scientist?"

"That nerdy scientist, my friend"—he sneered and pressed the key end into the flesh under her chin—"happens to hold a PhD in Marine Biology."

"So," Addie gasped, forcing the words out, "she told Crystal about it?"

"No, Crystal got the idea from a book she read."

"Don't tell me," she squeaked. "*State of Fear?*"

Patrick's body stiffened against hers. "How did you know?"

She tried to force out a laugh but choked.

"Yeah, the octopus venom was a brilliant idea. It's not common and would be harder to detect and trace. Her sister had the means of supplying it so . . ." His arm twitched with a slight shrug. "After they made the arrangements Crystal threw her copy of the book in someone's garbage can, so she couldn't be linked to it."

Addie's mind flashed to the copy one of her customers had brought into the store, and hoped that Crystal's prints would still be on it. "How did you do it?" Her foot slipped out from under her. She winced when the key jerked, scraping up her neck. "That toxin is lethal even to touch, from what I've heard."

"It was easy." She cringed when his hot breath drifted down the back of her shirt. "Her sister, Elise, told her how to handle it. I picked up lunch earlier than usual, about ten thirty; then Crystal doctored it according to instructions and was going to take it into Teresa about eleven, but then she discovered that Teresa already had a visitor. Your friend Jonathan." His weight shifted. Addie struggled to regain her footing. The key slipped, scraping down her throat to her collarbone. "Crystal got worried because she overheard their plan was to go for lunch. She had to stop it. We couldn't let this ruin our plans. She phoned Teresa and told her it was her birthday, and that she wanted Teresa to have lunch with her because she didn't know anyone else in town." He snickered. "She even said she was depressed about being alone and turned on the tears."

"And Teresa, being the kindhearted person she was, felt sorry for her and obliged." Addie managed to wheeze.

"Yup, Jonathan left right after that, and Crystal took in their lunch along with a bottle of whiskey to have a birthday drink with her."

"That way, when an autopsy was done the alcohol would show up in it, and there wouldn't be any questions, right?"

"That was until you started nosing around. Making the police doubt it was an accident like they'd thought." She fought the urge to heave at the stench of his rancid breath across her cheek. She winced and braced her foot against the desk leg. "How did you do it? How did you get Teresa in the stairwell?" She squirmed until her fingers eased some of the pressure from her throat.

"It was easy, after Teresa ate her doctored food. Crystal sent me a text that said *done*. I phoned Teresa and told her I needed her to come down to the event room. I told her the elevators were jammed with visitors, so I'd meet her at the stairwell entrance and explain the issue. By the time Teresa arrived at the bottom, the poison was kicking in. She was wobbly, had difficulty seeing and breathing." The cool, flat tone of his voice sent quivers up Addie's spine that niggled at the base of her skull. "I opened the door and just had to give her a little bump, sending her down the stairs to the basement level."

"Like you tried to do with me that day at the top of the stairs?"

"That was one of the warnings I gave you. I wanted you to see how easily accidents can happen so you'd back off and realize there was no need to be poking around."

"What happened then?"

His arm tightened his hold across her chest. "Crystal raced down the stairs, got the keys from me, and went back up to search Teresa's office to see if there was a copy of the ledgers."

"Did she find them?" Addie grunted under the pressure on her windpipe.

"No, she tore the office apart, but there was nothing. She figured she must have been too late and Teresa had already passed them on, maybe to that Jonathan fellow. She knew she'd have to start playing with him after that to find out if he had them."

"What then?" Addie pulled at his hand tightening around her throat.

"Crystal cleaned up the office, grabbed the sushi containers and the book out of the case, and then hid them in my office. She was supposed to text me when it was all clear and I'd meet her in the stairwell to return the keys to Teresa's wrist."

"But she'd forgotten the keys in the cabinet and left the office unlocked and had to go back in, right? But then"—Addie groaned—"I showed up before that could happen?"

"Yeah," he huffed. "I hadn't counted on you bringing the certificate in that day. I tried to convince you to give the papers to me, but no," he hissed, and droplets spattered across her cheek. "You had to hand it to her in person, didn't you, and mess up a perfectly good plan?" His grip on her throat tightened and squeezed.

"I had to text Crystal and warn her that you were on your way up. She was still in my office locking up the book, so I told her to stay put and watch until you went into Teresa's office, and then she ran to the desk so she could text me when you left and tell me you were on your way back down."

"Is that when she went back in and took the envelope?" Addie nodded, attempting to turn her head to avoid his putrid breath and spittle on her face. "You knew from what I told you that that you'd need the appraisal to get top dollar for the book when you sold it."

"Every dollar counts." He snorted. "But just my luck you used the staircase after you left instead of the elevator and found her body." He wheezed, pressing his weapon harder into her neck. "You have no idea how much your arrival screwed up a well-laid plan, do you?" He jerked her hard against him.

"Don't forget about the two coffee cups they'd had a drink in that Crystal forgot to grab from the trash can. Or was that part of the plan, to throw off the investigation, too?'

He laughed. "No, but it turned out all right at first, didn't it? The police, including you, assumed she was drunk and fell." His voice tightened. "Damn that lipstick, though."

She wedged a finger under his hand and swallowed hard. "But then there was still the little matter of the keys in the lock, which of course you couldn't let Crystal remove after in case I'd seen them."

"You're right. It was a silver lining in disguise, though. I did get the documents you dropped off. Except for the fact that the key would have been back on her wrist if you hadn't shown up when you did and a lot of unnecessary questions could have been avoided."

"Why are you telling me all this, Patrick?" His hand

shifted, pinching her skin. "Aren't you afraid I'm going to talk?"

His raspy laugh echoed in her ear, sending prickles across her shoulders. "I told you there was no way out." He pressed the fistful of keys hard against her jugular and twisted. "Besides, this is kind of fun. Like a cat playing with its prey before the final blow, and remember, you brought this on yourself when you didn't heed the message on your blackboard." He jerked her down toward the floor.

She braced and anchored her back leg, managing to remain upright. He yanked on her again. A key tip bit into her chin. Her front foot thrashed in the air and her boot toe clanged against a metal trash can beside the desk. She was not about die tonight, not here, like this. She'd darn well make sure of that, or . . . she swallowed hard. At least she'd die fighting. She tightened her leg muscle, kicked hard, and sent the can clattering across the room crashing into the door. Patrick recoiled, releasing his grip on her throat. She elbowed backward, striking him hard in the ribs, propelled herself around the desk, and flung the door open. "Marc!"

Chapter 33

Marc seized her wrist and whipped her behind him. She bounced off Jerry's chest and thudded against the corridor wall.

"Freeze!" Marc commanded. His and Jerry's guns held steady on Patrick.

The sound of heavy boots stomped down the hall toward her. With a trembling hand, she pointed two more officers to the open door and sucked in a strangled breath. She closed her eyes against the rising panic. The sound of handcuffs snapping closed brought her back to reality. Marc's matter-of-fact voice inside the office reading Patrick his rights echoed in her ears; then the two officers appeared and escorted Patrick down the hall.

"It's over," she murmured. Her body numb from head to toe, she slid down the wall to the floor and jumped when a hand touched her knee.

"Whoa. Steady now. It's done, over." Marc's soothing voice calmed her nervous tension as he crouched down beside her.

A smile tickled the corners of her lips. "Well, hello there. What brings you by today?" An anxious giggle bubbled at the back of her throat.

"What am I going to do with you?" His hand swept strands of hair from her face, but his thumb lingered on her jaw, stroking her bruised chin and mottled throat. "You're darn lucky that you at least told Serena where you were going and hadn't sworn her to secrecy when I went looking for you." He pressed his lips tight. His eyes darkened when they focused on her neck. "When will you learn that your best teachers are your last mistakes? You keep making the same ones over and over again."

"Well, you know me." She shrugged. "If there's a knot, I have to unravel it and see where the threads lead."

He locked his eyes on hers. "One day, I might not get here in time to rescue you."

"Rescue me?" An indignant gasp escaped her throat. "I was on my way out the door when you happened by. I think I did pretty well on my own, thank you very much." She glowered at him and choked back something between a laugh and a sob as her insides still shook with residual fear. "And . . . and why were you looking for me?"

"Because I wanted to show you"—he fished his phone out of his pocket and swiped at the screen—"this . . ."

She glanced at a photo of Crystal, aka Amy Miller, and waved it off. "Pffft, old news."

"Okay, I can see you have a bit of a story to tell me. But maybe I do know something that you don't?" He gave her an exaggerated wink.

"I doubt it, but you can try if you like," she grinned.

"You see, since Crystal—err, Amy—was already

flagged as a person of interest, my buddy in the FBI sent me the photo along with a complete list of names that popped up with it, aka Shannon Jenkins, aka Jenifer Rollins, aka Tracy Bower, who are all none other than Amy Miller, ecoterrorist, and all wanted on fraud and embezzlement charges across the Midwest." Her brows shot up. "And you haven't heard the best part yet."

"I'm afraid to ask." She hung her head between her knees.

He ruffled her hair. "Patrick's real name is Craig Saunders. He has a number of aliases, too, and is wanted on the same warrants. He and Crystal were partners and have been for years."

"That I did know." His brow creased. "I mean, not his alias names, but the fact they were partners. I suspected those two knew each other right from the second she told me at Catherine's brunch that she was from the Midwest, and then again when I saw them at dinner at the Grey Gull. Things looked a little too cozy for them having just started to work together, and he confirmed it to me just a few minutes ago. Right in there." She smiled broadly, pointing to the office. "While *I* got a *full* confession out of him, based on following *my* gut and *my* theories."

Marc's lips tightened. "I guess I should have viewed your theories more as a lead on the hard evidence that I keep going on about"—he glanced down at his cap in his hand, and his voice lowered—"and not have been so dismissive of them."

A toothy grin crossed her face. "Chief Chandler, are you actually saying that my theories might be valid at times?"

His face flushed. "Um, well . . ."

"You are, aren't you?" She playfully slapped his

knee. "Imagine what we could do if we actually worked *together*."

"And we will, after you graduate from the police academy. That is, if you live long enough"—his head gestured toward Patrick's office—"and don't have some madman kill you before then."

She wrinkled up her face and poked her tongue out at him. "Help me." She held out her hand. "I need to stand. I think I've cramped up."

"Thank God, my knees were giving way, squatting like that."

"Remember, neither of us are sixteen anymore." With his help, she hobbled to her feet. "The adrenaline is wearing off and this"—she pointed to the welts on her throat—"is starting to smart. I need to go home and pour a stiff drink." She started down the hall.

"Not so fast." He grabbed her arm and tilted her head up, inspecting her neck. "I don't see any blood, and you seem to be speaking okay, so it's not urgent. If you want, you can go down to emergency and get checked out after, but I need a full statement about what happened here tonight."

She groaned and flopped down on the bench by the elevator. "Okay, but be gentle, I'm not sure how much I can take right now."

"I'm always gentle." A smile tickled the corners of his mouth as he sat down. She gave him a shoulder bump and laughed. He did a snorty-smirky thing and pulled his notepad and pen from his pocket, balanced it on his knee, and waited.

When she finished regaling the evening's events, she rubbed her burning neck and leaned back against the wall. "He really believed I wouldn't get out of there alive, didn't he?" She looked at Marc. "Why else would he be so smug about it all and brag to me about his accomplishments?"

"I think he overestimated his skills and underestimated yours. But I'd say that by the look of the welts on your neck, you are darn lucky that you did survive." He squeezed her hand.

"Yeah." She shivered with the memory of the keys pressed against her throat. "But even with everything he said, I can't shake the feeling that there's still a missing detail in this case, and it's something important that's on my crime board." She leaned forward and rested her elbows on her knees. "It's right there in front of me, but I can't see it, and it's frustrating as heck."

"Don't beat yourself up. Thanks to your quick thinking in keeping him talking to get a confession, we can combine that with the lab results we have and then there's more than enough evidence for a couple of convictions."

"Yeah, but—"

"No yeah buts. You're not a cop. If there's anything else, we'll find it. That's *our* job, not yours." He snapped his notebook closed and pulled out his cell phone. "I'd better let my friend at the FBI know what happened and have him send an agent to pick up Crystal when she lands in the Cayman Islands."

She stood up and looked down at him, amazed by his thumb dexterity across the small keypad. Was this the same guy who feigned ignorance over doing an Internet search?

"My friend told me to thank you." He glanced at her. His lips curved up into a smile. She liked the way the corners of his eyes crinkled when he smiled at her. She grinned and pressed the elevator button.

Chapter 34

Addie absently toyed with strands of tinsel on the tree in her window display. Her gaze focused past it on the fluffy snowflakes that covered the grimy, snow-rutted streets, transforming them once again into an unblemished winter wonderland. It was a picture-perfect Christmas Eve.

"Addie?" Paige tapped her on the shoulder. Her blue eyes creased at the corners, revealing the hint of a twinkle.

"What's up?" Addie's eyes narrowed. "What are you hiding behind your back?" She craned her neck to sneak a peek.

Paige giggled and swerved, blocking her view. "Nothing." But the flush in her cheeks belied the word. "It's just that you said I could leave a bit early today, and Mom's out back in her car with Emma, so I was wondering, if—"

"Of course." Addie smiled. "I'll be closing soon and heading out myself."

Paige smiled and pulled a bakery box from behind her back. "These are for you from Mom."

"Really?" Addie took the box from her hands and peered through the cello window on the top. A chuckle formed low in her belly.

Paige's head tilted to the side. "I don't get the joke, but she said you might need a few of these over the holidays, and then she giggled."

"Your mother is a very wise and thoughtful woman." Addie clasped Paige's hand. "Please thank her for me. This box of gingerbread men means more to me than she'll ever know. She may have just saved my sanity through the holidays."

"Okay?" Paige eyed Addie curiously. "I'll tell her."

Addie retrieved a bulky envelope and a brightly wrapped package from under the counter and held them out to Paige. "This is for you. It's your well-deserved Christmas bonus." She handed her the envelope. "And this is for Emma. It's the primary-level copy of *A Christmas Carol* that I told you to take for her."

Paige chuckled. "With the laughy-snorty thing happening that day, I'd forgotten all about it. Thank you. I know Emma will love it." She peeked inside the envelope and gasped. "No, this is way too much."

"Nonsense. You earned every penny." Addie smiled.

Paige flung her arms around Addie's neck. "Thank you so much."

"You just have the best Christmas ever." Addie patted her back. "And don't forget to thank your mom for me."

"I won't." Paige grinned and headed toward the back door. "Merry Christmas," she called as the door closed.

The front door chimes rang out. Addie's heart sank

at the prospect of a late-day Christmas Eve customer. She wanted nothing more than to get home and start preparing for the Christmas dinner she was hosting for Serena and Zach tomorrow. She sucked in a deep breath, pasted the biggest smile on her face that she could muster, and swung around. "Catherine! What a pleasant surprise."

"Sorry to pop in so late, but I was next door buying some last-minute teas"—she held up a paper bag— "and Serena and I came up with a new plan for Christmas dinner."

"What have the two of you cooked up now?" Addie pinned her with a probing gaze.

Catherine returned her curiosity with a crooked smile but didn't say a word.

"Come on, you know you're going to tell me, so just spill it. Oh, wait"—Addie snapped her fingers—"Serena's sworn you to secrecy because she's invited you all to my place for dinner, right, and wanted it to be a surprise? Now that sounds like a Serena-type plan. Not that I would mind you joining our little group tomorrow," Addie chuckled, "but a heads-up would be nice."

"That's exactly . . . well . . . more or less what she wanted me to tell you, but I just couldn't give you that bad a fright on Christmas Eve." She laughed and snorted. Her eyes flashed wide, and her hand clamped her mouth. "I'm so sorry," she giggled. "I guess I'm feeling a little giddy this evening." Her eyes sparkled over her veiled mouth.

"Have you and Joyce been cooking with wine today?"

"No!" Catherine snorted another laugh. "Jonathan called, and he's alright and will be back as soon as he can." Tears shimmered in the corners of her eyes. "I'm just so relieved."

Addie swallowed hard. She'd completely forgotten Jonathan was still missing. Last night was such a blur, but one thing she did remember was that he didn't appear to be involved in any of it. She laid her hand on Catherine's arm. "Did . . . did he say when he'd be back? I really need to talk to him."

"Not exactly." Her dark shoulder-cropped hair swung with her headshake. "He said he had some loose ends to tie up and reports and such, but hoped he'd be finished up in time to take me to the New Year's Gala as we'd planned."

"The gala? So the hospital is still going forward with it?"

"Yes, that's something else I wanted to tell you. This morning Walter, the board chairman, called me and asked if I could take over the last-minute arrangements. He said Patrick wasn't able to carry on in his role?" Her brow rose questioningly.

"Right . . ." Addie glanced down at the floor. "I kind of heard something about that."

"His loss my gain, I guess." Catherine shrugged. "After being a volunteer at the hospital for all these years, it is kind of a feather in my cap," she grinned.

"And it's wonderful recognition for all your years of service, too. If I can be of any help, please let me know."

"That's . . . what I wanted to ask you about." Catherine arched a sly brow and winced. "Do you have another book you might be willing to donate to the auction?"

"For you, yes, I might even have one or two other Dickens books lying around." Addie smiled and took her friend's hand in hers.

"Perfect." Catherine pulled Addie in for a tight hug.

"Thanks, but I'd better run, got a houseful at home waiting for me." She started toward the door.

"Wait, you forgot to let me in on the new dinner plan that you and Serena hatched up. Or should I be asking what time I should expect you all tomorrow?"

"No." Catherine looked ready to laugh but a wide grin spread over her face instead. "You, she, and Zach will join us at *my* house for Christmas dinner tonight. We already have enough food to feed half the town, and Serena hasn't even picked up the turkey you asked her to get for yours tomorrow, so . . . the plan was born"—Addie opened her mouth to protest—"and I won't take no for an answer. Come over as soon as you've finished up here." Catherine waved over her shoulder, the doorbells jingling overhead. Addie could hear her laughing even after the door closed.

She grinned and wrapped her arms around her middle, hugging herself. Her little family here in Grey-borne Harbor had just gotten a whole lot bigger, and she loved it.

Humming a Christmas carol, she wove her way through the narrow aisles of bookcases and around the carved wooden post, uprighting toppled books on her way to the back room. She locked the alley door, eyed the crime board, and picked up the eraser to wipe it clean, but stopped. Her gaze focused on Jonathan's name. She shrugged and raised the brush. "So much for you being my number-one suspect." Her hand dropped to her side. But how could she have been so wrong about him with everything her gut told her?

Her lips set in a firm line. She studied the clues beside his name. If he wasn't off with Crystal on some romantic rendezvous, where was he and why had he disappeared? What was she missing? Her palm slapped the board. It was right here. She could feel it, but the answer remained just out of sight . . . just out of sight. She examined the clues again. *Australia*, and followed the link to Crystal's or Amy's-whatever-she's-called these-days sister, who lives in Australia. What did it mean?

Addie sat down on her desktop. Her gaze held fast on Jonathan's name. Could he have been the mysterious caller on the phone with Teresa who convinced her not to take the phony ledgers to the police, but why would he do that if he wasn't involved?

She raked her hands over her face. "How could I have been so wrong?" A loud thud behind her jerked her off her perch. "Marc?"

"Good afternoon." He grinned and leaned his hand on a black briefcase behind her on the desk. "What are you so wrong about?" He gestured to the board. "You got a confession and wrapped it up fairly well for us last night." His voice trailed off, muttering, "Although you could have been killed in the process, stubborn woman. . . ."

"For all the good it's done me." She glared at the board. "I still have one unanswered question."

"I don't see anything missing. You have notes about Patrick and suspecting him of stealing money. You have a question mark beside Crystal's name and her involvement. Also"—he pointed—"there's the notes about Amy Miller, ecoterrorist, and blue-ringed octopus toxin, and there's Marvin and his mob connections. But I especially like the line about Crystal's sister, the *nerdy scientist*," he laughed.

"Yeah, Crystal was sure smart at playing dumb and had me fooled with that one."

"I don't see why you're beating yourself up. It looks like you covered most everything we got them all on."

She scanned down the board and noted how all her dots did connect in the end, and grinned.

"The only thing missing is the information I got from my FBI friend, and you're not going to believe this." Addie bit her lip, hanging on every word. "It seems that last Christmas, Crystal, aka Amy, was in Australia for her sister's wedding to none other than Craig Saunders, aka Patrick Barton."

"What? He's married to Crystal's sister?"

Marc nodded smugly. "And the sister is none other than Elise Lockwood. She's actually Crystal's half sister and the leader of the ecoterrorist group Crystal, err, I mean Amy and Craig, had been embezzling money for all those years from various agencies. It was to support the family cause."

"Wow, have they been caught yet?"

He nodded, grinning. "Crystal, with the book in her possession by the way, was picked up by an agent along with her sister, who was there to meet her at the airport in the Cayman Islands. So, case closed." He leaned back against the desk, crossed his arms, and scanned the board. "Actually, your theories aren't that far off when I look at it now." He heaved out a deep breath, retrieved a toy deputy sheriff's star out of his pocket, and pinned it to her jacket lapel. "As usual, you were a big help in the end . . . infuriating as heck, but a help nonetheless."

She grinned down at the badge. "Are you actually complimenting me?"

"I wouldn't go that far. You still have one major mistake on the board, so maybe I should take that back." He held out his hand.

"No way"—her hand clamped over the badge—"this is mine." She examined the board. "Which one is wrong?"

He pointed to Jonathan's name.

"That's the part that I find hard to believe and can't figure out. I was so certain he was involved in all this somehow. I even thought that if it wasn't with Crystal, then it was with her sister, but you just shot that theory into outer space."

"He is involved, but not in the way you think."

"Explain, then." She wrapped her arms across her chest, staring at the board, strumming her fingers on her forearm. "Wait! I see it now." She poked her finger on the line beside Jonathan's name and the word *Australia*. "That's why he was there last year, for the wedding, wasn't it? But why? Who were they to him?" She searched his face for an answer. "Was he following them, is he actually an agent?"

Marc's hand scoured through his thick chestnut-brown hair. "What I can tell you is that he was the mysterious caller on the phone who told Teresa not to take the fixed books to the police until he got here. He and her used to work together, and he was afraid she might be in danger when he heard what was going on and who was involved." Marc's jaw tightened. "A decision he now regrets, to say the least."

Addie stared at his name. "I bet he does. That advice put her in even more danger."

"Yeah, but who was to know. Murder had never been part of this group's pattern in the past, and he got here as soon as he could."

"So, his entire visit was pre-arranged and had nothing to do with stopping by to wish me a Merry Christmas." She swallowed the lump growing in the back of her throat.

"Not completely." Marc's thumb wiped chalk dust from her chin. "He does care very much for you, but when she called him about what was going on, he had to come. It was the break he'd been looking for since last year when they fell off his radar, and the bonus for him was you were here, too."

"Wait!" She held up her hand. "The break he'd been looking for? Radar? So, you're saying I was right? He is an agent?" Her eyes widened. "And how do you know all this?"

He didn't reply, but she noted the way his eyes darkened. He opened the briefcase, withdrew a book, and placed it in her hand.

Chapter 35

Addie's mouth dropped. "What the . . . how did you get . . . ?" Her hand stroked over the red cloth cover. "I thought it was gone for good." She traced her fingers over the gold embossed title, *A Christmas Carol*. "Catherine's going to be thrilled to have it back for the auction. It should definitely help the foundation reach its goal to renovate the pediatric wing." She searched his face. "But how did you get it back so soon?"

To her surprise, he smiled. Just a little smile, and rested his hand on hers.

"But . . . but . . ." She blinked, then frowned. "Don't the authorities need it for evidence or something?"

"They have everything they need from it, a friend made certain of that." Marc's eyes flickered with mystery. "That friend also wanted me to give you this." He reached into his pocket and placed a flash drive in her hand.

"Wait, Jonathan? He gave these to you?" She turned the flash drive and book over in her hand. "I don't get it? So, you've seen him recently? Like in today, that recently?"

"He told me to tell you"—the corner of Marc's mouth twitched—"that this would explain everything, or as much as he can, anyway."

"I get the distinct feeling that all along you haven't been telling me everything you knew about him, have you?" Her gaze pierced his, but his tell was gone and his face masked. She looked down at the book. "Well, thank you. I don't know for sure how all this came about, but I do intend to get the whole story about him out of you at some point."

He placed his finger over her lips. "Shh, it's a secret."

"Like in top secret?"

"That . . . I can never tell." His finger lingered on her lips.

A wave swept through her and she steadied herself, her heart racing. She stared up into his soft-brown eyes as he leaned in closer. His finger tilted her chin upward. His lips brushed across hers. "Marc," she whispered.

He withdrew his lips from hers and cupped her face in his hands. A shy smile tugged at the corners of his mouth. "Did you just say *my* name?"

"Yes, I guess I did." She grinned up at him.

"Merry Christmas." He kissed the tip of her nose. "That's the best present I've ever received," he whispered into her hair. "But I'm afraid I have to go now. I'm on duty tonight. Have a wonderful Christmas, Addie." He kissed the top of her head. "I'll see you around soon?" She nodded. He picked up his bag, turned to go, and stopped. "Um, hello, Simon."

"I . . . ah." Simon's face reddened. "I knocked, but I

guess you didn't hear me." His shoulders twitched with a slight shrug.

Marc puffed out his chest when he pushed past him in the doorway. The front door bells announced his departure.

"I didn't hear the door when you came in," Addie said.

"I guess you were busy." He fumbled with a small, silver-foiled box in his hands. "I just came by to give you this." A flick of pain sparked in his eyes as he held out the gift.

She prayed her eyes conveyed what her heart felt. She could never voice an apology for him having witnessed what had just occurred between Marc and her. Hand trembling, she lifted the lid from the box. She plucked out a small white ceramic bird dangling from a red ribbon. "It's beautiful," she whispered.

"It's a turtle dove," his voice wavered. "It symbolizes love and faithfulness, and is also said to soothe the soul and ease a troubled mind."

"I love it. Thank you." She fought the tears welling up behind her eyes.

He ran his hand through his thick black hair and blew out a shallow breath. "It's also a symbol that love is always near." His lips turned up at the corners, suggesting a hint of a smile.

She swallowed and looked away, rubbing her fingers over the smooth varnish finish of the doorframe. "So, is Courtney waiting outside for you?"

"We never even got through our second date."

"You did leave her at the curbside, then?"

His head tilted to the side. "What?"

"Nothing," she muttered, toying with the bird in her hand.

"In truth, spending any time at all with her made me realize I still want exactly the same thing I wanted since you and I first met."

Her heart did a tiny flip in her chest.

He wrapped long strands of her hair around his fingers and danced her backward against the doorframe. He drew her to him. His lips brushed hers with whisper-like caresses; then he kissed her like she'd never been kissed before. He withdrew his lips. Her mouth hung slightly open, wanting more, but he rested his damp brow against hers. "Merry Christmas." He kissed her forehead before hurrying toward the door without as much as a glance back. She braced herself against the doorframe, trying to catch her breath.

Serena was so, so wrong. Addie paced around the store quite certain her head would explode. "Make him kiss you," she muttered mockingly, "and then you can decide which one of them you're really interested in." She slammed a book upright, sending two more toppling to the side. "Well, it didn't work, my dear friend. I'm more confused than ever." She scrubbed her hands over her face. "Tomorrow, I'll think about it tomorrow."

She plopped down on a counter stool, swung her opened laptop toward her, and shoved the flash drive into the port. Immediately, the smiling face of Jonathan greeted her on her screen. Her eyes narrowed, and she turned up the volume.

"Addie, there is so much I want to tell you, but unfortunately I can't, not only for my protection but also for yours. But please trust me when I say none of what you think you know about me is true."

Those words echoed in her mind. She gnawed on her bottom lip. As her father always used to say, "Follow your gut instincts," and she had until her mind got in the way regarding Jonathan and who and what he was. She studied his eyes in the video, looking for a hint, a tell . . . something, anything that would confirm to her what her gut had originally felt about his true identity.

Marc had neither denied nor confirmed her suspicions about him tonight when she brought it up. That was a good starting point, but she needed more. She pressed repeat and play over and over, scanning his face, the background in the video, the lighting, every detail she could take in, but saw nothing, no clues.

Then she remembered what David had said after one of Jonathan's flyby visits. "Some things couldn't be shared because they were top secret, and some things couldn't even be spoken about because they were above that classification." At the time, she had thought he was talking about one of his cases, or a book he'd read, but now? Maybe it was something else. Had Jonathan shared his true identity finally with his son on one of his later visits? Is that why in the end David appeared to have forgiven him for all those years of grief? She hit play again and sat back.

"What is true is that I know my son loved you very much. As you did and still do him." Addie drew in a deep breath to squelch the sob that rose up in the back of her throat. "I've also witnessed firsthand how his memory has stopped you from moving forward in matters of the heart." He leaned closer to the camera, his smoky-gray eyes imploring her. "Never forget him, but it's time for you to leave David's ghost in the past, where it belongs." Addie's chest constricted and she sucked in a little breath.

"To borrow the words of an old Irish saying . . . *Death leaves a heartache no one can heal. Love leaves a memory no one can steal.* Remember that David will always be with you in a special place in your heart. No one will ever take that away from you. However, I also know my son would only want you to find happiness now in the present and in your future. You're a lucky girl to have both Marc and Simon in your life, two fine men who care for you a great deal. Now, it's time for you to decide. Do you want your present to remain haunted by your past ghosts, or do you want to take a step into your new future with one of them?" A smile skipped across his lips. "Merry Christmas," he said, and with his fingers, he blew her a kiss. "Until next time, my dear." He gave her a playful wink and grinned. The last thing she saw before the screen went black was a sparkle to his eyes that she'd never seen before.

She sucked in an uneven breath and folded her lips together to keep her tears in check. A sensation of being watched niggled her mind. She ran to the display window and pressed her face against the cold glass. Past the falling snowflakes glistening under the streetlights, a dark figure stood across the road. "Merry Christmas," she whispered, and returned the wink with a wobbly smile. The man in black tipped his hat, turned, and vanished into the park.

Addie placed one foot in front of the other. Her back foot propelled her skate style up the slippery sidewalk toward Catherine's front door. Both feet slid out from under her when she skidded over a patch of ice buried under the snow. Her arms flailed, her legs sprawled in different directions, and she corkscrewed toward a snowbank and landed on her butt.

Chin-deep in the snow, she tossed her head back and laughed. Where was Simon when she needed him to catch her? She struggled to get to her feet and brushed the snow from her wool coat, still giggling. She was fully prepared to give her performance a curtsey should there be a witness in the house to her calamity and glanced at the front picture window . . . her heart fluttered an extra beat. Zach, his arm draped across Serena's shoulders, leaned over Jack and a spiky-red-headed Adel on the piano bench as they all belted out a tune.

In spite of Jack Frost's kisses across her cheeks and the freezing snow wedged in her cuffs, up her back and down her collar, it couldn't take away from the warmth bubbling through her at that moment. With the sight of her friends gathered together in the living room, the Christmas lights strung around the windows and porch appeared to shine brighter tonight. Catherine spotted her through the glass and waved. Tears of happiness formed in Addie's eyes. Standing out here on the sidewalk, it was as though the ghosts of her Christmas past were giving her a glimpse of her Christmas present.

Drawn in by the sounds of love and laughter ringing out from behind the door that Catherine held open for her, she made her way up the steps. Behind her, a car horn beeped from the street, and she turned. Through the gently falling snowflakes and past the reflection from the Christmas lights glistening off the snow-covered tree boughs was Marc's cruiser stopped on the road. He waved and smiled before he continued along the street. Was that a peek behind the veil into her Christmas future? Addie grinned and stepped across the threshold. What could be more perfect than spending Christmas surrounded by people she loved?